True, he kissed me, but he was teasing. Wasn't he?

There was one thing to do, and Jane did it, thinking through all the reasons that she could not be in love with Mr. Scipio Butterworth. First, there is that name, she told herself, then smiled, despite her misery. But it suits him somehow.

What he is, and always will be, is a mill owner, a man with his eye on the ledger. She paused and waited for this thought to disgust her, but to her further irritation, it did not.

Well, then, if his status does not repel you, she told herself, begin with the essential difficulty: he is too old for you. She sighed and wrapped the blanket tighter around her shoulders. Except that he is enthusiastic and has not put on any pounds.

He is already talking about buying another mill, and you announced to him that you were looking for a husband who would devote much attention to you. He would never have the time.

It was easy to think, but she knew in her heart that he would always find time—if he loved her. . . .

Miss Milton Speaks Her Mind

CARLA KELLY

A SIGNET BOOK

SIGNET
Published by the Penguin Group
Penguin Putnam Inc., 375 Hudson Street,
New York, New York 10014, U.S.A.
Penguin Books Ltd, 27 Wrights Lane,
London W8 5TZ, England
Penguin Books Australia Ltd,
Ringwood, Victoria, Australia
Penguin Books Canada Ltd, 10 Alcorn Avenue,
Toronto, Ontario, Canada M4V 3B2
Penguin Books (N.Z.) Ltd, 182–190 Wairau Road,
Auckland 10, New Zealand

Penguin Books Ltd, Registered Offices:
Harmondsworth, Middlesex, England

First published by Signet, an imprint of Dutton NAL,
a member of Penguin Putnam Inc.

First Printing, November, 1998
10 9 8 7 6 5 4 3 2 1

With love to the wonderful members
of the Ozarks Romance Authors,
Springfield, Missouri

"If thou do ill, the joy fades, not the pains;
If well, the pain doth fail, the joy remains."

—George Herbert
(1593–1633)

Chapter One

Andrew Stover looked up from the atlas he was perusing. "Miss Mitten, is it possible to dread winter even before it gets here?"

Although she knew that her cousin Lady Carruthers would never approve, Jane Milton had allowed Andrew to spread out the atlas—a cumbersome book at best—on the floor close to the fireplace. He was watching her now as she sat close to the window, mending Lord Denby's favorite nightshirt, one that he wore almost all the time now, since he had confined himself to his bed. "It is possible to dread the coming of winter," she agreed, and then glanced at the calendar, "even though it is only October." She anchored the needle in the flannel. "And what does this have to do with finding the Pennsylvania town located where the Allegheny and Monongahela meet to form the Ohio?"

Andrew propped his chin on his palm. "It has nothing to do, I suppose. Pittsburgh," he said, but there was no pleasure in his answer. He rolled onto his back to contemplate the plaster furbelows in the ceiling. "Miss Mitten, I do not want to spend another winter like last winter."

"Nor do I," Jane Milton replied quietly as she addressed herself to the nightshirt again. "Question two concerns the mountain range mentioned in the Proclamation of 1763. Do apply yourself, Andrew, or Lady Carruthers will sentence you to the vicar's school."

He turned back to stare at the map of the United States on the next page. She watched him a moment, assessing him, as she had done since he was placed in her arms as a baby. He was almost twelve now, and rarely needed a reminder to blow his nose, or tie his shoes. *You really need a visit to a tailor, Andrew,* she thought. *I wonder how long I will need to spend convincing Lady Carruthers to grudge you some new trousers? I can't even convince her that I need a new cloak.*

Andrew was requesting her attention again. Jane dragged her thoughts to the spot on the map where he pointed. "I think that it is the Appalachian Mountains, Miss Mitten."

"Milton," she said absently as she pulled out the needle again. "*I* do not mind that you call me Miss Mitten—heaven knows you have been doing it for years, my dear—but Lady Carruthers objects. Yes, it is the Appalachian Mountains. Apparently the British tried to protect the colonists by denying them access, but the Americans took exception to it."

Andrew pushed the atlas aside. "I think they were just tired of being told what to do."

"What is there left to teach you?" Jane teased. "You have certainly reduced the history of the colonial rebellion to its least common denominator, Andrew!" She put down the nightshirt again.

"Do you ever get tired of being told what to do, or does it not bother grown-ups?"

"I suppose it does not bother me, Andrew," she replied, standing up. "If you were to take a turn about the lawn now, I am certain that you could make more sense of Americans afterwards, my dear."

Amused at how quickly he could move when he was released from his studies, Jane Milton stood at the window and watched her charge kick leaves that one of the groundsmen had painstakingly piled that morning. She watched Andrew Stover become a distant figure, and wondered to herself if she had ever minded being told what to do. *It is my natural state,* she concluded. She looked over at the nightshirt she should be mending, and felt a twinge because she was seated so idly at present. *I always do as I am told,* she reflected. *I never complain or call attention to myself, or expect that my stipend should be paid on time. I am the perfect poor relation.*

She heard footsteps in the hall and tensed herself for the briefest moment before she recognized them. She smiled when Stanton came into the library. "Come in, sir," she called. "Do save me from revolutionary thoughts brought about by staring at this confounded map of North America."

He dropped his butler's demeanor long enough to stare at her in mock horror, then smiled back. "Are you ready to rebel and spend your afternoon complaining that the last box of sweets from Cormier's is gone?"

She looked at Lord Denby's butler with sympathy, grateful that his lot was not hers. "Stanton, is my dear cousin Lady Carruthers showing signs of another bolt to London? I know there are other boxes of those sweets she craves."

The butler fixed his attention on a particularly interesting bit of parquet in the floor. "Well, let us say that she cannot find any. This must mean she will leave us soon for the comforts of Cecil's encumbered chambers on Curzon Street."

Jane looked at the butler with perfect understanding, and he gazed back, the portrait of innocence. "Stanton, how do you engineer these thefts?" she asked simply. "Whatever would I do without you?"

It was not a question that required an answer, considering the level of their confederacy through the years, but he surprised her this afternoon. He regarded her with total serenity. "It is merely that Lord Denby was complaining to me that you never laugh anymore, and I thought that perhaps his sister's removal might make a difference in your state of mind."

I *am* surprised, she thought. "You are kind to think of me, but I doubt her removal will make a difference," she said simply.

"Then you are the one in need of a change of scenery," he replied, not noticeably troubled by her response. "Why do you not go in pursuit of your charge, Miss Milton? I recommend a slow chase, the kind that Nathanael Greene used on Lord Denby in the Carolinas."

"Oh dear! Is Lord Denby reminiscing about the American rebellion? I wish he would not," she said with some exasperation. "It only makes him overheated, and then he will not sleep, and you are up, or I am up."

"Go outside, Miss Milton; it will do you good."

"What is it about butlers?" Jane murmured as she drew her cloak tighter about her and let the wind push her. Could it be that he has seen the side of me that no one sees, not even Andrew?

Oh, especially not Andrew, she thought, as she hurried from the house with more relief than she would have owned to, if someone had asked her. It would never do for Andrew to know how sorely I miss his father, or how many tears I have really cried in this long, long year. Jane ventured a kick or two at the leaves. "It will take more than a change of scenery for me, Stanton," she said as she looked down. "I need a new life."

If Lady Carruthers is thinking about leaving her brother Lord Denby on his sickbed, she will be packing now, and not watching to see what Andrew and I are doing, Jane thought, as she headed toward the lake. Not that she—or anyone—cares about Andrew and his education.

Despite the gloom that refused to lift all the way and never would, she feared, Jane did feel a release of tension in her shoulders as she walked to the water. She breathed deep of the turned-over earth and the smell of burning leaves coming across the water from Mr. Butterworth's outbuildings. The harvest was nearly done; trust her cousin Lady Carruthers to bolt to the city when there was a harvest dinner to plan for the tenants, and leave the work to her. Not that it would be a jolly celebration, not with young Lord Canfield cold in the tomb these ten months only, and old Lord Denby determined now to pick his own stubborn route to decline and death. Besides a bountiful harvest that almost seemed a mockery, there was the prospect of Cecil Carruthers coming for Christmas.

"That will be dreadful indeed," she murmured, thinking of his visit after Blair's death, all solicitude and hypocrisy, with a certain smugness when he looked at Blair's son. He had certainly made no effort to disguise the fact that he thought he should become the next Lord Denby, and not Andrew.

I wonder if he can actually change the succession? she thought, and not for the first time; far from it. She did not know if the tenants at Denby were farsighted; for their sakes, she hoped otherwise. If I know Cecil (and I think I do), if he becomes Lord Denby there will be no harvest festival, and then no harvest at all. The estate will be sold to pay his debts, and everyone will be turned off.

She sat on a bench facing the terrace, enjoying the view of formal garden, even if it had grown scraggly and untended during a year of neglect. "Must everything mourn at Denby?" the vicar asked her once, on one of his weekly visits of comfort that never failed to set her teeth tight together. "I do believe, my dear Miss Milton, that as a cousin of the late Lord Canfield—God rest his soul—you should be setting a better example of bravery and good cheer. My dear, a year has passed since Waterloo. Can you not think of your neighbors now?"

We have become a neighborhood reproach, she thought, as clouds rushed to cover the sun. Here it is, fifteen months after Waterloo, and no one in Yorkshire wishes to be reminded of death, least of all our vicar, whose inadequacies quite amaze me. People are getting tired of us, and the black wreath that remains on the front door. They want to celebrate peace, and we are an unwelcome reminder that not everyone is happy.

She frowned as she twisted the fringe of her black shawl between her fingers. Trust Blair Stover to have no idea when it was time to leave this life. My dear cousin, you were never on time to anything in any one of your thirty-four years, and once there, you always outstayed your welcome. "I don't begrudge you a minute of it, though," she said out loud. "If it was never your most endearing trait, at least you were consistent. You were not even on time for your own death."

The wind carried away her words. I wonder which is worse, she thought, immediate death on the field, or that protracted, agonizing, half-living, half-dying that ended, in our case, ten months after Waterloo? She remembered—or more honestly, she could not forget—the still days of June, when news of the approaching battle reached Denby.

Belgium was close, so the wait for more news was short. Lieutenant Colonel Blair Stover, Viscount Canfield, of the Yorkshire Sixth Foot, was on no one's butcher bill, so they could all swallow a huge sigh and continue breathing. But then June passed and there was no direct news from him, no letter to share with the neighbors or the vicar. Lord Denby had taken his carriage to London and Horse Guards for news of his son, and had returned home to Yorkshire to retire to his chamber, old suddenly. He left it to Stanton to tell her and Andrew that he had learned nothing.

Through August, they had all shut their ears to the gaiety from neighboring estates when sons returned. The pain became fierce when friends looked away in church, or avoided their eyes at what few country gatherings they felt obligated to attend. She did not know how Andrew was absorbing all this misery; no one at Stover Hall ever disclosed much.

News came at the end of August. After the battle, Lieutenant

Colonel Stover had been left in a farmhouse on the road to Wavre. They learned that he had been detached to Blücher's corps as liaison, and then wounded and left behind as the army moved. Not until two months later had the farmer thought him well enough to withstand the journey of sixty miles to allied headquarters in Ostend.

"And then you came home to us," she whispered. The wind did not pick up her words this time, but left them all around her like a shroud.

"Miss Mitten, you are so easy to surprise!"

Andrew stood next to her, his hair smelling more of sunshine now, even though the October wind had a sharpish bite. "You did not even hear me," he scolded, even as he leaned against her and her arm went around him automatically.

"I suppose I did not hear you."

"Are you thinking of my father?" he asked.

"I am."

"Do you miss him?"

"I do."

It was not something Jane could ever tell anyone, especially not over dinner that night, when Lady Denby stretched the outward boundaries of her patience with complaints over her missing sweets. She accused Andrew of stealing them, which he firmly denied, all the while not taking his eyes from his plate of ragout.

"You see there, Jane, he will not even look at me when I accuse him!" she stated finally, the loose flesh under her chin wobbling in indignation. "That is the sign of a criminal mind!"

"It is no such thing, Lady Denby," Jane said calmly. "I wish that you would not accuse him."

Andrew looked at his aunt then, narrowing his eyes and pursing his lips in a way that reminded her of his father. Oh, please do not, she told him silently. She held her breath then, knowing that Lady Denby's next comment would make Andrew return his gaze to the plate in front of him.

"Cousin, why you persist in thinking that he is any relation at all to my late nephew I cannot fathom," Lady Denby said, in a loud whisper, dabbing at her dry eyes.

"Because he *is* Blair's son," Jane said quietly, when she really wanted to fling a spoonful of that fricassee onto the bare expanse of Lady Carruthers' bosom that seemed such a mockery of the mourning she wore.

"Some say," the woman muttered, staring at the boy, who was looking at his plate again, his cheeks flushed.

Oh, cousin, you exasperate me, Jane thought as she rested her arm along the back of Andrew's chair, just barely touching his shoulders. Do you think he is deaf? Or as cotton-headed as your own son?

"What a shame that the boy is too old to take his meals in the nursery anymore," Lady Carruthers said. "He has no conversation, Jane. You could at least have been teaching him something, in all these years. I do not know why you have turned out so badly, considering that we have tried to give you every advantage."

Jane sighed with relief. Thank thee, God, for turning the attack to me, she prayed silently, grateful for divine intervention. "I know I am a disappointment to you, Lady Carruthers," she murmured. "I suppose things have turned out about how you have predicted, have they not?"

I am so good at this, Jane thought, as Lady Carruthers, like an old bloodhound on a new scent, went baying after her shortcomings, leaving Andrew alone to choke down the rest of dinner. I could not have borne this twelve years ago, Jane told herself as she calmly finished her own meal, nodded serenely for the footman to remove their plates, and then took herself and Andrew from the dining saloon with something close to grace. Of course, twelve years ago Andrew was a motherless infant. Who would have credited him with the audacity to thrive?

Her mental commentary took her through the remainder of Lady Carruthers' scold, and allowed Andrew to escape to his own room. She sat mending in silence while Lady Carruthers cheated at solitaire, and sighed her way through the weight of the world and the general unfairness of things and people. Her eyes on Lord Denby's nightshirt, Jane knew her cousin's complaint so well that she only had to nod once or twice in the right place and murmur an occasional apology. And when Lady Carruthers had finished cataloging her complaints, there would be only the indignant slap of cards on the table.

When Lady Denby was silent, Jane waited for that relief to settle on her as it always did. To her discomfort, this night was different; she felt only dissatisfaction that she was so compliant, and that Lady Denby had been so pointed in her attack of Andrew at the dinner table. *I wonder if she is beginning to believe that her brother really does plan to die,* she thought as she knotted the thread, cut it, and shook out the nightshirt in her lap. *If my cousin is seriously listening to her brother, then she is plotting for Cecil, that blockhead. And if that is the case, then Andrew must be brought to ruin. Then what? Have we not endured enough trouble of late?*

The thought propelled her to her feet, which caused Lady Carruthers to look up in surprise from her contemplation of the game spread out before her. "You have not even called for tea yet," the woman said, turning even this simple request into an accusation.

"No, I have not," Jane said, stuffing her scissors into their case. "I leave that to you tonight, Lady Carruthers. I have not looked in on Lord Denby all day."

Jane left the drawing room without saying good night, and, she realized as she hurried down the hall, without her usual solicitous inquiry after Lady Carruthers, and her final, "Is there anything I can do for you?" which always brought some last-minute request, generally of a picayune nature which did nothing beyond reinforcing that tyrant's supremacy. *Please be better, Lord Denby,* she said to herself as she knocked softly on the door and let herself into the bedchamber. *I would like there to be some good reason for all the scolds I will get tomorrow morning because of my precipitate departure from your sister's presence.*

Stanton sat beside the bed, impeccable as always, but with closed eyes. To her amusement, the man in the bed put his finger to his lips. *I will take it as a good omen, my lord, that you have retained your sense of humor through another long day much like the one before it,* Jane thought. She tiptoed forward and placed the nightshirt on Lord Denby's bed.

"Shall I send Andrew in to wish you good night?" she asked as she always did, knowing the reply, but asking anyway.

"No, Jane, no," he replied as always. "You know my feelings on the subject."

"Yes, sir," she whispered back, wishing as always that he would not be so unkind as to consider his grandson a "subject," and not a little boy. "And how do you do, sir?"

He did as always, as far as she could tell, managing somehow to lie in bed straight like a soldier should, his bedclothes in order and not twisted about from the restlessness of disease or even discomfort. Blair had been like that, she thought suddenly, organized and military until the final month when he quit caring and gave his wounds permission to overrun his own superbly maintained defenses.

"I am going to die," Lord Denby told her, his voice less soft now and his eyes on the sleeping butler. "I wish you would believe me."

"We are all going to die, sir," she replied, surprising herself for the second time this evening with a touch more asperity in her voice than customary. "Mr. Lowe is convinced that you will feel much better if you take an interest in your surroundings."

I wish you would get angry enough at me to get out of bed, she thought, as the head of her family merely glared back. I can always rouse your sister to unimagined flights of fury with far less provocation.

"An interest in my surroundings? Mr. Lowe would have us believe that is the height of medical achievement?"

Well, I will take that as a slight improvement, she thought. You almost sound jocular, Lord Denby. I'm certain the mood will pass. "I suppose we are lucky, my lord," she replied, with just the hint of a smile. "Stanton, did we disturb you?"

The butler was awake now, and looking from her to his master. "Miss Milton, you don't disturb me," he said, the lightness of his words telling her that he had been listening to their casual banter. "My lord, didn't you tell me only this morning that there is no pleasure greater than waking to the sight of a sweet-faced lady?"

"It is merely Jane," Lord Denby grumbled, but Jane could hear that same lighter tone. Or do I imagine it, she asked herself. No, I will be the optimist this evening. He is getting better. Maybe tomorrow he will be more charitable about his grandson. Maybe something will be different.

"Do you know, Stanton, she almost smiled," Lord Denby said.

"I would smile more if you decided to throw back the covers tomorrow morning and send the footman running to the stable to call for your horse, sir," she said.

He only fixed her with his usual eagle stare. "Jane, you are the silliest member of this family. Go away now."

She left then, after a nod in the butler's direction, and the proper curtsy to the family head. I will try again tomorrow, she thought. Tomorrow has to be different.

And if it is not? She stopped in the hall and leaned against the wall, closing her eyes against the pain of the regularity of her days. This is a strange night, she thought. One would think when I try to jolly Lord Denby that I am only trying to jolly myself. One would think.

Andrew was already asleep when she let herself into his room. A reminiscence of the American war by one of Lord Denby's old comrades was lying open on his chest. With a pang that she had been too late this night to read with him, Jane took it carefully from him, marked his place, and stood looking down.

"I suppose you are too old to be read to," she said softly, "but, my dear, if everyone else must suffer me in this household, so must you, as well." She kissed him on the forehead, grateful that he was asleep and would take no exception to this small sign of her great affection. My dearest, have you any idea of the depths of my love? I scarcely do.

It was a thought she took to bed unwillingly, knowing that in the strange honesty of sleep and dreams, she would dream of his father with more regret than she knew she could ever acknowledge in the light of day. For all that it had been a good day—Lady Carruthers had been distracted from spending all evening complaining about Andrew, and Lord Denby seemed almost inclined to good cheer—she knew that she would awake far too early, and in tears.

She said her prayers on her knees as always, then laid herself down, already dreading the sorrow of her sleep and the pain each wakening brought, a private agony to be worked through before she dared show herself to anyone in the morning, a sweet-faced woman.

It is not winter I so much dread, she thought as her eyes closed in resignation more than sleep; it is every day.

Chapter Two

She woke too early, jolted awake and staring at something that was not there, alert to the smallest sounds. There were none, of course. She tried to relax, remembering a time—it had been years—when she could roll over, snuggle down deeper in the mattress, and return herself to slumber. As she lay there in the dark, Jane tried to remember just how long ago that had been. She thought first of the workhouse, something she never cared to reflect on, but which occasionally surfaced like a piece of shrapnel embedded deep in flesh that works its way to the top of the skin.

No, it was not the workhouse. She never woke there one second sooner than needed, mainly because even at age eight or nine—was it twenty years ago now?—she went to sleep exhausted and clung to every particle of sleep grudged to her.

The years in Dame Chaffee's School for Young Ladies? Jane almost smiled into the darkness, remembering her years of growth and how hungry she always was, even though Eliza Chaffee could never be accused of setting a stingy table. I have never wanted for appetite, she thought, though Lady Carruthers scolds when I take second helpings. It must be a particular trial to her that I never put on weight.

"No, indeed, not at the Dame's school," she said as she sat up in bed. "You were hungry, Jane, but you slept well." She never woke early at school, especially after she was seventeen and put in charge of the littlest girls who boarded there. She did smile then, remembering her cherubs, who were probably even now preparing for come-outs in London. Has it been so long? she asked herself with a pang. My dears, you all ran me ragged at Dame Chaffee's. Now I suppose you will dance merry tunes for husbands or lovers—perhaps both. I wonder, do you ever think of me?

Jane knew that no one did, and there was nothing in her thoughts of ill-use or self pity. Lady Carruthers had been telling her for years that she had nothing to recommend herself, and Jane could find no argument.

"Except for Andrew," she amended, as she always did. "Andrew would miss me." She sighed and closed her eyes as she wrapped her arms around her knees, perfectly comfortable, even if the sun was not up. That was it; from the moment Andrew had been put in her arms when she was almost eighteen, she never slept soundly again. It has been nearly twelve years, she told herself in dismay. *Am I so old? Better still, was I ever young?*

For all that she was the poor relation, she had believed Blair Stover—more properly Viscount Canfield from one of their family's numerous honors—when he had put his small son in her arms, winked at her in that way of his, and said, "Janey, just keep an eye on him for a little while, won't you? Lucinda claims that if she cannot bolt to Leeds to peruse the silk warehouses, she will dissolve."

Strange that after all these years she could remember that plea from Blair. Home to Denby from Dame Chaffee's and waiting for her first position in a household, she had been only too pleased to take the infant in her arms, enjoy the sweet smell of him, and watch him quite carefully during the day of Lord and Lady Canfield's expedition to Leeds, the first after Lucinda's confinement.

Jane looked out the window and was rewarded with the sight of dawn glowing dull red to the east. "Oh, it will rain today," she said out loud, straightening out her legs and tucking the coverlet tighter. "Andrew will be so disappointed."

She kept her gaze on the window, remembering that she had been sitting in the window seat at dusk with her knees up and Andrew, burped and fed, regarding her with sleepy eyes from his resting spot on her stomach, when a messenger arrived on horseback from Leeds. Not enough years had passed for her to forget Lady Carruthers' shrieks from the front hall, the long silence, and then the butler's heavy tread on the stairs.

"I put you right here on my bed, Andrew," she said, as though he were there. "You were six weeks old, and I laid you down right there, and opened that door to such awful news."

The butler had been unable to speak. She thought about him, dead these several years, recalling vividly the way his mouth had opened and closed, and the way he had crumbled into tears before her eyes. Never before or since could she remember a butler succumbing so entirely to grief, and as she sat in bed, the memory made her tuck the covers tighter.

When he could not speak, she shouldered her way past him and ran down the stairs where the footman—butler now—was attempting to revive Lady Carruthers. "Stanton," was all she said. She could still see Stanton gentling Lady Carruthers' head back to the floor and rising to grab her by the shoulders. Standing there so close to her, he told her of the contents of the note that rested by Lady Carruthers' hand, fluttering a little from the breeze let in by the still-open door.

She had heard him in shock and horror, and then released herself from his grasp to retrieve the note, as though she did not believe his words. She recognized her cousin Blair's untidy scrawl, and how the words "accident" and "near death" leaped out at her like imps.

I suppose I could have made some effort to revive Lady Carruthers, she thought, but felt no more regret now than she had all those years ago. Instead, she had pulled herself hand over hand up the stairs again, hardly noticing Lord Denby's rush down them, and then the sound of his carriage leaving the estate with the crack of a whip and the sudden grind of gravel on the front driveway. She had returned silently to her room and picked up the baby, as though to shelter him from the news that had changed his young world even before he was aware of it.

Messengers had come and gone those next two days, but she knew nothing of Andrew's young mother. Even then, Lady Carruthers had been disinclined to grudge her any civility, and she had not the heart to ask. She should have known that Lady Carruthers would later throw it back in her face that she was callous and had a heart of stone, but at the time, she only wondered and grieved deep inside herself, and held the baby.

Two days later, Lord Denby and his son returned to Stover Hall in a carriage swathed in black. Ignoring everyone, Blair had let himself into her room to hold out his arms for his son and sit with him in silence.

Jane got out of bed and lit the lamp on her bureau, welcoming the little light that forced the demons back into the shadows. She sat in the chair that Blair had sat in so many years ago with his small son resting along his legs. His voice a perfect monotone, he had told her how Lucinda, her arms full of packages, had looked both ways before attempting to cross the High Street, and then stepped out directly in front of a mailcoach.

"She knew it was there, Janey, she had to know," he had told her. "She was so happy to be back in the shops again! I think she just forgot what she was doing. I had turned to speak to an acquaintance. Janey, the last thing she said to me was 'Oh, I hope it will hurry by and not spatter me with mud.' And then she just . . . just walked in front of it!"

Watching the lamplight, Jane knew that no amount of years would ever dim the amazed grief in her cousin's voice. It had been forceful enough to wake his son, who stirred, made little mewing sounds, and then cried. She had taken the baby from him to caress into sleep again.

"Why did she do that, Janey? Did she just not realize? Was she that excited?"

She had never questioned the strangeness of Lady Lucinda's death, because she knew the impulsive nature of the dear creature who had captured her cousin's heart, and both of them so young. When the rumors started about suicide and worse, Jane had simply closed her ears; she knew the truth. Wrapped up in her excitement and pleasure, Lucinda had walked before she thought, and her fatal steps so many years ago had, in their own odd way, dragged them all after her.

The worse horror to Jane was that the poor woman had lingered in such pain for two days. His own voice destroyed with grief, Blair told her how Lucy had patted her deathbed, as though searching for her baby.

"Oh God, Jane, I remember how she used to wake up at night and pat our own bed, hunting for Andrew," he told her. "She laughed about it, and assured me that this must be an instinct mothers had. My God, Jane, she would not stop patting that bloody bed, and then digging into the mattress with her fingers! I will hear that sound forever."

And so I became your mother, Andrew, she thought, as she made her bed. She must have been a few moments later rising than usual, because she was still sitting on her bed in her chemise and petticoat when the second upstairs maid tiptoed in with the copper can of hot water.

"Miss Mitten, I wish you would sleep longer!" Becky said, as she set down the can.

It was their little joke, begun when Becky arrived from the workhouse as the new 'tween stairs girl, terrified and tongue-tied, even as she had come from there herself, all those years ago. No one else would bother to put the child at ease, so Jane did, with the result that led Lady Carruthers to announce with some satisfaction to dinner guests one night that, "It takes a servant to deal with a servant, I suppose." No matter; Lady Carruthers' words no longer flayed her, as they once would have. Becky could never do enough for her and Andrew, and that was enough result from a little kindness.

"You know I cannot sleep longer," Jane replied, providing her share of the tease. "You must wake up before you ever go to sleep, to catch me, my dear!" She stood up to twist her hair into its usual tidy knot. A pin here, a pin there; she scarcely had to look into the glass, except that Becky was watching.

The maid sighed, then looked around before she spoke. "I don't care what Lady Carruthers says, miss, *I* wish you would not wear those dratted caps, because your hair is so beautiful."

"Lady Carruthers says that I need the dignity," Jane said, as she settled her cap at its customary angle. "You are a dear, though."

She buttoned her dress thoughtfully, mindful of the mirror as she seldom was. It was nice hair, thick and black and so unlike Lady Carruthers' thinning brown hair. No argument with her figure, either; Lady Carruthers regularly cast her glances that could only be called envious. Or her grace; Blair had even once told his ill-starred Lucinda that she could copy his cousin's graceful way of getting from room to room without mishap to furniture or dignity. (Jane had scolded Blair then, reminding him that any woman seven months gone with child had gravity troubles that would baffle even Sir Isaac Newton.)

There was a time when mirrors interested her, and she thought of it now, that year she was sixteen and completing her final year before she began to teach the younger girls. Dame Chaffee's pimply son, home from Cambridge for some infraction, had composed a poem to her "eyes of sea foam green, sprung from limping pools where Venus rose," or some such nonsense created when he should have been repenting with his books. She was certain he meant "limpid," but at sixteen, a poem was a poem.

By seventeen she was too busy to think about poems, and

chose from then on not to give much heed to her own reflection, no matter how sea foam green her eyes, or even how glorious her skin. No more poems found their way under her door; she would have been certain they were intended for someone else, had one appeared.

But that was years ago, she reminded herself as she quit her room that morning. "No, no, Jane, do be honest," she said under her breath. "As of next January, you will be thirty, and it will be twelve years."

She hurried toward Lord Denby's room, intending only to look in, and see if he needed anything, but she could not face the smell of the sickroom. Instead, she stopped on impulse, looked around, and let herself into Blair's room.

To her surprise, the draperies were open. She almost exclaimed, before she thought, that it was too much light for an invalid, even if it was the October sun, which steadily lost its strength. She gritted her teeth and reminded herself that Blair Stover, Viscount Canfield, Lieutenant Colonel of the Sixth Foot, slept in the Denby family vault.

She knew that she could never perch upon that bed again, so she settled herself on the campaign chest at the foot of it. The bedding had been stripped from the mattress, and the whole thing covered with a spread, and she wondered why no one had thought to burn the wretched mattress and replace it with a new one.

Jane looked around, afraid for one irrational moment that nothing had been done since that horrid death in the early hours six months ago. She relaxed; all the bloody cotton wadding was gone, as well as the useless medications that had lined the table beside the bed, and the puny edition of *Rudge's Medicament* that she had ripped through frantically in those last moments of his life.

She knew the pillows were gone and burned, because after Mr. Lowe's early-morning arrival and official pronouncement of death (as though anyone could still be alive with what remained of his blood spread like a rug on the floor), she had marched downstairs with the sodden pillows in her arms, and quick-stepped them across the endless lawn to the fenced area where the gardener burned old leaves.

The door opened and she looked around in surprise. "Well, Stanton," she said, "I thought I had sneaked in here unaware."

Lord Denby's butler closed the door behind him and joined her on the campaign chest, obviously as unwilling to sit on the bed as she was, even after six months.

"What did you do with *Rudge's Medicament*?" she asked suddenly.

"Burned it, Miss Mitten," he replied just as promptly. He coughed. "Your . . . your fingerprints were all over it."

She nodded. Of course he had; she had even asked him about it before. How strange she must have looked when they found her there, Lord Canfield dead and her sitting there so calmly. She colored from the remembrance of her earlier panic that no one had seen, she who had not panicked for one moment when it mattered, especially when Mr. Lowe had told her exactly what would finally happen. He had been far too right, but this was nothing to be thinking of now.

"And how is our difficult patient this morning?" she asked as she headed to the door, allowing the butler no choice but to follow.

"Mr. Lowe is right now patting him here and there and checking for soundness of wind."

"It is so early!" she exclaimed. "We may have taken him on because of his enthusiasm for modern medicine, but I think Mr. Lowe tries too hard."

Stanton smiled, and she knew he appreciated her humor, especially when she knew how glum she must have looked sitting there on Blair's old campaign chest. "He knocked at the servants' entrance at an obscenely early hour and informed me that he had just seen the grocer's wife through a tedious confinement and would I mind if he killed two birds with one stone before he went home."

"Mr. Lowe is such an economy," she said with a smile of her own. "I cannot imagine that your master is being even slightly polite at this early hour."

"He is not," Stanton agreed cheerfully. "When our good doctor is through prodding him, I will sweeten Lord Denby with an offering from the publisher." He twinkled his eyes at her. "It arrived last night, Miss Milton."

"Oh, that will be just the thing!"

This is news indeed, she thought as she followed the butler to the breakfast room. A parcel wrapped in brown paper rested on the sideboard next to the bacon. She looked at it hopefully, noticing that the string was not bound tight. Drat, she thought, after another look. There is wax and a seal; we dare not.

She carefully avoided looking at the package as she put together her breakfast from the sideboard and then smiled her thanks to Stanton, who pulled her chair out for her. She tinkered with the bacon, then cleared her throat. She was rewarded with an eager look from the butler.

She selected her words carefully. "Do you know, Stanton, how disappointed Lord Denby would be if you took that package to him and it turned out to be the wrong book?" She knew better than to look him in the eye; they had conspired on too many previous occasions to have any scruples left. "These mistakes do happen, especially if it is a busy publishing house, I would suspect."

"It could send him into a deep decline from which he would never recover," he said.

Jane nodded. "And that would mean Cecil would encroach on the premises and likely go through all the silver drawers and get his slimy fingermarks on everything." (This for the benefit of the footman who stood behind her, and who she knew took especial pride in the Denby silver.)

Barnaby put down his napkin. "Reeves, I do believe we had better take a look at that package. If only someone here had a knife."

Reeves did. Two strides took the footman to the sideboard, and one quick motion from the knife that he always carried inside his livery rendered the package open. He handed the books to Jane. "Reeves, this is a relief to my heart," she murmured, still not daring to look at her confederate, who had occupied himself with straightening the plates.

She turned the pages, enjoying the fragrance of leather, and admiring the beautiful type. The backaches and eyestrain she had endured while copying the older essays weren't even a memory any more, not with this volume before her. "This is an achievement, Stanton," she said, handing him a copy. "Now officers everywhere can read about how to conduct themselves in foreign lands to the credit of the Empire. What a virtuous example for their men! I am proud to have been connected in some small way with its publication." She picked up another copy. "Of course, Lady Carruthers will claim all the credit and tell her friends that the idea of compiling her brother's essays was her idea, but we can still enjoy it right now."

After another moment admiring the book, and the reminder from Stanton that her egg was getting cold, Jane ate half of it. "Just think! This might be enough of a restorative to blast Lord Denby right out of that sickroom."

"And how would I earn a living then, Miss Milton?" said a voice behind her. "You know that my specialty of diseases of the rich enables me to labor among those not so blessed with the coin of the realm. Really, Miss Milton, where is your philanthropy?"

She turned around to see Mr. Lowe, who set his black bag on a chair by the door, nodded to Reeves, and began his own assault upon the sideboard. "There is always Mr. Butterworth next door," she reminded the physician as he sat next to her.

"Far too healthy to suit a doctor. In all his years in this district he has never been a patient of mine," Mr. Lowe said.

"Sir, how does our Lord Denby do this morning?"

The doctor made another face. "He is still determined to die, but I have yet to establish what his chief complaint is. Do pass the marmalade, Miss Milton."

She handed him the marmalade and another copy of the essays. The physician looked at the title on the spine. "*On the Deportment of Officers in Foreign Lands.* So there it is at last." He spooned marmalade onto his toast. "How fitting that England's most venerated warrior should pass on his advice to the officer corps." He ate his toast with complete satisfaction and reached for his teacup. "Jane and Stanton, this is your work, of course." He beamed at her. "My dear, if you even got one-tenth the credit for anything you have done around here . . ." His voice trailed off. He shrugged and took a sip.

"It is not credit we yearn for, Mr. Lowe," she told him, picking up the book he had set down. "I wish I could think of some way to use this book to propel him from bed."

Jane expected no answer, and she was surprised when the butler cleared his throat. "Beg pardon, Miss Milton, but what would you think if the publisher were to hold a small party here for Lord Denby? You know, a little affair to introduce his book."

"Such things are done in London, I believe," the doctor commented.

"But not here in Yorkshire," she suggested, her voice cautious

enough to disgust her. Lord, I am sounding like my cousin Lady
Carruthers, with a reason for every bit of laziness that afflicts
her, she scolded herself. "And yet, we could probably do whatever we wanted, to celebrate this publishing event," she
amended. "Who would stop us?"

"It could be a reunion, Miss Milton," Stanton said. "We could
invite all his comrades in arms from the American war. There
must be ten or twenty of them left." He opened the book and
thumbed to an early chapter. "Remember this essay, where he
exhorts all young officers to remember their own mothers and
wives, when quartering themselves in civilian homes?"

She remembered it well from transcribing it last summer, and
her own blushes of the story of Lieutenant Jeremy Dill, and his
unfortunate encounter with tar and feathers, all because the mis-
tress of the house where he was quartered had presented her
twelve-months' absent husband with a bawling, wriggling token
of British affection. With a smile, she turned to the essay's con-
clusion and cleared her throat: " 'And so, sirs, take advice from
Lieutenant Dill's cautionary tale and limit your interest in the
local flora and fauna to an occasional walk in the woods to cat-
alog the cedar waxwing, or hairy-beaked teal. Avoid, as you
would the plague, the walk upstairs to admire the early rising
buxom landlady!' " She looked at the physician. "Oh, dear, it
does seem out of place among his serious essays, doesn't it?"

"And all the more delightful, Miss Milton," said the doctor, as
he stood up and reached for his bag. "Particularly when one con-
siders Lord Denby's own exemplary character, and the particularly hilarious contrast that this represents. I think a reunion of
those American war veterans on the occasion of this book's release might be just the thing to interest Lord Denby in living
again. They will at least have a laugh or two." To Jane's dismay,
he put the back of his hand against her forehead and just as
quickly withdrew it. "And so might you, my dear. Let me know
what you decide."

The doctor nodded to them both and left. She finished her
breakfast in silence, not without noticing the butler's occasional
glances in her direction, and his inclination to be on the verge of
speech. "Do tell, Stanton," she said at last, exasperated with
him. "Am I becoming so forbidding that you cannot speak
around me?"

"You've been a trifle touchy for months on end now, miss,"

he said, then wiped his hands with a napkin. "Not that I do not understand but . . ." He sighed. "I think a reunion would be fun for all of us."

Jane regarded him in more silence, noticing how quiet the house was. With scarcely any effort, she could hear the clock ticking in the next room. "Perhaps you are right. Let us put it to Lord Denby this morning." She twinkled her eyes at him. "And his tart-tongued lazy relative!"

Chapter Three

"Lord Denby, we are the bearers of tea and toast and rather good news," Stanton said as he set the breakfast tray beside the bed.

To Jane's amusement, Lord Denby opened one eye and then the other. "A delegation," he murmured. "And of course, my own devoted sister."

Is there something dryer than usual in your voice, dear sir? Jane asked herself. Here Lady Carruthers sits, all solicitude, but how delicious it would be if you knew that she never exerts herself beyond arriving the moment before you wake up.

Jane had to turn her head to hide her smile. "Agnes, the doctor beat you in here this morning!" Lord Denby was saying as Barnaby helped him into a sitting position and layered pillows behind him. "Possibly in future, since I know your early-morning habit, you can save yourself the trouble of trying to appear so interested in my welfare."

Lady Carruthers gasped, but maintained her calm. "My, but we are in a good mood this morning," she managed to say.

"You, too, my dear?" he said, accepting a napkin from his butler. "Ah, thank you, Stanton. Agnes, do you ever just long for horse meat some morning? Or something equally mystifying, cooked over a campfire? I do. But, sister, here *we* have lovely, lovely porridge."

"I was referring to *you,* Charles," she said, with far less accommodation in her voice.

"Oh," he said. "I am never quite sure, what with *we—this* and *we—that.* My dear Jane, what is that book you have clutched to your bosom? Something I should see?"

"Indeed it is, my lord," she replied, handing it to him. "Stanton and I took the liberty of opening it." Her smile deepened, "to spare you the pain of a misplaced address."

"Both of you are conniving rogues," he said. To Jane's pleasure, Lord Denby turned the pages slowly. "One of Blair's better ideas, wouldn't you say?" he asked as he set the book by his side.

"He had them regularly," Stanton replied. "Even up to the last, my lord."

"A number of good ideas," she said.

"We have an idea, sir," Stanton began.

"I trust it will be nothing strenuous," Lady Carruthers said. She rose to fluff her brother's pillows.

"There is some exertion involved," Jane said, "but it doesn't follow that . . ."

"I am continually amazed that in all your years of service that you have never grasped the simplest notion of leaving people in peace," Lady Carruthers declared, two spots of color rising in her cheeks as though slapped on by imps. "How dare you?"

"Leave it alone, Agnes," Lord Denby said.

To her relief, the butler wedged in his conversation before Lady Carruthers could draw a deep breath. "My lord, we are suggesting a reunion of your brothers in arms from that American unpleasantness as a way to share the book with them, and renew old acquaintance."

Lady Carruthers gasped. "You have both lost your minds! I am still astounded that my dear brother did not perish from the exertion of compiling that book, and done while his son was dying!"

Very well, cousin, take an agitated turn about the room and throw your arms about, and sigh two or three times, Jane thought. Excellent, excellent. And *I* am astounded how little you realize your brother's disgust of theatrics. She looked at Lord Denby. "We could begin writing your old comrades now, and plan the reunion for spring."

"Only think how your brother officers would relish the opportunity to give proper attention to the one man in the entire army who has done more to improve the morals of the common soldier, than anyone since . . . since . . . oh, Hannibal at least," the butler concluded, leaning forward and speaking softly as Lady Carruthers paced about, her own audience.

Lord Denby laughed out loud, which caused his sister to stop in midstride and stare at him. "And who is so bold as to predict that I will still be alive when spring comes?"

"I am," Jane said. "You know it will be a treat to share this event with the men who helped you formulate your ideas that have since influenced an entire army. Only last night, Andrew was reading a reminiscence from . . ." She stopped, but not in time. I am a blockhead, she scolded herself, as Lady Carruthers jumped in with both feet.

"Andrew should be reading Greek and Latin with the other boys at the vicar's school, and not lurid stories about wretched Americans," Lady Carruthers snapped. "Jane refuses to listen, even though I have told her and told her."

"Jane, he is almost twelve and should have been at Latin School a year ago," Lord Denby said.

"My lord, the other boys are unkind. The rumors . . ."

". . . are only that," Lord Denby concluded, and his tone was final. "It will toughen him."

It would if he had another ally in this house besides someone of no consequence, she thought. "The term has already begun," she began, knowing before she started how feeble her argument was, but unable to resist the attempt. "Would it not be better to wait until . . ."

"Now, Jane, now."

"Yes, my lord." She rearranged the napkin to cover Lord Denby's nightshirt. "Sir, about the reunion."

"Are you determined to put me in an early grave?" Lord Denby asked, but Jane could hear the humor in his voice.

"The very idea!" Lady Carruthers said.

Oh, we play a wily game, Jane told herself as she glanced at Stanton. Lady Carruthers would not know humor if it introduced itself and gave her references. How delicious that she is going to lose this round, and doesn't even know it yet. "Actually, sir, I . . . we . . . thought rather to divert your mind from your ailments. And aren't writers of books vain creatures, who like to share their words with captive audiences? A reunion will trap them here."

He laughed again, took a bite of porridge, and made a face at his butler. "Stanton, cold porridge is a nasty business."

"Indeed it is, sir. I will get you some horse meat instead," the butler replied with a straight face, while Lady Carruthers gasped. "Cooked over a cedar chip fire. A reunion would be almost as good."

Lord Denby reached for his porridge again. "Very well, you two. I am convinced. Let us have a reunion." He took another bite. "Oh, do not puff up so, Agnes! It could be fun!"

Two steps forward, one step backward, Jane thought as she tightened her cloak around her. We will blast Lord Denby out of that bed yet, but Andrew must suffer the purgatory of Latin School among little boys full of their parents' rumors.

She had hoped for Andrew's company on the walk into Denby, but she was not surprised that he declined. "You are a better teacher, Miss Mitten," he said in protest when she gave him the bad news.

"I cannot teach you Latin or Greek," she had reminded him, "and you are nearly twelve." And this is not the issue, but I will not trample your dignity into the ground by reminding you of it, she had promised herself.

"Do you think . . ." he began, then stopped to pick his words carefully. "Are Lord Kettering's sons in that class?"

"I believe so, my dear."

"And the Castlereagh twins?"

"Probably. You are all of much the same age. Sir Harry's sons, as well."

"I had thought them already at Eton or Harrow," Andrew had said, after a long pause that she did not rush to fill.

We are so polite! Jane told herself as she hurried toward the vicar's house. Lady Carruthers is gloating over our discomfort, and we are trying so hard not to show it. And I am wondering, how many of those neighborhood rumors are ones that she sent spinning on their way around the district to damage the reputation of a poor woman long dead, and her child.

The thought was so distasteful that she stopped walking. What is the fascination people have with gossiping about others? she asked herself, and not for the first time. Why are some so busily engaged in bringing others low? "And those who cannot defend themselves," she said out loud, and quite unable to hide her disgust.

She could never put her finger on the rumor—where it had

started, and how it had grown into something so horrible that Andrew would all of his young life shy away from the neighbor boys who should have been his friends. Through the years, she wondered if she could have scotched it, but her own powerlessness made such an undertaking seem impossible. Had I said anything, no one would have believed me. There were enough rumors circulating about my own days in the workhouse, she thought.

As it was, when Andrew was placed in her arms, and then remained there because of the events of that awful day in Leeds, she had been far too occupied with Andrew to listen to idle rumor. When she finally settled into a routine with her new charge, Jane could only wonder at the baseness of some people, and the things they gossiped about when boredom overtook them.

She heard the rumor first from Stanton, who took her aside one afternoon while Andrew slept. His eyes averted, blushing with embarrassment, Stanton had stopped her on the landing and whispered what he had heard from the village of Denby, how word was out that dear Lady Canfield had run mad and stepped in front of the mailcoach to end her life. "That is absurd," she had whispered back, appalled by the suggestion.

"Miss Milton, it is worse," the footman had continued, taking her arm with no apology, so intent was he to convey the whole distress of the situation. "You will own that Lord and Lady Canfield did marry in some haste and that . . ." He paused and blushed some more. "Well, she quickly found herself . . . you know."

"I do know," she had told him, blushing herself, but relieving him of the necessity of spelling out how quickly—and with what shy delight—Blair had announced that his bride was increasing.

"And you know, of course, that Lady Canfield's family was much under the hatches until Lord Canfield married her and relieved their anxieties with a spot of ready cash."

"These things happen, Stanton," she had reminded him.

"I know, but, Miss Milton, she had had an earlier suitor whom she much favored. You remember?"

Of course she did, even though all anyone at Stover Hall knew was that he was the scoundrel who had caused Blair endless frets. "Why must my dear Lucinda allow that vagabond to pursue her?" he had protested to her one evening, when his own wooing appeared to be going nowhere.

She had been at Dame Chaffee's School as a teacher during Blair's courtship and only heard the anguished details in bits and pieces during holidays home, but she remembered well the day that Blair had written her to announce that Lucinda had consented to be wed. " 'Constancy appears to have won out over profligacy,' " he had announced in one of his infrequent letters to her. 'Lucinda will not allow even a month to pass now before we are married.'

She stopped again, remembering her conversation with the footman, how he had informed her, with more blushes and stammerings, that the rumor circulating about Blair's late wife included an unlooked-for pregnancy with the scoundrel, who had immediately disappeared, and how the family had rushed her into marriage with Blair to avoid scandal.

"That is preposterous," she had assured the footman, who could only nod his head in sad agreement. "I agree of course, Miss Milton, but that is the rumor. The upshot is that Lady Canfield was so overcome with shame at having duped her husband that she stepped in front of the mailcoach to put a period to her existence." He had finally turned mournful eyes upon her. "According to gossip then, the child is certainly not a son of Lord Canfield."

It was too astounding to believe, and in her own naïveté—she blushed even now to remember it—she had been quick to assure the worried footman that the whole evil-minded tale was so ridiculous that it would sink under its own weight. "You're good to tell me, Stanton, but do believe me when I say that in a fortnight, it will have been forgotten."

The bell in the church rang and Jane started walking again, intent on a moment in private with the vicar before duties at Evensong called him away. "I was so certain that no one could possibly be so small-souled as to believe such a taradiddle," she said out loud as she hurried toward the vicarage.

To her dismay, the rumor had only thickened like some evil pudding, wrapped in cheesecloth and allowed to steam until it was fully ripe. Blair was often away with the army, but when she took Andrew to church, Jane could not overlook how intently everyone gazed at the child. To her further dismay, Andrew did not appear to resemble Blair.

"And that is how a story starts," she told the vicar a half hour later over tea. "Since you are fairly new to this district, I wanted you to know why I have avoided placing Andrew in your charge for Latin School. They are only rumors, and not to be believed."

"Oh, I would never . . ." In a nervous rush, the vicar poured his tea. "And yet, Miss Milton, it is common knowledge in the village that Lord Denby himself treats his grandson with indifference, and that his sister's son goes about preening himself to become Lord Denby, when Andrew's claims are brushed aside."

"I know," Jane said, unable to finish her tea. "How sad it is that people who should know better have doubts."

"And you have none?" he asked, with all the tone of the confessional.

"None, sir," she said firmly. "Lord and Lady Canfield were quite happy with each other. Her death was just a horrible accident."

He waited a long moment to comment, and her heart sank. "It must be as you say then," he replied finally. "Still, the other boys only repeat what they hear." He looked at the clock then, and to Jane's critical eye, seemed relieved that Evensong was upon them and he had an excuse to hurry her along. "I can promise you that he will be treated equally and fairly in my classroom, but I cannot vouch for what boys will do, when the lessons are done."

"I suppose you cannot," she said, resisting an urge to grab him by his neckcloth and shake him until his prominent Adam's apple rattled.

"Miss Milton, I have a duty to everyone in my parish."

And that is the best I can get from that thin-livered vicar, she thought, cross with herself as she hurried home. "And even if every dreadful part of that odious rumor were true, why would anyone want to gloat over it and injure the heart of a little boy? I do not understand Christians!"

"Nor I, Miss Milton, but then neither did Nero!"

She stopped, turned around in embarrassment, and then smiled with relief. "Oh, thank the Lord it is you, Mr. Butterworth!" she exclaimed. "At least you will not tell the world that the old maid at Stover Hall talks to herself."

Whatever am I saying? she thought, surprised at herself. And here was Mr. Butterworth, slightly out of breath, carrying an umbrella that was now extended over her, as well. She looked at him in surprise, wondering why he stood there in the rain in his shirtsleeves and waistcoat.

She knew him well. His Christian name was general knowledge in the regions about because it was such an amusing one: Scipio Africanus. When she thought about it, she wondered what someone with a name like that would actually be *called.* Andrew had suggested "Sippy" once, and that had sent them both into such a fit of the giggles that Lady Carruthers had scolded her for an entire day on why women in charge of children should not be so silly.

Unlike some of the district's gentler folk, she never regretted his arrival in the neighborhood. When someone had purchased the Mott estate after old Lord Mott had been gone from it for a decade, Lady Carruthers had taken it upon herself to find out the origins of the new owner. The unwelcome tidings that he was a mill owner from Huddersfield—that most inelegant of towns—launched her into a month of spasms. Jane doubted even now, ten years after the event, that Lady Carruthers had entirely recovered. As it was, she certainly never extended an invitation to Mr. Butterworth to take his mutton with them.

"Miss Milton, won't you come inside until the rain lets up?"

She had a ready excuse on her lips—it was late, she was expected at Stover Hall—and she would have delivered it, if she had not looked down at Mr. Butterworth's feet.

He was wearing house slippers of such a virulent shade of lime green yarn that the colors almost spoke to her. "Sir, what on *earth* are you doing out here worrying about me, when your feet are . . . my goodness, Mr. Butterworth, but that is an . . . an exceptional color."

He merely smiled and offered her his arm, and for some unaccountable reason, she took it. He will catch his death if I make him stand outside in the rain and argue about whether I should come inside, she rationalized as she let him hurry her along the lane toward the house. Heaven knows he is not a young man, even if he is not precisely old, either.

He did pause for a moment to raise up one slipper from the wet gravel of the lane. "My dear niece made these for me last Christmas. My sister teases me that they were only just Amanda's practice piece, but I think them quite acceptable."

"They are, indeed," she replied, as she allowed herself to be led where she had never gone before. "Am I to assume that you saw me from your window and thought I needed rescuing so badly that you would risk a present from a niece?"

She had never thought herself a witty person, but Mr. Butterworth threw back his head and laughed, which meant that the umbrella went, too, and the rain pelted on her forehead again.

"Oh, I am a poor Sir Galahad, indeed, Miss Milton," he said, when he straightened the umbrella. "But yes, that is it entirely."

She smiled at him, thinking that no one in England looked less like Sir Galahad than Scipio Africanus Butterworth. She thought he might have over forty years to his credit, but she could not be sure. She was not tall, but standing this close to Mr. Butterworth, she felt even shorter than usual. He was taller even than Lord Denby, and massive without being fat. He could have been intimidating, had his general demeanor been less kind. Years ago over dinner at Stover Hall, Blair had declared that the Almighty had obviously broken the mold with the mill owner. She thought that unfair, and so informed her cousin with a vehemence that surprised her.

She thought of that now, as she found herself being led up the Butterworth lane to the front door. He was directing some pleasantry to her, but all she could see was what she always saw about him: the brownest of eyes with their glance of utter enthusiasm belonging to a far younger man. He also looked so benign, a trait she had never much associated with the district's general opinion of mill owners.

This perpetual air of good feeling had always amazed her about him and nothing had intervened in the ten years of their acquaintance to change that. Although Lady Carruthers had sniffed that their new neighbor "smelled of the shop" and that he would never be permitted to pollute the Stover environs, their equals in the village of Denby had not been so scrupulous.

Lady Carruthers had always blamed Blair for seeing that Mr. Butterworth was named to the board of directors of the town's charity hospital. "But, Aunt, he donates far more than anyone else, and twice as much as we do," Blair had pointed out, on one of his infrequent furloughs home from the army. "I'm too far away most of the time to do my duty, and do you know, I think that someone with management skills would be a welcome addition. Besides, he had added. "He isn't the sort of man I would like to argue with, for all that he is so pleasant."

That Mr. Butterworth proved to be a tremendous asset to the

board only increased Lady Carruthers' determination never to allow him to set one foot over the threshold of Stover. Their equals made up for her stricture, allowing the mill owner entrance into Denby society, or at least enough of it to suit themselves, and flatter the prevailing mood of equality that sometimes surfaced, even so far removed as they were from actual London politics. He came to christenings, kissed babies, donated generously to the parish at Christmas, let fox hunters ride over his extensive acres, and sponsored the annual hunt dinner.

She smiled, thinking of the innumerable times at those dinners and assemblies where Lord Denby would take Mr. Butterworth aside and argue that the lake on Mr. Butterworth's estate had been surveyed improperly and really belonged to Denby. It would do him good to argue with Mr. Butterworth again, she thought.

The lane was not long, and she wished it were longer, as she relished every step of the way to the door. For years she had admired the pleasant overhang of leaf and tree which was far more elegant than Stover Hall's approach, even if much shorter. The leaves were turning color now, and the whole picture lifted her heart. "I could never tire of this," she said simply, as she walked beside Mr. Butterworth. She could not help noticing that he had shortened his rather daunting stride to match her steps. "Do you know, sir, that Blair used to get so impatient with me when I had to skip to keep up with him?"

"Silly chuff," he said, with his usual air of complacency. "Why on earth would a man want to hurry along a woman of good sense? Savor the moment, I say."

She smiled at him, but he only sighed and tucked her arm deeper within the crook of his own. "Was a time, Miss Milton, that you would have laughed at a statement like that," he admonished.

"Nothing seems so funny anymore," she said finally, as she walked up the steps with him, comfortable in the thought that he would not scold her for melancholy, or command her to buck up and think of others. Thank goodness you saw me from the window, she thought.

And now Jane stood in front of his door, which was opened magically, as she had known somehow it would be, by a butler who must have had hearing acuity exceeding that of gossips or springer spaniels. "Excellent, excellent, Marsh," Mr. Butterworth was saying. "We'll be having tea, if you will be so kind."

She sighed and pulled her cloak tighter around her. ". . . I had tea at the vicar's, and . . ."

". . . and then you have not had tea . . ." he interrupted. "Tea and cakes, Miss Milton, the gooier the better, and you can tell me why you were pacing in front of my property . . ."

". . . Oh, I couldn't have been actually *pacing*," she interrupted, exasperated with herself.

"You were," he said firmly, ". . . talking only to yourself, when surely you must have some inkling that I have always shown myself willing to listen."

She stood there in the doorway, neither in nor out, struck by the truth of what he had just said. While he took her arm and encouraged her over the threshold, and then lifted her sopping cloak from her shoulders and handed it to the butler, she thought about all the times he had approached her at one village gathering or another. He was always willing to let her chat about Andrew, and never seemed bored by what Lady Carruthers sniffed at as her totally inadequate social sense. And always there were his wonderful brown eyes, and the excitement that seemed to jump from him like little sparks.

I have been missing you, she thought suddenly as she took his proffered arm again and let him lead her toward the sitting room. All the months of Blair's illness, then mourning, came to her now in a rush of feeling that brought unexpected tears to her eyes. She looked away in embarrassment.

"You may find a dry place in the laundry for Miss Milton's cloak," he was saying smoothly, as though she had turned away to admire his wallpaper.

"I'm not staying long," she told the butler, who only smiled and nodded and bore off her cloak anyway. "Even the butler does not listen to me," she said as Mr. Butterworth showed her upstairs and into the sitting room that overlooked the front entrance. She went directly to the window, hoping to give herself a moment to regain her composure. It would be dark soon, she thought, but with only a little sadness. Another year has turned. She heard someone open the door. "And when I turn around, I will see the footman bearing irresistibles. Ah, yes. Not a moment too soon."

With a smile, she allowed Mr. Butterworth to direct her to a chair and preside over the pouring of the tea, as though the house were hers. She knew his sugar requirements from the long practice of watching him at other gatherings, and added three lumps before handing over the cup and saucer. "Lovely china, Mr. Butterworth," she commented.

He accepted the cup from her. "It is nice, isn't it?" he agreed, then smiled at her. "Those of us who smell of the shop are conspicuous consumers."

It was their little joke through the years. She sipped her tea, savoring it before she even tasted it, because she knew from the servants that Mr. Butterworth only bought the best. She thought of Andrew, who, when he was five and introduced to Mr. Butterworth for the first time, sniffed the air around the man and announced to his astounded aunt, "He smells just fine. Far better than Lord Marchant."

"You're thinking of Andrew," Mr. Butterworth said, offering her a plateful of pastries which she had no intention of refusing.

"I am," she agreed, slipping off her wet shoes, which the footman promptly placed before the fireplace. She looked at her friend, admiring the tapestry of his waistcoat, and for the millionth time the wonderful scent of the lavender-noted cologne he wore. She had never imagined another man could have carried off that fragrance, but it never failed with Mr. Butterworth. She doubted he had ever smelled of the shop. "I suppose I always am thinking of Andrew, am I not, sir? Does this make me boring?"

He smiled and shook his head. "Only think how many times I have been diverted at Denby's social events by your breathless tales of teeth falling out, and limbs abused by tumbles from trees!" He leaned toward her, and she was struck all over again by his grace, despite his size. "If I were to have a wish, Miss Milton, it would be that you thought a little more of yourself, oh, just every now and then."

"That has never been a habit of mine," she reminded him. "You are kind to give me tea, Mr. Butterworth."

She was sure she would not have said anything more than that, if he had not looked at her in that interested way of his. If there was a kindlier expression on the planet, she did not know of it. His spectacles were slightly askew, as usual, and his eyes behind them invited disclosure. She had seen that expression at any number of gatherings, but there was something about it this time, that was taxing her to her heart's limit.

She set down her cup, and thought of all the times she had almost told him everything in her heart. Eat something, Jane, she thought in desperation. It is what you always do at gatherings when you invariably find him at your elbow, and then have to pry yourself away after an hour's conversation, before Lady Carruthers notices, and you know you have a scolding in store.

She reached for a pastry, determined to keep her own counsel, as she always did. Instead, she clasped her hands in her lap and took a deep breath, even as the more reluctant side of her nature tugged at her to stop. She cleared her throat.

"Mr. Butterworth, why must things be so difficult?" she asked, and then the words seemed to tumble out. "Blair is six months dead and Lord Denby is hovering on the brink of . . . of . . . I have no idea what! We're trying to arrange a simple reunion of his brother officers, and Lady Carruthers is making things so hard. She insists that if I am to actually win a point for a change and hold this reunion—which she is opposed to because it sounds like exertion—then I must give up something else, which, in this case, happens to be Andrew."

She glanced at him, alarmed at her hemorrhage of words, but his expression did not change. "To hold this reunion, apparently I must sacrifice Andrew to the vicar's Latin School, which is inhabited entirely by twerpy little heathens who only want to tease him about his dead mama, even though so many years have passed. Oh! It is all so impossible!"

Her voice rang in the tidy apartment, and she opened her eyes wide in amazement. "Did all of that just come out of my mouth?" she asked.

Mr. Butterworth nodded. "I believe it did." To her heart's relief, he sheltered her dignity by taking off his spectacles to clean them. He directed all his attention to this homely detail, and even hummed under his breath. "Do you feel better?" he asked after he replaced his spectacles. "If it will help I will challenge Lady Carruthers to a duel and shoot her dead. Ah, I was waiting for that smile."

He rose to stand by the window, rocking back and forth on his heels. She finished the pastry, wondering how low her credit was now, after such an outburst. Lady Carruthers is right, she thought mournfully; I have no countenance. "I know I have agitated you and I apologize," she said, her voice quiet. "Thank you for listening, though."

"Pretty petty of me," he murmured. "You and Andrew suffer, and I listen and offer pastry."

Surprised, Jane looked at him. I should leave, she thought, but joined him at the window. "I didn't mean to give you a fit of the megrims, too," she said.

"Just a little one, Miss Milton," he said after a long moment. "So there is to be a reunion?"

She knew a change of subject when she heard one, and grasped at it with both hands. "Yes! We—Stanton and I—did anyone ever have a better confederate?—are conspiring to draw together next spring Lord Denby's comrades from the American War."

"For the purpose of . . ." Mr. Butterworth began.

". . . of . . . of . . . oh, I suppose we want to blast Lord Denby out of bed, and into taking more of an interest in things again," she said. "After all, it was in America that he began focusing his thoughts on the conduct of soldiers in wartime occupation that have so signally affected all levels of military life."

Mr. Butterworth made a noncommittal sound in his throat. "So you feel that something extra is needed to prop up Lord Denby?"

"It is our hope," she said simply.

"But what if he really wishes to die?" he asked her. "A man ought to have some say in the matter, wouldn't you agree?"

Trust a mill owner to find the practical warp in this weaving, she thought. "Sir, he is only sixty!" she protested.

He smiled at her. "Cheer up, Jane Milton!" he said. "I think it is a wonderful idea, and I await the day . . . no, the very moment . . . when Lord Denby will throw back his covers, storm over to whatever social gathering where I am to be found, and assure me that a proper survey of my estate would return my lake to Stover Hall, once and for all!"

"It *has* been a while since he has bothered you about that, hasn't it?" she said. "It used to be his chiefest amusement." She shook her head. "You see how low we have fallen."

Mr. Butterworth was silent for another long minute, and then he clapped his hands together. "A reunion it should be then, Miss Milton. If he is in a sufficiently weakened state, he will be indifferent if you bring over the invitations so I can help write them, too." He touched her shoulder. "If you will not allow me to shoot Lady Carruthers, and the vicar, too, as well as all those pesky Latin scholars, we can at least gorge on pastry and umbrage!"

"And plot revolutions of our own. Done, sir," she replied, holding out her hand to him. He surprised her by kissing her fingers.

She had no time to be embarrassed, because then Marsh was there with her cloak, quite dry and even warm. She allowed the butler to swirl it around her shoulders, and then permitted Mr. Butterworth to escort her to the entrance. "I will be over soon then, once we have composed an invitation. At least one of the letters, maybe more, must go all the way to Canada, so we cannot waste a moment," she said.

"You know I would happily call for my carriage," he told her as they stood at the open door. "It hardly seems sporting to rescue you on the road in front of my house and then send you out again."

"Of course you can, sir. It is only misting now, and I do not require an escort. She pointed to his feet. "I would not have you utterly destroying last year's Christmas present."

He laughed in that hearty way of his that seemed to fill the room. "I forgot all about these!" He leaned closer, his finger to his lips. "Do not tell Lady Carruthers. She will have another charge about mill owners to lay at my door."

"That you are eccentric?" she teased, as the rain spotted his spectacles.

"That will be the kindest thing she says." He squinted into the rain, which was spotting his glasses. "Do tell Andrew that I will be happy to help him with his Latin, should he need some brushing up. Good night, Miss Milton, and thank you."

She tugged her cloak tighter. "For what, sir? For letting me speak my mind?"

"That is it, my dear Miss Milton. Someday—if you are really good—I will tell you what is on mine."

Chapter Four

They began the following Monday, after Andrew's incarceration in the vicar's Latin School. The way was paved by Lady Denby's abrupt departure for London and a visit with her son. "Or 'Cecil the Silly, the queerest leaf on anyone's family tree,' "

Jane told Mr. Butterworth as he sat her down at the desk, which he had moved to take advantage of the best morning light. "That was what Blair used to call him."

Mr. Butterworth stood over the wastebasket, shaving the last quill into a finer point. "I rejoice then, that my diminished status as mill owner in this fine neighborhood has kept me from claiming a closer acquaintance with so *rara* an *avis*."

She twinkled her eyes at him. "Oh, excellent, excellent man! We should have engaged you as Andrew's Latin teacher." She frowned. "I did hate to leave him there today."

"Buck up, Miss Milton," he said, his voice mild. "Growing up is difficult, but not impossible."

"For him or me, sir?" she asked.

He touched her shoulder. "Correct me if I am wrong, but since you have, in all but actual fact, been this lad's mother since almost his birth, we will allow some misgivings on your part."

With their heads together, she and Mr. Butterworth composed an invitation that was more of a letter, informing Lord Denby's former brothers-in-arms of the book, and his desire to see them all once more. "We don't want to be too morbid," Jane said. "They should be informed of his son's death—those who do not know—and our ardent hope that such a reunion will bring Lord Denby the cheer so sadly lacking from his life, of late." My life, too, she thought, swallowing down an enormous lump.

To her relief, Mr. Butterworth took the narrative from her. "We will invite them to spend a day or two here at Denby in . . . when do you think, Stanton?"

"The middle of April, sir," he said after a moment's thought, then looked at Jane. "What about it, Miss Milton?"

Thank you both again for sparing me, she thought. "That would be good. By then some will be returning from the London Season, and others will be heading for their summer pursuits." She glanced at the directions on the list. "And considering that this is October, it will provide adequate time for those far away to reply. Except possibly those here in Canada." She looked closer. "My word, Connecticut, United States?"

Stanton took the list from her and held it at arm's length to read the name where she pointed. "Edward Bingham, Hartford, Connecticut."

"After all these years, how on earth does Lord Denby have his direction?" Mr. Butterworth asked.

"Lord Ware—you remember Lord Ware from the funeral—has kept in touch with Bingham through the years," Stanton explained, handing back the list. "I suppose that is why it is among Lord Denby's directions. Apparently Ware, Lord Denby, and Bingham were lieutenants together before a change in orders sent Lord Denby as adjutant to Lord Cornwallis in Charleston. The other two sailed to New York to wait attendance on Lord Clinton." He accepted the quills from Mr. Butterworth. "We can assume that Bingham preferred life among the rebels."

"I don't know that it's worth the bother to write to him," she said as she opened the bottle of ink before her.

"Oh, I would," Stanton said. "He could be the most interesting participant of all, should he show up."

"Which is unlikely," Jane said. "Fresh ink, Mr. Butterworth? Lord Denby will have to repent some day of his constantly nagging about your lake, especially since you are treating us so well!"

The first letter did not suit her. "I do not want them to think we are on our last legs, Mr. Butterworth," she told him when she realized he was watching her hesitation. "I am determined that this is going to be a pleasant experience for Lord Denby. If only we did not have to keep reminding him how pleasant!"

He wouldn't hear of their return to Denby for lunch, cheerfully ignoring their protests at his efforts on their behalf. "Cook would be disappointed if I did not occasionally bring someone here to test a new receipt," he said, when she attempted a half-hearted argument.

Stanton did take his leave, but insisted that she remain. "Lord Denby expects me to serve him his gruel and tea, but you needn't dance attendance," he assured her.

"I could never protest too much," she said as Mr. Butterworth seated her in the breakfast room. The draperies were open to the warmth of the October sun. She accepted the dish that he handed to her, reminding herself that while others in the district had welcomed this good man to meals, and probably dined here, those at Denby had not, on the poor excuse that he "smelled of the shop."

Chagrined at herself, she looked about her at the wonderful ivy wallpaper that pulled the outdoors inside, and the expanse of glass that warmed the room, even in mid-October. She was comfortable right down to her toes with a sense of well-being that startled her with its suddenness. *This suits me far more than Stover Hall.* She picked up her fork. *No wonder it is so easy to speak my mind here.*

Mr. Butterworth lifted the lid from the soup tureen. "It is nothing more exciting than navy bean soup," he admitted with a shake of his head, as he filled a bowl for her. "We mill owners are too commonplace for hummingbird tongue."

She breathed deep of the fragrance of beans and ham. *I could almost eat,* she thought, even though she made no move to pick up the spoon. *I must, or he will think that I am an indifferent guest.* She stared at the soup, realizing for the first time that since Blair's death she had stopped eating luncheon. No one ever commented at Stover, but here there was only Mr. Butterworth, and she knew he was watching her.

He sat beside her instead of across the table. "Food's not much fun anymore, Miss Milton?" he asked gently, even as he took her spoon and put it in the bowl for her.

Even though she did nothing more than watch him stir the soup as though to tempt her appetite, she knew that somewhere a page had turned in her book of life. *I need a friend,* she thought suddenly. *Andrew is in school where I fear he will be mistreated, Blair is dead, there is a reunion to plan, I am nearly thirty, and I need a friend.*

"Nothing is fun anymore," she said. She hesitated, waiting for him to move away in embarrassment. After Blair's funeral she had tried to talk to the vicar, but he had been more concerned for Lord Denby. There was Andrew to comfort, made all the more difficult because she did not know how much comfort he needed. *Now here I am, sitting at my neighbor's table for a perfectly prosaic luncheon, and I am about to fly into a thousand tiny pieces,* she thought. *He will think I am a lunatic.* "Nothing," she concluded, and picked up the spoon.

"Then we will have to change that, Miss Milton," he said. "Now eat your soup and let us return to the invitations."

She did as he said, disinclined to say more, since she had already said too much. While Mr. Butterworth ate another bowl of soup, Jane worked her way around a strawberry tart. *I am so good at creating the illusion of eating,* she thought, observing to herself that she had quite mastered the art of plying knife and fork to no effect. *I need a friend,* she thought again, as she put down her fork. She took a deep breath.

"Mr. Butterworth, can we be friends?" She thought it would sound dreadfully forward, and cause her neighbor to fall off his chair. Nothing of the kind happened.

"We will speak our minds to each other. I find that agreeable, Miss Milton."

So it is, she thought, as she allowed him to pull back her chair. As he escorted her back to the desk in the sitting room, she was hard-pressed to recall a time when she had been on such terms with anyone. Only at the very end of his life had Blair entrusted her with his thoughts, and by then, they were only regrets. She sighed and turned her attention to the invitations before her.

Jane worked steadily, her mind on the task before her, until she noticed that the light was changing in the room. She put down the quill and flexed her fingers, then rose to look out the window.

"It is too early for Andrew," Mr. Butterworth said, and she realized with a start that he was sitting at the other desk in the room, one with pigeonholes and papers. She supposed that he had been there all afternoon.

"Do you run your mill from here?" she asked, not ignoring his comment, but interested in a desk so cluttered. There was a wooden basket marked "In," and another marked "Out," and a large inkwell. "I have never seen anyone engaged in actual business before," she said.

He gestured at the desk. "Then look here, Miss Jane Milton. My brother-in-law is my junior partner. He sends me weekly reports and only troubles me with those problems he cannot solve himself. I go home one week in the month. In this way, we have managed to keep our crass commerce flowing through the empire."

"Why do you live here?" she asked, coming around the desk to look over his shoulder. "I should think it would be easier for you to be closer to Huddersfield."

"I choose it," he said, closing the ledger in front of him. "The village is quiet, the air is better, and I choose it."

"What is that like, I wonder," she said. "To choose something, I mean, and then to do it?" she added, when he looked at her in surprise. "And do not be so astonished! I doubt one female in three has much choice in anything she does."

She thought he would laugh, but he only frowned, and then went to stand beside the window. "Now you are watching for

Andrew, sir," she accused him. "He already knows that I am a worrywart, Mr. Butterworth, but I do not think he suspects such a thing of you. Come away, sir!"

He shook his head, but said nothing, and she was content to watch him there. She was deciding that he was handsome in an impressive sort of way when he turned to her and gestured toward the door. "My dear Miss Milton, let us rummage about belowstairs and locate some refreshment for Andrew when he arrives. If I remember right—can it be over thirty years ago that I was ten?—Latin is a fatiguing business."

The kitchen was quite the place she thought it would be, with a cook up to her elbows in flour, and the scullery maid paring potatoes. What surprised her was the light in the room, let in by large windows and accentuated by pale yellow paint. "Such a pleasant kitchen," she whispered to him. "Sir, did you do all this?"

Mr. Butterworth nodded, and smiled at the scullery maid, who was beaming at him and sitting up straighter as she worked on the mound of potatoes. "Moira, you are an expert with that knife," he said, and then, "Mrs. Chatham, do your exertions point to kidney pie for dinner? You are a pearl beyond price."

Jane tried to imagine Lady Carruthers even going belowstairs and then speaking to a scullery maid, and could not. *Heaven knows she did not speak to me*, she thought, watching while Mr. Butterworth engaged his cook in earnest conversation. He was joined by the butler and footman, who each seemed to have a morsel to contribute. *I wonder if it is like this belowstairs at Stover*, she thought.

After a few minutes, everyone returned to their duties. Jane picked up the tray, smiling her thanks to Mrs. Chatham. Mr. Butterworth held open the door and admonished her to mind her steps as she walked upstairs. *I wonder if he even knows about me*, she thought, then decided to plunge ahead.

"Did you know, Mr. Butterworth, that I came to Stover Hall through the scullery?" she said as she set the tray on the table in the sitting room. "In a letter, Lord Denby told his sister—Lady Carruthers, of course—to retrieve me from the workhouse, but he neglected to add that I was meant to be upstairs, and not belowstairs, so down I went."

"I've heard those rumors," he replied, giving her his full attention, in that way of his that she always found perfectly gratifying. "If I may ask, how did you find yourself in a workhouse in the first place?"

"No one has ever wanted to know," she said, wishing that her uncertainty did not show. "Are you certain . . ."

"I am certain, Miss Milton," he said. "In fact, I am firm upon the matter."

"My mother was a Stover on a modest branch of the family tree. She made an improvident marriage. My father left us when I was five." My, I sound so casual, she marveled to herself. "After Mama had contrived and schemed and then sold everything of any value to keep us afloat, she locked the door and we walked to the Leeds workhouse."

"Why did she not apply to her Stover relatives instead?" Mr. Butterworth asked, seating himself beside her.

"Pride, sir. Her father had made no bones about his distaste for the marriage, and on the Milton side, I can only assume that there were grave reservations, as well. And I suppose people said things they could not retract."

As she watched his face, she could not overlook his expression. "People do that, don't they?" he commented, after a moment.

"Have you ever been in a workhouse, Mr. Butterworth?" she asked suddenly.

"No," he said, and he looked at her in that kindly way that had sparked her earlier truth telling. "I cannot imagine that it was a place for children. Were you separated from your mother?"

She nodded, and found herself hardly able to speak of it, even after so long. "I suppose that is one reason I have coddled Andrew all these years," she said finally. "Every child needs a mother. I saw her once a week." She paused a moment, then spoke when he looked at her. "She died there when she was 27. Her grave is number 248."

"I do not understand," he said.

"No one gets an actual headstone, Mr. Butterworth," she explained, pleased with her control. "That would be an expense."

Mr. Butterworth nodded, in a way that she found most sympathetic, and yet without embarrassing her, then turned his attention to the window, where he had taken himself. "But why the scullery, Miss Milton?" he asked.

I shall pick my way delicately here, she thought, and I have no actual proof that Lady Carruthers meant harm. "Lord Denby was away with his regiment in Canada when he heard the news of my mother's death. He has always taken seriously his duties as head of the family." Jane sighed, joining him at the window. "I do not believe his sister precisely understood his orders about retrieving me from the workhouse, and so I went to the scullery."

She allowed herself a glance at his face, and was surprised to see such an expression of dismay. "Mr. Butterworth, it was not onerous, not after a workhouse!" Jane you silly, she scolded herself, that bit of artless conversation did nothing to brighten Mr. Butterworth's day. "This will amuse you, sir," she added. "That first night when I scraped the pots, I saved the burned-on bits to eat later." She stopped as his expression of dismay deepened. "I . . . I only meant it to amuse you, sir," she concluded.

She stared out the window, too, remembering how Stanton, the footman then, had pitched into the other maids when they found her little stash of leavings and teased her. I have never thanked him for that, she thought. He would only be embarrassed if I reminded him now.

"Damn," Mr. Butterworth said.

She had never heard him swear. Startled, she looked where he pointed. Andrew came up the lane from the high road, head down, eyes on the gravel bits that he kicked along in front of him. "I don't think he had a good day," she said softly. "Oh, Mr. Butterworth!"

He said nothing, but put his hand on her shoulder and kept it there as they stood in the late-afternoon shadow at the window and watched. I wonder what taunts he has endured today, she thought, inclining her head toward Mr. Butterworth's hand until she remembered. I think I know how cruel children can be.

She knew that Andrew must not see her own distress, and steeled herself to greet him cheerfully. "I will not be a ninny about this," she murmured.

Mr. Butterworth tightened his grip on her shoulder. "Good show, miss—have I heard him call you Miss Mitten?"

She nodded. "You have," she replied, her voice soft. She looked out the window again. "Oh, Mr. Butterworth, I think I am going to cry!"

"Mustn't do that, Miss Mitten," Mr. Butterworth said. She didn't look at him, because to her ears, his voice didn't sound all that calm either. He removed his hand from her shoulder, his hesitation almost palpable to her. "What . . . what would Lord Denby do if you refused to return Andrew to Latin School?"

She stared at him, her tears forgotten. "I dare not disobey!" she declared. She heard the front door open, and then close quietly. "Lord Denby would . . . would . . ."

"Would what, Miss Mitten?" the mill owner asked as he crossed to the sitting room door. "With your skills, you could easily find other employment, should he ask you to leave." He looked at her, his hand on the knob. "Someplace where you needn't keep wearing black, and where there isn't still a black wreath on the door, six months after the fact."

She could think of nothing to say, and still he regarded her. "Or perhaps *you* prefer this, Miss Milton."

"Actually, I have never thought of it that way," she said, when he appeared to expect some conversation from her, even as his hand rested on the knob and she could hear Andrew's footsteps on the parquet. "I could never leave Andrew!" she burst out, then put her hand to her mouth.

If the mill owner was surprised at her outburst, he didn't show it. "Take him with you," was his mild comment as he opened the door. "Andrew, come in! From the looks of things, your day has been a grind. Oh, laddie, no tears now!"

After a silent dinner that evening with no company but Andrew, who wouldn't even look up from his plate, Jane continued to sit at the dining table. She knew Andrew was watching her, but to her further dismay, he did not fidget. He sat as quietly as she, resignation announcing itself in every line of his body.

"What happened, my dear?" she asked finally. She was not sure that he would answer. After his tears in Mr. Butterworth's sitting room, they had walked home in silence. "I want to know," she said, and folded her hands in front of her on the table. "In fact, I insist upon it."

He looked at her, and she could tell she had surprised him by the unexpected iron in her voice. "I didn't do too badly, Miss Mitten," he said, his voice so low that she had to lean forward to hear him across the table. "I think I could almost like Latin."

"Mr. Butterworth does," she said, striving for calmness in her voice. "He claims to still have his Latin texts and glosses from his grammar school days."

Andrew got up from his chair and came to sit beside her.

Wordlessly, she put out both her hands to him and he grasped them. "Miss Mitten, I was afraid at first, but nothing happened." He shuddered, and tightened his grip on her hands. "Really, I did, and then when I went to the door to leave, Lord Kettering's son—the one with spots and bad teeth—told me to look both ways when I crossed the street so I wouldn't get squashed flat like my mother."

He started to cry and Jane pulled him onto her lap, holding him close to her. "Everyone laughed," he said when he could speak again.

"The vicar did nothing?"

Andrew shook his head. "He even smiled before he turned his head away and pretended it didn't happen." He sighed and leaned against her. "Miss Mitten, do you ever hear people laugh, long after they have stopped laughing?"

"Oh, yes," she said, remembering all over again the event in the scullery she had described only that afternoon to Mr. Butterworth: the maids' laughter as they uncovered her pitiful handkerchief of scraps. She thought of the butler as well, and kissed the top of Andrew's head. "But I had a champion, my dear, and he made them stop."

"I wish I had a champion, Miss Mitten."

My dear, you do, she thought, although I have been too timid by half. She kissed Andrew again and then pulled him gently away from her so she could see into his eyes. "Andrew, you are not returning to the vicar's Latin School," she said. "I will arrange something else. Wash your face now and get into your nightshirt, and I will come up and read to you."

She could almost feel the weight lift from him and sink onto her own shoulders. "I will blame you entirely, Mr. Butterworth," she murmured out loud as Andrew left the room. "And if I lose whatever standing I have in this house, you will have to find me a situation elsewhere."

She sat another quarter hour in the dining room, watching the hands of the clock and wondering why she had promised any such thing to Andrew. She rose finally, and then sat back down again because her ankles seemed weak. "It is merely your spine, Jane Milton," she told herself. "Push off now." She walked slowly upstairs to Lord Denby's room.

Stanton answered her knock. "Is something wrong, Miss Mitten?" he asked, and she knew that even the slow walk from the dining table to Lord Denby's chambers had not erased the unease on her face.

"No, Stanton, nothing is wrong," she replied. "Well, there is a small matter, but it is something I have determined to ask . . . no, to tell . . . Lord Denby, and it will only take a moment. Is he still awake?"

The butler nodded. "He was looking at the book again." He shook his head. "Do you know, he reads that first essay over and over. You know, the silly story about Lieutenant Jeremy Dill and the amorous landlady. I wonder why?"

"I cannot imagine, Stanton, particularly since his own life is so spotless of moral wrong," she replied. "Except . . ." She could not finish, wondering what to make of a man who believed rumors about his own grandson.

She took her accustomed place beside Lord Denby's bed, grateful again that his sister had gone to London. If only she will stay away until Christmas, Jane thought, as she watched Lord Denby, who lay before her with his eyes closed. She could not help but think of Blair, and the days and nights she had sat at his bedside. I do not care for deathbed watches, she decided.

"Lord Denby?" she began. "I have something particular to say to you."

She did not know if he slept, so she kept her voice low. He opened his eyes immediately.

"You don't have to shout, Jane," he said.

"I'm not shouting, my lord," she replied, almost more amused than afraid. "I am merely speaking firmly."

"Well, you don't do that very often," he retorted.

She took a deep breath. "Lord Denby, I have decided that Andrew is not returning to the vicar's Latin School. The other boys were rude to him about his mother, and I do not care if you think I am coddling him, but he will not be sent back for more abuse, not from little twerps who only repeat the gossip their parents inflict upon them." She would have said more, except that she was out of breath. She sat back, amazed at herself and afraid to look at Lord Denby.

When a minute passed and he said nothing, she looked at him and braced herself. To her further amazement, his eyes were closed and there was even a peaceful expression on his face. Dear God, I have killed him, she thought in horror as she reached for his wrist to take his pulse.

To her relief, it beat quite steadily. She cleared her throat. "I thought you might have some commentary on the matter, Lord Denby," she said at last, when he seemed disinclined to contribute anything.

He opened his eyes again. "I don't know why you should expect such a thing, Jane, since you appear to have reached a decision and have only come to inform me of it."

She glanced at Stanton, who appeared as surprised as she was. "You're not going to insist that I send Andrew back?" she asked, when she could not contain herself.

Lord Denby shrugged. "You would probably only remove Andrew again, and then march in here with another ultimatum. Do as you wish, Jane, but I do expect Andrew to be ready for Harrow in a year or two."

Don't stop now, Jane, she thought. "I do not think it will be Harrow, my lord," she said. "Lord Kettering's horrid sons are going there soon enough. Imagine the tales that would precede Andrew's entrance! We will think of something else, my lord."

"*You* will," he said in that tone of voice she recalled from better times, then closed his eyes again with a finality that she could not ignore, not even in her present state of command.

I suppose I will, she thought, as she smiled at Stanton's wide-open eyes and let herself quietly from the room. And now I must write a letter to Mr. Butterworth, telling him that I have taken his advice and done something different, and as a consequence, he should drag down his Latin glosses from the attic. "After all, Mr. Butterworth," she said as she pulled her chair up to her writing desk and straightened the sheet of paper in front of her, "you have far too much leisure for a man your age."

Because it was only nine o'clock, she summoned the footman and directed him to take the letter next door. "You needn't wait for a reply," she told him, smiling to herself.

All this decision in one day has quite worn me out she thought later, after listening to Andrew read, and then hearing his prayers, which included Mr. Butterworth this night.

"I don't have to go back?" he asked her, anxious, as she closed the draperies.

"No. We will continue at Sunday services, of course, but you needn't have another thing to do with the vicar," she said. She paused at his bedside. "I do want you to keep it firmly in your mind that what happened to your mother was a terrible accident, and nothing more. If you are teased, you will have to learn to bear it."

She kissed him good night and went to her room. There now, Mr. Butterworth, she thought, I have done some different things today. I do not know how pleased you will be that I have all but ordered you into being Andrew's Latin teacher. See what happens when I speak my mind?

Chapter Five

If she had ever had any doubts, as she stood at Mr. Butterworth's front door with Andrew the next morning, Jane knew that Lady Carruthers was entirely wrong about the mill owner. Sir, you are a wonderful gentleman, she thought as she looked at the white square of paper tacked to the door.

"It is in Latin, Miss Mitten," Andrew said. He looked at her with some uncertainty. "Do you think he means for me to translate it?"

"I am certain that is what he means, my dear," she replied. "Find your gloss."

She sat on the front step as Andrew thumbed through the book. She lifted her face to the wind that blew down off the Pennines behind them, scattering leaves along the immaculate lane. She thought of the invitations meant for Canada and the United States, sent on their way that morning with a frank from Lord Denby. She would compose the others during the remainder of the week; they had not so far to travel.

Already she was pleased with herself over the invitations. When she went to see Lord Denby that morning, he was propped up in bed and reading the newspaper, something she had not seen him do in several months. She hoped he would ask her what arrangements she had made for Andrew, but he did not. His curiosity was directed toward her correspondence, and she told him of the letters going to his former companions now in North America.

"Bingham, too?" he had murmured when she told him. "I doubt he will come."

He made no more comment, until she was ready to leave the room. "You're returning to Butterworth's today? And with Andrew?"

There, sir, you *are* interested, she thought with a feeling close to triumph. "Yes, I am. He offered to teach Andrew Latin, and I know what an economy that is. Perhaps even Lady Carruthers will not object when she returns."

"Of course my sister will," he had replied, and rattled the paper for emphasis. "If we choose to tell her."

Andrew chuckled, and she glanced at him over her shoulder. He gestured at the gloss, then tucked it under his arm with his other books. "Miss Mitten, it says we are to come right inside without waiting. " *'Sine esperando,'* or something like."

When they came inside, Mr. Butterworth's butler bowed and handed Andrew a card on a silver salver. Mystified, he picked it up and then grinned. "Better hand me the gloss again, Miss Mitten," he said as he opened the note. He was so intent on translating this next passage that he hardly noticed when she peeled his overcoat off him and handed it to Marsh with a smile. The butler unbent enough to remark, "I am not sure, Miss Milton, who is enjoying this more, Andrew or Mr. Butterworth."

Or me, she thought, as Andrew exclaimed in triumph and hurried to the library. She followed. Mr. Butterworth sat at the desk with a Latin book open in front of him. By the time she arrived, Andrew was already seated down in the chair opposite. The mill owner nodded to her and directed his pupil to open the book in front of him.

"Miss Milton, we will dismiss you to the sitting room, where you can continue those invitations." He smiled at Andrew. "Lord Canfield here and I have a rendezvous with Julius Caesar in Gaul. Do excuse us."

With a smile, she let herself out of the library and was soon seated in front of a pleasant fire, where the invitations awaited. She was deep into them an hour later when Mr. Butterworth joined her.

"I am nearly half done," she announced, putting down the pen to flex her fingers. "Sir, I suspect you went to some trouble to find a dip pen. I hear they are all the rage in London."

Mr. Butterworth looked over her shoulder. "Writes well,

doesn't it? What a modern idea, and how smart I am. I shall order a dozen more for my mill offices." He bowed. "Madam, I am a selfish beast. Feathers make me sneeze, and I am lazy enough to put you to work, testing the newfangled invention for me."

Jane touched his arm. "You are nothing but kindness, Mr. Butterworth." She hesitated, then looked in his eyes. "I do not know how Andrew and I can intrude upon you like this for his education. I will simply have to think of something else."

He sat down in the chair that was pulled up beside the desk. "You will do nothing of the kind, Miss Milton. Actually, you have solved a dilemma of my own."

"That cannot possibly be the case, sir," she protested. "We are nothing but a burden! I plop my troubles in a messy little pile at your feet, and you ply me with lemon curd pastries and tempt me with modern pens."

The mill owner smiled at her, and she wondered how Lady Carruthers could ever think him common. He did look especially fine in that plain dark suit. She wasn't so sure about the waistcoat, but decided that bright green paisley may have been the exact touch. She took a deep breath; she could never fault his cologne.

"My dear Miss Milton, I could not be more serious about this. I have recently purchased another mill and . . ."

"Mr. Butterworth, we are twice the burden then!" she exclaimed in dismay, her well-being gone as quickly as it had come.

He laughed and took hold of her hand, giving it a slight tug before releasing it. "Miss Milton, the only thing that keeps you from being by far the prettiest woman in this district is your disturbing tendency to frown!"

And my almost thirty years, she thought, pleased in spite of herself, and hoping that she was not so simple as to blush at compliments from a man almost fifteen years her senior. "Try as I might sir, I cannot think how the addition of another mill, plus a schoolboy needing the remedy of Latin can possibly lighten your work," she said. "Perhaps I lack sufficient imagination."

"Yes, Miss Milton, I do fear your imagination has been stifled by too much confrontation with Lady Carruthers," he replied. "There! I was hoping you would smile!"

"How can I do otherwise, when you are so preposterous?" she asked.

"It is this way, my dear. The addition of another mill in Huddersfield means that I finally require the services of a secretary here. Now, do not frown! I have needed a secretary for several months, and have been too poky to stir myself about it until now."

"You are so busy," she began, but even to her ears, it sounded like a weak protest.

"Busy is what I like, Miss Milton, and you know it," he reminded her. "My secretary will handle any additional correspondence that the new mill generates, but I am certain that he will have extra time." He leaned closer and looked into her eyes, as though daring her to animadvert. "That was why I put off transferring Joseph Singletary here. He clerks in my other mill in Huddersfield. I happen to know that he took honors in Latin at school, and is just the tiniest bit bored by only secretarial duties. Andrew and Caesar will be just what he needs to round out his week."

"He should be on his way to Oxford then," Jane said.

"And he will be, when I figure out a way for one of his distant relatives to leave him a nest egg." He leaned back in triumph. "It takes even me time to think of everything, Miss Milton. Joe can handle my additional correspondence, which will not be onerous, and tutor a small boy who will find him quite a remarkable fellow, and far more fun than a mill owner whom he probably thinks is old enough to have accompanied Caesar's legions. Now you may applaud my good sense!"

She laughed and clapped her hands. "How will you create a distant wealthy relative, Mr. Butterworth? Mr. Butterworth?" She looked at him in alarm, surprised at the sudden tears in his eyes. "Are you well?"

He took her hand again, and could not speak for several moments. She wanted to dab at his eyes with her own handkerchief, but felt shy. Besides that, he was holding her hand, and she had no urge to pull her fingers away.

In another moment he was smiling at her. He released her fingers. "Miss Milton, I have not heard you laugh in months. That is all," he said as he stood up and moved to his own desk across the room. "If that is what a secretary and newfangled dip pens will do, why, we will plan surprises every week!"

"Thank you," she said simply. "I suppose now you will tell me that you will discover a distant nabob dangling from Mr. Singletary's family tree, or a buried Caribbean treasure, or Revolutionary War bonds next fall when the Long Term begins."

She knew he would smile at her own wit again, and he did. I think that exposing your own generosity is more than you care for, my dear Mr. Butterworth, she thought. I can keep this light. She folded a paper and sailed it across the room to him. He caught it in midair and returned it the same way.

"You are almost correct, Miss Milton," he said as he opened the ledger before him. "Mr. Singletary—who by the way will arrive by the end of the week—will indeed find good fortune by September next, and so will Andrew, if you will permit me some entanglement in his affairs. I believe that your charge will discover St. Stephen's in Scarborough far more to his liking than Harrow. It will not contain those little twits currently applying themselves at the vicar's Latin School, who are probably more than eager to spread rumors enough to blight Andrew's existence. St. Stephen's is *my* school; I am a trustee, and it will be an economy over Harrow, so Lady Carruthers will dare not complain."

"Why are you managing Andrew's affairs, sir?" she asked suddenly. "No one has ever taken an interest in them before."

He opened his eyes wide and stared at her until she laughed again. "Miss Milton, you *are* going to tell me what you think!" he declared. "I thought that you would retreat and become missish after our little heart to heart yesterday. Thank God I was wrong."

"You were wrong," she agreed. "After I told Lord Denby what I thought last night, and sent that note to you, I knew that I had no shame left, sir!" This is the right touch, she thought, pleased with herself. And my word, but it feels good to say what I think. I shall continue. "You are amazing, sir."

He settled back in his chair with a smile on his face as he directed his attention to the ledger. "Amazing, eh? Now, hush. I have mills to run."

She straightened the paper missile on her desk, dipped the pen in the ink, and wrote, "Thank you!" on one of its wings. When it dried, she sailed it back, enjoyed his chuckle, and turned her mind to the reunion invitations.

It came sailing back with "You're welcome," written on

the other fold. Impulsively, she blew a kiss in the mill owner's direction, felt the warmth of his laugh, and returned to the invitations.

They were done by the end of the week. She had no more excuse to visit, and so she told Mr. Butterworth as she sealed the last invitation and waited for the wax to cool.

"I refuse to accept that, Miss Mitten," he said, with typical good humor. "Joe Singletary is arriving tomorrow or Sunday, so you must return on Monday to meet him, and see if he passes muster."

"Very well, sir," she agreed, admiring the invitations. "Thank you for the use of your lovely sitting room, the extravagant luncheons . . ."

"I must eat, too," he interrupted, and winked at her.

". . . the dip pens, fresh ink and paper," she continued, then clasped her hands in front of her. "But I will wager you have no idea what else has happened this week, sir."

He closed the ledger in front of him with a certain finality. "You have decided that I am a superior man," he quizzed.

"I already knew that, Mr. Butterworth," she said serenely, and felt a certain delight when he blushed. "Lord Denby is starting to grumble and complain because I was not at Stover Hall this week." She gestured to the invitations. "What is even better, he began complaining again about you and your ham-handed, mill owner's way of buying this estate right out from under his nose ten years ago!"

Mr. Butterworth rolled his eyes. "After it had sat vacant for years and sprung more leaks than an East India merchant's dinghy!" He rubbed his hands together, and she almost laughed at the look in his eyes. "Did he squawk about the survey and assure you that he was robbed of my pretty little lake?"

"The very thing, sir," she replied, looking around for her reticule and bonnet. "Stanton is so proud of himself and his reunion idea. He is practically crowing about the fact that Lord Denby is grouchy now and taking a real interest in things again. Even you."

She found her reticule, and Mr. Butterworth retrieved her bonnet from the bust of Julius Caesar where Andrew regularly hung it each morning. He set the bonnet carefully on her head.

"Actually, my dear, if we are to be plain speakers, I suspect that Lord Denby is a grouch because you are not there."

"That is a strange notion," Jane contradicted as she tied the ribbands. "No one ever misses me." No, that is not true, she thought. They miss me if there is something disagreeable to do, like sitting up with Blair while he lies dying. She frowned into the mirror over the fireplace as she realized that she had not thought about Lord Canfield for an entire week. How odd. "They do not miss me, Mr. Butterworth," she repeated.

"I cannot agree," he said. He handed her the invitations and walked with her to the library. "I'll wager that you are the heart and soul of the place, Miss Milton."

It was so absurd that she stopped. "You cannot be serious, sir," she said finally, when she could almost feel the blush spreading up from her bosom to her face.

To her relief, the mill owner did not pursue the matter. He shrugged and held open the library door for her. "My mother—you would have liked her, Miss Milton—was much that way. I do not recall Mama ever raising her voice, or even stating her opinions much in a far too opinionated household." He sighed. "But I do not suppose I have felt much peace since she left us, my dear. I never knew how necessary she was to me until it was too late to tell her."

Then we are all fools together, she thought, you and me, and Blair, and probably Lord Denby, for all I know. "You should marry, Mr. Butterworth," she said impulsively, motioning to Andrew that it was time to leave.

"So should you, Miss Milton," he replied just as quickly. "Andrew, have you finished the entire page? You will make Mr. Singletary's life a heaven on earth. Let us go over it." He winked at her. "Miss Mitten can wait, for it is what she is best at, so she tells me."

This is odd, she thought in confusion as she watched the two of them, their heads together, discussing Andrew's page of the Gallic *Commentaries*. She retreated to the window seat and perched herself there, letters in her lap, as she watched the last of the leaves drift in spirals from the elm outside the window. As she watched, the rain began, and then slanted sideways as the wind roared down from the Pennines. It will be so long until spring, she thought, and felt a familiar prickling behind her eyelids. Why did Blair have to wait until the last day of his life to tell me he loved me? How could he have been so stupid?

She leaned her forehead against the windowpane, grateful for the cold glass. The rain beat against it, and the drops pulsed against her face through the glass. How good this feels, she thought.

She sat up and looked around, hoping that Mr. Butterworth and Andrew were still occupied with the translation. But no, Andrew was pulling on his coat and chattering in that animated fashion he never used at Denby, and the mill owner was watching her. Don't ask me anything, she thought.

He saw them to the front door, speaking of inconsequentials, and informed her that Marsh had already called for the carriage, when she pulled up the hood of her cloak.

"Sir, it is only a brief walk past the lake," she protested. "You know how brief. Lord Denby claims it is his!"

Mr. Butterworth smiled. "I won't have you catching the cold, or getting those invitations wet and start the ink running, my dear Miss Mitten."

When the carriage arrived, Andrew darted out and leaped inside. The mill owner took the umbrella from his butler and held it over her as she moved at a more sedate pace. "Seriously, Miss Milton, I have wondered these ten years why you are still a single lady," he said after he helped her inside.

She seated herself and leaned forward. "Mr. Butterworth, no one has ever asked me to be otherwise." She sat back. "You have no such excuse, sir."

"No, I have not," he agreed. "You would call me an idiot if I presented the lame excuse that I am too involved in cotton mills. 'No one is that busy,' you would tell me, wouldn't you, now that we have decided to be truth tellers, eh, Miss Milton?"

She shook her head, wishing that he would hurry inside before he took a chill. Now is the time to return a quizzing answer, she thought, except that I am never clever enough to think of one. "I know how time gets away from us, Mr. Butterworth," she said quietly. "Twelve years ago, Andrew was a baby in my arms, and now he is preparing for school away from me. I don't know when it all happened. Lord Denby is contemplating a reunion of old men who were sprigs in the American Revolution. And Blair is dead . . ." She turned away to search her reticule for a handkerchief.

The carriage jostled, and the door closed, and Mr. Butter-worth surprised her by seating himself next to her. "It's getting dark, Andrew, and one must beware of road agents between my house and Stover," he explained. "You need me."

Andrew only laughed and stared out the window again at the rain. "If an agent tells us to stand and deliver, sir, I can surren-der Caesar's *Commentaries*."

Mr. Butterworth laughed. He put his arm around Jane and held her close to him. "Have a good cry tonight, Miss Milton," he whispered in her ear, "then dry your eyes and plan this re-union."

She nodded, and blew her nose, grateful to lean against his comforting bulk. "I am being missish," she said in apology.

"I don't care," Mr. Butterworth replied serenely. "If you think Lord Denby could stand the strain, invite me over some after-noon to drink tea and play cribbage with him." He turned to look at her. "Just tell him that I have missed his visits of complaint about the lake and will bring the quarrel to him, for a change."

"I'll do it," she said, drying her eyes, "on one condition."

"Which is . . ."

"That you make some push to meet an agreeable lady of sense—I do not care if it is here or in Huddersfield—and waste no more of your own time."

"That's a straightforward request," he said. "I shall think about it, Miss Milton."

She sighed, and made no objection as his arm continued firm about her shoulders. "I do not know that I have ever leaned on anyone before, sir," she whispered. "You are not uncomfort-able?"

He shook his head. "Miss Milton, you are totty-headed if you think that I am uncomfortable."

That is honest enough, she thought with amusement as the carriage passed down the grander lane of Stover. To her way of thinking, the trees were not so finely shaped as Mr. Butter-worth's. How that must chafe Lord Denby, she told herself. And how much prettier this park would look with Mr. Butterworth's lake attached. She began to laugh softly, so Andrew could not hear.

The mill owner looked at her. "Now what is so amusing?"

"I was thinking of your lake, sir, which Lord Denby covets. None of us seem to get what we want, do we?" She leaned closer. "I want Andrew to be happy, and Lord Denby to go about living again. Lord Denby—when he isn't wanting to die—wants your lake. Stanton and I are foisting a reunion on him." She looked at him, then followed his gaze to the front door as they pulled up before it, and the mourning wreath, which even now dripped black dye onto the stoop. "Do you want me to remove that, Mr. Butterworth?" she asked.

"It would be a good start," he answered as the carriage stopped. "Shall I do it now?"

He opened the door and Andrew hurried out, after promising to be on time Monday morning to meet Mr. Singletary. Jane sat where she was, contemplating the wreath, then looked at the mill owner. "Not yet, please," she said. "Let me think about it some more. I mean, I should consult Lord Denby."

Mr. Butterworth nodded and left the carriage first, so he could help her down. "The rain has stopped," he said as she took his hand to steady herself.

"See there, sir," she told him. "You could have saved yourself the exertion of a carriage ride. We could have walked. After all, who puts you out more than Andrew and I? I am almost embarrassed."

He bowed over her hand and kissed her fingers. "My dear Miss Milton, just invite me to tea now and then. If my presence doesn't send Lord Denby into the boughs every so often, then I am scarcely worth my salt as a neighbor, and he is too far gone to be resuscitated! Good day, my dear. Have a thought about yourself once in a while."

She nodded. "I suppose you will give me no peace until I do, sir." She took his arm to detain him. "In all my quizzing, I have not been thoughtful enough to ask you what it is you want. You have been so kind to me, that I wish it were in my power to grant whatever it is."

He shrugged and she released his arm. "Miss Milton, where is your imagination? Surely Lady Carruthers has gone on and on about how disgustingly, unwholesomely wealthy I am, and that I must lack for nothing! How could I need anything?"

"That is no answer," she said as he climbed into the carriage again, then lowered the glass.

"My dear, I will tell you what *I* want when you decide what *you* want."

She frowned at him, and stepped away from the carriage as

the coachman mounted to the box again. "You know that I am most concerned about Andrew's welfare and Lord Denby's state of mind and health. I want them to be happy."

"Which tells me nothing about *you*, Miss Milton," he replied. "Do think about yourself, when you can fit it into your schedule."

Chapter Six

What do I want? It was food for thought, but surprisingly simple to push to the back of her mind as October turned to November and then December, and the postman brought replies to her invitations. Lord Denby surprised her one morning by pacing back and forth in his nightshirt and robe in the foyer, waiting for the postman. "I'm expecting some important papers from my solicitor in Leeds," he said, before she had a chance to say anything. "I'll let you know if any letters come for someone else." She had the good sense to withdraw from the foyer, on the excuse that she was just passing through on her way to go over the week's menus with Cook.

"You wait now, Stanton. I will go upstairs with the latest post, and he will be quite casual, even though he is just almost jumping about, wanting to know whom I have heard from," she told the butler belowstairs as she drank tea with him.

"He's pleased then?"

"Oh, yes," she assured him. "He's even planning who will sleep in what room, and debating whether or not he should encourage them to bring along their old uniforms!"

Between morning walks to Mr. Butterworth's house to deposit Andrew into the tutelage of Mr. Singletary—an amiable young man of no particular background, but with vast supplies of both character and intelligence—she spent time belowstairs with Stanton, making plans for the reunion.

"It is never too soon to plan menus," she told Mr. Butterworth when he came over, as he often did now, for cribbage with Lord Denby. "Everyone who is able is making plans, sir, and I mean for this to be an event." She made a face. "He even wondered if we could procure a rather disgusting creature called a possum, for the evening we have a Carolina menu."

"You don't want one," Mr. Butterworth assured her. "I believe those bags of guts with snouts were only eaten to assuage the outer extremities of starvation." He patted his waistcoat. "A good haunch of venison should serve rustic purposes, Miss Milton."

She was content to agree with him. In fact, Jane, she reminded herself that evening as she was brushing her hair, you are becoming remarkably complacent, where Mr. Butterworth is concerned. She shrugged at her reflection. His ideas for the reunion are always so good that I feel no qualms in going along without a murmur, she explained to her image. I wonder if I am relishing the novelty of having someone else make decisions around here.

She couldn't deny that his frequent presence on the estate was having the desired effect on Lord Denby. She smiled, thinking of the cribbage games that were so often detouring into loud discussion on Lord Denby's part. She could not remember Mr. Butterworth raising his voice, but when he left in the afternoon, and she went to visit Lord Denby, he always seemed more alert.

Only today, Lord Denby had thrown off the blanket she liked to spread over his legs when he sat in his chair, and walked up and down in front of his window, exclaiming about Mr. Butterworth and his liberal tendencies. "It's downright dangerous, Jane, when a man thinks he can buy a cotton mill, educate some rabble to run it, pay them more than other mill owners, and expect to get any work out of them!"

"So *that's* what he does," she murmured, as she folded the unneeded blanket over the chair and then scooped the pegs back into their pouch. "Oh, dear, and he is losing money by being kind?"

She smiled at her mirror image, remembering how Lord Denby had stopped his marching about to stare at her. "No, no, Jane! That's the deuce of it!" he had exclaimed, with quite the power of his former arguments. "He *makes* money! I don't understand it, either," he concluded, with a shake of his head. "Republican tendencies will ruin a nation faster than a good dose of plague."

"My lord, some would say that the United States is a case for disagreement," she had ventured, but Lord Denby only shook his head again and continued his pacing, muttering under his breath about the "evils of democracy" and a "ramshackle experiment."

"He even went so far as to tell me that he hoped Edward Bingham would come from Connecticut for the reunion, so they could have a rousing debate," she told Mr. Butterworth the next morning as he walked her to the door, after she had brought Andrew. "Mr. Butterworth, I believe he is having more fun with this than any puny wrangling over your lake." She put her hand on his arm. "Do you really run your factories along republican lines?"

"Guilty as charged," he replied cheerfully, as he tucked her arm through his and left the house with her. "We prefer to call them utilitarian lines, however. I'll walk you to the edge of the lake, Miss Milton, provided Lord Denby has not mined it and posted a patrol to keep me off disputed boundaries."

She laughed. "Only because it has not occurred to him yet, sir!" She stopped to look him full in the face. "Mr. Butterworth, thank you for replenishing his supply of umbrage."

He inclined his head toward hers in a little bow. "What an odd compliment, Miss Milton. It will go right to my head."

"I doubt that, sir," she teased. "You have far more on your brain than frivolities."

"Indeed I do, my dear," he said, and started her in motion again. "I am only doing what others are attempting in Scotland and Birmingham. I do believe that kindness is a far more useful incentive than niggardly wages, overwork, and humiliation." He looked at her. "Is this scary democracy? I prefer to think of such revolutionary ideas as Christian kindness."

"Mr. Butterworth, you are a rare man, indeed," she said.

"I know," he replied, giving her a nudge when she laughed. "Miss Milton, your laughter is a tonic!"

"Oh, dear! Lady Carruthers claims it is unrefined." She sighed. "Which brings me to a far less sanguine matter: We received a post from her yesterday evening."

"And?" he prompted.

"And she and Cecil will be here in two weeks—two weeks!—to celebrate Christmas with us."

They walked along in silence for a few minutes. "This is not precisely good tidings of great joy, I gather," he said when they reached the edge of the lake.

"Not at all," Jane said, removing her arm from his grip and pulling her cloak tighter. "She will ride me unmercifully if I allow Andrew to continue Latin School at your home, and twit me day and night if she knows it was my idea that you visit Lord Denby."

"Only if you allow her to trouble you, Miss Milton," the mill owner said, as unperturbed as if she had told him that the leaves had left the trees. "Good day, now, my dear Miss Milton. I trust you can navigate the perimeter of *my* lake."

She did, walking slowly and leaning into the wind. You are right, of course, Mr. Butterworth, she decided as she rounded the lake and stood too soon before the side entrance to Stover again. I do allow people to trouble me, and I say nothing.

The notion made her quiet through dinner. A couple of discreet coughs from Stanton reminded her to eat, and she smiled her thanks at him, secretly amused that he must dread as much as she did Cook's fits of depression when he carried uneaten food belowstairs. "I do not believe that Lord Denby pays you enough," she told him after Andrew excused himself. "You are the soul of diplomacy."

He bowed and then smiled at her, which delighted her because he so seldom unbent from his butler's demeanor. "No, Miss Milton. I am merely a coward where Cook is concerned," he said as he directed the footman to carry out the tray.

I suppose we all suffer our tyrannies, she told herself as they walked upstairs to Lord Denby's chamber. Except for you, sir, she thought, standing beside the bed and looking down on Lord Denby, who slept. Who could possibly ride roughshod over you?

"I am quite at leisure this evening," she whispered to Stanton, "so you needn't sit here with him." She made herself comfortable and picked up her mending. The letters are mailed, the arrangements made—as far as we are able—for the events this spring. She looked up at the window, black now with night coming earlier and earlier. The more I plan, the closer spring will seem, she told herself.

The butler did not leave, and Jane looked at him. "Is something wrong?" she whispered.

He shook his head slowly, as though he was undecided how

to answer her, then leaned closer to whisper in her ear. "He got another letter from Lady Carruthers this afternoon, reminding him that she and Cecil would be here soon." He hesitated when Lord Denby stirred in his sleep. "I think it sets him off, Miss Milton, just thinking about her arrival."

It sets me off, too, she admitted to herself as Stanton let himself out of the room without a sound. She yanked one of Andrew's socks over the darning egg and sewed vigorously, her lips set in a tight line. She sewed until the hole in the heel had far too many darning stitches to fit comfortably into any shoe Andrew owned. "Drat!" she said out loud.

"My dear cousin, we will have no wooden swearing."

Guilty, she looked at Lord Denby, who was watching her. "I didn't mean to wake you, my lord," she said.

He closed his eyes again. "You didn't really," he murmured. "Don't know why I feel so tired today."

It is because you cannot bear the thought of your sister back so soon, she told herself, or her son Cecil and the way he oozes around, taking inventory on everything he plans to inherit someday, if Andrew's claims can be brushed aside. She thought of Mr. Butterworth and his truth telling. "Do you know, my lord, if you made it perfectly plain to Cecil that Andrew truly is your grandson and will be the next Lord Denby, I know he would not plague you further."

There, she had said it. Jane clipped the thread from the sock and kneaded the sock between suddenly icy fingers. Moments passed; the clock on the mantelpiece seemed to tick louder with each second it marked. Startled, she looked at the clock and wondered when it would explode with the noise and throw itself facedown on the carpet, gears and sprockets whirring everywhere.

"I know nothing of the kind, Jane," he said finally, his eyes still closed.

Well that is final, she thought, shocked. "My lord, you know that Blair was never in doubt," she said gently, wanting to touch him, but repulsed somehow, which only shocked her more.

"Blair was in love, Jane," he replied, then made a dismissive gesture, as though to ward off further questions. "If you had ever been in love, you would understand that it throws reason right out the door with the slops."

I beg to differ, she thought, rising and then thrusting her

mending back in the basket. "My lord, I know that you were very much in love with Lady Denby, for Blair . . . Blair told me. And you have never been one to throw reason away."

He closed his eyes again and put his arm across his eyes in a gesture of rejection she could not ignore. "Perhaps we never really know each other as well as we think we do, my dear. Good night now. I do not require tending."

She remained where she was until his breathing was regular—whether he was fooling her or not, she could not tell—then rose to go. From the lifelong habit of doing for others, she pulled up the coverlet from the foot of the bed, moving aside the book that was there. It was the copy of his essays. Out of curiosity, she opened the book at the place marked with a scrap of paper, then closed it, wondering why he never seemed to get beyond that first humorous essay about Lieutenant Jeremy Dill and his brush with the amorous New York Royalist. Perhaps we do not know each other, she thought, as she left the room.

It pained her to watch Lord Denby withdraw to his bed again and keep to it with a vengeance, the closer Lady Carruthers' arrival loomed. Jane received her own peremptory letter, telling her to make sure that the second-best chamber was aired and the sheets dry. " 'I would be chagrined if Cecil should contract a putrid sore throat or bilious fever at this most joyful time of year, and I know you share my sentiments (or at least you should),' " she read out loud a week later when she allowed Mr. Butterworth to escort her and Andrew home from his lessons. Andrew had run on ahead, and was waving at her even now from the side door at Denby. She pocketed the letter and returned his wave. "If I had any brains at all, I would take to my bed, too, Mr. Butterworth!"

He shook his head. "Not you, my dear."

He stopped at the place where he usually relinquished his grip on her arm, but instead of releasing her, stood looking into the water of his lake. She did not mind, beyond the fact that the wind was picking up and Lady Carruthers' third-best cloak had never been warm. She made a slight gesture, but Mr. Butterworth might have been in another country, for all that he noticed. "Sir, I must be going now," she said at last.

He looked at her in surprise, as though she had recalled him from a distant field, but he did not loosen his grip. "Miss Milton, what you suffer from is an acute sense of duty."

"Sir?" she asked, more amused than surprised at the serious-ness of his tone.

He started in motion again, but not toward Denby. He led her to a bench and sat down with her. "You would never take to your bed, because that would leave Andrew defenseless," he said, as calmly as though they discussed the rising wind. "I think, my dear, that under your somewhat bland demeanor, you are quite a tiger, at least as far as that little scamp is concerned."

She didn't know whether to be offended or delighted. "Bland, sir?" she asked.

He nodded toward Denby. "In the name of rescuing you from a workhouse, those relatives of yours have turned you into a ser-vant, Miss Milton. They suck hours and hours of work from you, tending Andrew, soothing Lord Denby, and—God rest his soul—caring for Lord Canfield when no one else would . . ."

". . . or could . . ." she said quickly, before she thought.

He looked at her for a long moment and she prayed that he would not ask. "They give you nothing in return," he concluded.

Spoken like that, even in Mr. Butterworth's quiet way, it sounded so harsh. There must be something my Stover cousins have given me, she thought, frowning at the mill owner. "I have a place to live, sir, and . . ." She stopped, unable to think of any-thing else. "Oh, dear, Mr. Butterworth," she said softly. She sat next to him in silence.

"Miss Milton, even a hedgehog has a place to live," he said at last. "A place to hang his . . . his hedges, if you will." He gave her arm, still tucked through his, a little thump. "What would you like, Miss Milton? Do speak your mind."

"A family of my own, sir," she said without thinking further. "Babies just far enough apart so the neighbors don't laugh, a place for Andrew to stay during school holidays, a husband who cannot begin to do enough for me, and . . . and a red cloak three times as thick as this one!"

It sounded so funny, hanging in the afternoon air between them, that she gasped at her own effrontery. Gently, she took her arm from his and stood up. "Please overlook that, Mr. Butter-worth, I blame my outburst on your absurd questions! You have just furnished me with sufficient amusement to see me back to Stover . . ."

". . . and enough to get you through an evening with Lady Carruthers?" he asked, interrupting her. "I couldn't bring myself to tell you earlier, but I noticed a post chaise traveling the lane while you were reading my newspaper and waiting for Andrew and Joe to finish with Caesar."

"Oh drat, they are early! Cecil must be hiding from his creditors!" Jane exclaimed. She plopped down on the bench again, startled by the sudden weakness in her legs. "I don't know if it's enough," she said, suddenly hollow inside. "Tell me something else absurd to make me laugh, Mr. Butterworth."

He was silent for a long while, and Jane had not the heart to look at him. I must hurry, she thought, rising again suddenly. Andrew must be facing her awfulness without me. "Mr. Butterworth, I must . . ." She stopped and looked at him. "Is something the matter, sir?" she asked.

He was dabbing at his eye with a paisley handkerchief that perfectly matched his overpowering waistcoat. "I am certain it is some fluff blown into my eye from Lord Denby's odious yews," he said in a moment after returning the handkerchief to his breast pocket with a certain flourish that she defied any Bond Street beau to imitate. "My dear Miss Milton, I haven't said anything absurd yet! Why do you insist that a husband and babies are so out of reach?"

In all their years of acquaintance, she had never heard such a personal question from the mill owner. I brought it on myself, she thought, excusing his own lapse of manners. Oh, and did I actually say "babies" instead of "children"? I certainly did not mean to be so suggestive. He is blind indeed, if he thinks I need to clarify my situation. "Mr. Butterworth, you know me quite well enough to know that I have no fortune and no prospects!" she exclaimed, her stomach made even more hollow by the bleak expression in the mill owner's eyes. What kind eyes he has, she thought, happy to forget her own awkwardness for a moment. Surely they are his best feature. Here he stands in this cold wind, and he has forgotten his hat. "I wish you would not worry about me," she said finally, then surprised herself by standing on tiptoe to kiss his cold cheek. "I could use that red cloak, however! Now go indoors and do not worry about me and Lady Carruthers. I am used to her."

"And that is entirely the problem!" he called after her. "God grant you a little less complacency for the holidays!"

How odd, she thought, as she kept her head down against the wind and ran toward the side entrance. He must be feeling a little bilious from all those pastries he ate while Andrew wrestled with Caesar's legions. What a shame that someone with such a kind heart and so much to offer never married. "Jane, it is your duty to remind him to look about for matrimonial prospects when he is in Huddersfield for Christmas," she murmured as she looked back toward the lake. "My duty!" She laughed softly to herself. "You have my measure like no one else, Mr. Butterworth. Duty *is* my dilemma." She squinted to see him through the little distance and the gathering dusk. The mill owner stood there still at the edge of the lake. How is it that you know me so well? she thought. Do go inside, sir, and spare yourself death by pneumonia. Who else can say absurdities, even when you claim you are serious, and make me laugh?

No more than five minutes into Lady Carruthers' visit, Jane realized with a pang that she should have stayed at the lake with Mr. Butterworth. The hall was empty when she let herself in through the side door and she knew she had closed it quietly behind her, but there was Lady Carruthers coming toward her. Jane removed her cloak and folded it carefully over her arm, reminding herself not to let Lady Carruthers frighten her into agitation. Now, should I call her cousin, or is Lady Carruthers more appropriate tonight? she asked herself as her relative came nearer. Perhaps Your Worship? That absurdity made her smile, which proved, she soon discovered, to be another mistake.

"I cannot imagine how you have the effrontery to laugh in my face, Jane," was Lady Carruthers' greeting after a month of absence.

Jane considered. Ordinarily, the thing to do was duck her head and remain silent, or so experience had trained her. If I were to talk back to her, I wonder what she would do? she thought, considering the matter for a long moment while Lady Carruthers fumed.

"People often smile, Lady Carruthers," she said calmly, even as her knees smote together. "I hear it is done, on occasion, when relatives see each other again after some time has elapsed. Good evening, cousin. I trust you had a pleasant journey from London."

She nearly stepped back when Lady Carruthers gasped, but stood her ground, ready to dig her toes into the parquet, if she needed to.

"Of all the . . ."

Jane waited. Nerve? Rag manners? Turkish treatment? she thought, filling in the text in her mind as her own amusement deepened. *Or can you not go on because I've said nothing you can attack without appearing distinctly ungenerous, eh? It must have been a more horrible ride than usual, cuz, if you cannot think of a single thing to bait me with.* Of course, any carriage journey with Cecil would be purgatory past bearing. Amazed at herself, and giving all the credit to Mr. Butterworth, she looked around elaborately. "And where is my cousin Cecil, madam? Please don't disappoint me by telling me that he chose to stay in London."

There now, I have delivered that with total aplomb, she thought, as she watched her cousin's face grow beet red and then resume its customary pallor. *Even you will not accuse me of sarcasm, because I have said nothing unseemly. Oh, three cheers for a bland demeanor, Mr. Butterworth, you dear fellow!*

"Poor Cecil is lying down with a sick headache," Lady Carruthers said. "I blame the wretched postilions, who did not tie down his smaller traveling case." She paused for what seemed to Jane to be dramatic effect, even though her audience was only one. "It was dumped in the snow this side of Leeds, and his lace and neckcloths have suffered real indignities. As a consequence, he has taken to his bed."

I shall go into whoops, Jane thought, as she tightened her lips together. "I cannot imagine such a mishap," she said, when she was able.

Lady Carruthers looked at her with an expression that Jane could not recognize. *She thinks I am in agreement with her,* she realized finally, struck almost to openmouthed amazement by this blinding epiphany. *For years I have hung my head and stammered around this dragon, when all I needed to do was look her in the eye and deliver my sarcasm with a straight face. I cannot wait to write a note to Mr. Butterworth.* "Oh, my," she said faintly, not even realizing that she had spoken out loud, until Lady Carruthers nodded.

"It was a dreadful thing, indeed, Jane," she said. "Cecil had scolded and scolded them to tie down his luggage just so, and then this happens. I cannot understand why he has all the misfortune."

Oh, I can, Jane thought suddenly. *It is the revenge of the powerless, cousin, can't you see?* Cecil probably pranced about, wringing his hands and rolling his eyes, and cajoling and threatening their jobs. The postilions dare not talk back in kind, so they manage to drop his traveling case in the snow and blame it on winter and travel conditions. "There was probably a quantity of mud, too, wasn't there, where the case fell off?" she said, controlling her voice by the force of her will and praying that she sounded sympathetic.

Lady Carruthers nodded. "It was as though the coachman found the worst place on the entire Great North Road to stop the post chaise and clear the mud from the horses' hooves." She shook her head. "My dear baby has such wretched luck. And so I told the butler. What's his name . . ."

"Stanton, ma'am," Jane said, linking her arm through her cousin's and pulling her gently along the corridor. "Did . . . did Cecil rehearse all his troubles to Stanton?"

"Oh, yes, and to the footman, as well. There may even have been that wretched upstairs maid peeping about and spying on her betters." Lady Carruthers stopped. "That was over an hour ago, and do you think the servants have made a single push to bring him bouillon, a tisane, and a simple can of hot water? I requested it specifically. In fact, I demanded it."

Stanton, you are a sly dog, she thought, barely able to contain herself. "Perhaps if you had not demanded it, cousin . . ." she ventured.

Lady Carruthers removed her arm from the crook of Jane's elbow. "Jane Milton, stupidities like that will always brand you as workhouse. You will never know how to deal with servants!"

Jane had to duck her head then to hide her smile. "That is it," she said, her voice soft. "I tell them please and thank you like a ninny." And I always have hot water and whatever else I wish, she thought. "Thank you for the education, cousin. Do excuse me for a moment. I must check on Lord Denby."

She escaped up the stairs, raising her skirts and taking them two at a time, even as she heard Lady Carruthers' gasp of disapproval. "Jane, I despair of your improvement!" her cousin called after her.

"And so do I," Jane murmured. The upstairs linen closet door was open, so she ducked inside. Stanton stood there examining the shelves where the sheets were stored. With a wave of her hand to him, she sat on the stool by the towels, grabbed one, and laughed into it. If the butler was surprised, he did not indicate it, but continued his perusal of the shelves.

She wiped her eyes on her sleeve after another moment and

then watched him. "Stanton, is there something I can help you find? I probably know those shelves as well as you do."

"You probably do," he agreed, his voice serene. "I have come from the Honorable Cecil Carruthers' room, where he tells me that his sheets are too scratchy, and insists that I do something before he breaks out in hives because his skin is so delicate." He peered at her from around a mound of sheets. "I disremember how long it takes for him to throw out spots, Miss Milton," he continued, the picture of placid demeanor. "Was it ten minutes or twenty minutes?"

"Ten, I think," she replied, laughter bubbling up inside her again.

The butler slapped his forehead. "Oh dear! I know I have been here at least fifteen minutes! How thoughtless."

"Stanton, you are amazing," she said. "I think you will find the sheets you want over there next to the burlap bags and hair shirts. And do you plan to see that he gets only tepid shaving water?"

He bowed. "If he is extremely lucky, Miss Milton, it will not have chunks of ice floating in it. We are washing his muddy neckcloths and lace right now, but I greatly fear for them. And as for his bouillon?" He shrugged. "I cannot imagine why that is taking so long."

Very well, sir, she thought, getting off the stool, if you are so composed, I can be, too. "Perhaps too much wind down the chimney is making the stove draw strangely," she said.

"I am certain that is it." He sighed. "And now Lord Denby swears that he will remain in bed until he dies."

She giggled, then covered her mouth with her hand. "I cannot blame him. I wonder, Stanton, do you think he will take an interest in things again when Lady Carruthers and Cecil leave?"

"I wouldn't know, Miss Milton," he said.

There was a long pause. She looked at the butler, and wondered why, like the other upstairs inmates, she had never taken his full measure. I have always had allies in this house, she thought, even in the worst moments. "I am certain that he will, Stanton. You are a wonder, sir!"

He bowed again. "We only do what we can, Miss Milton." After another careful perusal of the shelves that threatened to send her into a fit of laughter, the butler selected some sheets. From a distant room, Jane could hear a bell jangling. "I thought

I heard something, Miss Milton," he said, pausing to listen and then simply amazing her with a long, slow wink. "No, must've been the wind." He shook his head. "I am certain the stove is not drawing properly now. Oh, dear."

With the slightest of smiles, he nodded to her and went to the door. "Miss Milton, I do believe that Lord Denby received a letter from Mr. Butterworth next door, inviting you and Andrew to spend Christmas in Huddersfield with him at his sister's family home. Lord Denby would like to talk to you about that, and he told me to mention it to you."

She left the linen room with the butler, her heart in perfect charity with him. Down the hall in the opposite direction, the bell jangled more fiercely. "Perhaps I should see to Cecil," she offered, holding out her arms for the sheets. She ran her hand over the fabric. "These feel like sandpaper! Stanton, did you hear me?"

"Actually, no, Miss Milton," he replied. "Did you say something?"

She shook her head. "Nothing of importance. Do check on Lord Denby and tell him I will be with him directly." She waited while he bowed to her. "And, Stanton . . ."

"Yes, Miss Milton?"

"I doubt there is a thing wrong with Huddersfield," she told him. "Surely you are not as big a snob about mill towns as Lady Carruthers!"

He did not even pretend to look shocked. In fact, she was amazed that a man could raise his eyebrows so high without really changing his expression. "Never," he said succinctly.

I can hardly wait to dash off a note to Mr. Butterworth this evening and tell him how much I have learned, she told herself, and then another thought took hold. "Do you know, Stanton, in the—oh, my, has it been twenty years since we have known each other?"

"I believe it has been, Miss Milton. I was a footman then."

He was smiling now, and she could not help but notice how it animated his eyes. What a handsome man, she thought. "All these years, and I do not even know your Christian name," she concluded simply.

"It is Oliver, Miss Milton."

"Then Merry Christmas, Oliver."

Chapter Seven

In her heart of hearts, she knew she would rather crawl the
length of the driveway on ground glass than knock on Cecil's
door, but she knew—even if Mr. Butterworth did not—that duty
counted for something. From the frantic sound of the handbell,
she knew that Cecil Carruthers was not noticeably enfeebled.

"Cecil?" she asked, peering into the room. He had been
propped up on his elbow, but when he saw her, to Jane's intense
amusement, he collapsed back onto the mattress and the bell
dropped from nerveless fingers.

"I thought help would never come," he managed, when she
tiptoed closer.

"Oh, Cecil, it was only your traveling case," she said, noticing that there was no fire in the hearth yet, and that the draperies
were still open, even though the afternoon had waned into dusk.
She closed them, grateful that she had never given the servants
cause to ignore her. Cecil, I predict you will have a dreadful
Christmas, she thought, without a shred of remorse. "Don't you
have a valet?"

The slight figure under the covers moved only a little. "I have
been abandoned, cuz," he said, hand to forehead, "and all because I was a little behind with his wages."

"How little, Cecil?" she inquired as she laid a fire.

"Eight months is all. I ask you, Jane, where is loyalty these
days?"

"Where, indeed?" she echoed, her heart sinking. If this
excuse for a human ever gets his hands on Lord Denby's estate,
we are all doomed, she thought. The solicitors might as well put
everyone on the estate in a wicker basket and send us over those
falls on the Canadian border.

"Come closer, Jane, and feel my forehead," her cousin
begged.

She watched the fire a moment to make sure that it was burning properly, and went to the bed. Cecil Carruthers lay there, his
hand delicately to his chest, the picture of put-upon humanity.

He looked enough like his cousin Blair to make her stand there a moment, unwilling to touch him. I have done this too often, she thought, finally placing the back of her hand against his head. He was not so much like Blair, she told herself, reconsidering. He is rather like Blair done in watercolors and then blotted and smudged until only a shadow remained. Or Blair with all the blood drained from him. She took her hand away quickly.

"Is it that bad?" he asked in alarm.

"There is nothing wrong with you that a little sal volatile in porter would not cure," she replied, going to the door, wanting to be away from him. "Let me see what I can find." She left before he could begin his protest, but before she was many steps down the corridor, the bell began to jangle again.

It was almost a relief to step into Lord Denby's room and sit down beside his bed. She took his hand, admiring, as she always did, the handsome veins so well-defined. "I cannot have you taking to your bed again, my lord," she said, leaning forward to rest her cheek against his hand for a moment. "Not when you have been doing so well."

He sighed. "My sister was in here earlier," he said.

She could not help but notice the dismay in his voice. "I am certain she wanted to wish you a good evening, my lord," she said, sitting up straight again.

"No, my dear, she wanted to rehearse for me all of Cecil's woes and beg for an advance upon his next quarter's allowance," he said, the exhaustion unmistakable in his voice. "I told her that I would."

And he will only beg for more next time, and more, until he has your estate and he ruins us all, she thought, looking around the room because she could not bear to gaze at Lord Denby so helpless again, when only yesterday he was arguing with Mr. Butterworth. All she achieved was a reminder of how shabby the place was becoming. There is no firm hand at Denby anymore, she realized.

"Stanton said that you received a note from Mr. Butterworth," she prompted, wanting to change the subject.

He turned his head toward a letter lying on the night table. "It is some sheer nonsense about inviting you and Andrew to spend Christmas at his sister's home near Huddersfield." With an effort he turned upon his side and faced the wall. "Of course you will answer and give your regrets."

"Of course I will," she echoed. "Good night, my lord." She picked up the letter, the paper familiar to her fingers because it was the same stationery she had used for the reunion invitations. She hesitated at the door. "Perhaps things will seem better in the morning, my lord."

"Is she going away then?" he asked hopefully.

"No, my lord. She and Cecil are here for Christmas." His sigh went on so long that she wanted to cover her ears. So much for loving relatives, she told herself as she left the room quietly.

It doesn't have to be this way, she wanted to shout as she hurried down the hall. "But how do you know that, Jane Milton?" she asked out loud as she stopped before the door to Blair's room, then went inside. How do I know? she wondered as she moved, sure of herself, in the dark room as she had done so many times during that last winter and spring, when the light had finally begun to bother his eyes. She found the box of sulphurs where they always were, and lit the candle.

She sat on the chair next to the bed, as she had sat so often during the months when he loitered between life and death. The room was peaceful now, smelling of mint and balsam that Lady Carruthers had insisted on placing about. It was a good idea, she thought, breathing in the fragrance. I should tell her; everyone likes a compliment.

There was a sound in the doorway, and it did not surprise her to see Andrew. She motioned him in, and he leaned against her chair. In another moment his arm was around her shoulder. Without a word she took hold of his hand as it lay on her shoulder.

"Do you miss him, Miss Mitten?" he asked, his voice as quiet as the room.

She nodded, unable to speak.

"I think I would miss him more, if I knew him better," Andrew said.

Jane looked at him in surprise, and then she thought about what he had said. "It was the war that took him away, my dear. If you want to blame someone, blame Napoleon."

To her further surprise, he shook his head, and then after a moment's hesitation perched himself on the bed so he was facing her. "Other fathers came home once in a while, Miss Mitten," he said, as though the words were being dragged from him. He leaned toward her. "Miss Mitten, do you think he believed those stories about my mother, too?"

She leaped from her chair and sat beside him, both arms around him. "I am sure he did not!" she exclaimed.

"Then why did he never come home?" he asked, his eyes big with a question that she could not answer.

"There is so much we do not know," she replied, knowing that it was an unsatisfactory tack, but unable to think of another. She held her breath, hoping that he would not ask anything else. He sighed, and settled against her. "I wish that you had let me sit with him, too," he said softly.

Oh, you do not, she thought. Besides, I promised.

"I . . . I could have told him that I loved him."

Touched, she looked at Andrew, thinking of the other boys his age in the district, and how childish they seemed by comparison. Andrew, have you always been old? she thought, even as she knew the answer.

"He knows you loved him, my dear," she replied.

The boy nodded and got off the bed. He looked at it a moment, then patted the pillow. "Maybe so, but there is something in the telling, isn't there, Miss Mitten?" He nodded to her and left the room.

Silent, she sat in the chair again, unwilling to leave the room, unwilling to fetch sal volatile and face Cecil again, or even to pick up a pen and turn down Mr. Butterworth's kind offer. She heard another sound behind her, and smiled. There *is* something in the telling, she thought. I suppose it won't hurt to tell you, my dear. Mr. Butterworth says I should speak my mind, and it matters, you know.

"My dear boy, do you know, before he died your father told me that he loved me." It seemed easy to say just then, and a weight lifted from her shoulders. You are so right, Mr. Butterworth, she told herself. I should speak my mind more often.

Her blood turned to chunks as she heard someone clapping behind her. Jane whirled around, hardly breathing, to see Lady Carruthers standing in the room. "Oh, I thought you were . . ." she began, and then stopped, as the applause continued. "Please don't do that," she begged.

Lady Carruthers laughed and stopped clapping. "Jane, trust you to believe a delirious man," she said. "Lord, I do not know when I have been so diverted. I simply must share this with Cecil. He needs a good laugh!" She was still laughing when she turned on her heel and left the room.

Jane was awake all night, hands clenched at her sides, staring at the ceiling in her room, wishing for morning to come, and then dreading it, because that would mean another encounter with Lady Carruthers. "No, Mr. Butterworth, I cannot speak my mind around Lady Carruthers," she said out loud, when it seemed that morning would never come. "I must leave this place."

When she could not stand another moment of lying in her bed, she got up and dressed quickly, her fingers clumsy. She was tying her shoes when she stopped, her hand on the lace. And where will I go? she thought in despair. Where am I free from relatives? I could never leave Andrew. It was almost the last thing Blair had said to her, his last thought, after he told her he loved her. "Watch him, Janie, as you always have," he had whispered, the words draining out of him like his own blood.

Jane shivered and finished tying her shoes. She snatched up her cloak and tiptoed from the house. In only a few minutes she was circling Mr. Butterworth's lake and then seating herself on a bench, shielded by trees from both houses. In exhaustion and perfect misery, she sat there through Lady Denby's departure for church. When the carriage was small in the distance, she trudged back to the house.

Andrew was gone, and Cecil, too. Jane marveled at her own insensitivity in exposing Blair's son to the full force of their dislike. I should have gone, she thought, lying down on her bed and drawing up her knees to her chest. No matter how bad it is, I should have gone. She slept then, too tired to do anything else.

She was vaguely aware when they returned from church, but she slept again, to be roused soon enough by the smallest knock on her door. "Come in," she said, pushing hair and sleep from her eyes.

Andrew, his face so pale that his lips were white, came into the room. She stared at him as he sat down in the chair in front of the fireplace. Horrified, she could tell that he was beyond tears. "Oh, Andrew, what did they say to you?" she said as she hurried to kneel beside the chair.

He shook his head. "Nothing to me," he said finally. "After church, my aunt asked the vicar how I was doing in Latin School."

Jane gasped. "Oh, God, I never thought of that! And . . . and did the vicar tell her about . . ." She couldn't finish.

Andrew nodded. "Mr. Butterworth was standing near." He

hung his head down and she watched the tears drop onto the arm of the chair. Wordlessly she pressed her hand against his head. "She said such terrible things to him, Miss Mitten!" He looked at her, his eyes red. "Called him common, and someone who pokes his nose where it doesn't belong, and . . . and words I never heard before." He sobbed into the arm of the chair. "All he was doing was teaching me Latin, Miss Mitten!"

Jane rested her cheek against his hair. "I know, Andrew. It's all my fault."

He shook his head. "No, it isn't. We didn't do anything wrong." He looked at her. "Do you think Mr. Butterworth will ever want to see us again?"

Not if he is as smart as I think he is, she thought, and then went all hollow inside. We will have no friends anymore, and I am to blame for speaking my mind. I should have known no good would come of it. "We can wish that he would, my dear," she replied, "although I would not hold out too much hope."

Andrew sighed. "Why does she care how I learn Latin? She never cares about anything else I do."

Andrew, if you only knew how many years I have been wondering why she dislikes me so much, Jane thought, as she got to her feet and found a handkerchief for the boy.

"I am sure it is she who has been telling everyone that my mama . . . Oh, Miss Mitten, suppose it is all true?" he burst out. "I do not understand!"

Her own heart full to bursting, Jane took him onto her lap and let him cry. "I don't understand, either," she murmured. And I do not understand why no one—Blair included—made any effort to scotch the rumors. She could not stop her own tears then. Am I the *only* one who ignored the rumors?

She forced herself to stop crying, and held Andrew close against her until his tears turned into hiccups, and then stopped. Calmly she wiped his face, kissed his forehead, then let him rest against her again. "My dear, I believe that your aunt wants our cousin Cecil to inherit Lord Denby's titles and estates," she told him.

"He can have them," Andrew replied promptly, his voice muffled against her breast. "I just want to learn my Latin, then go to school someplace where no one teases me." He pulled away from her. "That's not too much to ask, is it?" he questioned her, his voice anxious.

"No, it is not, my dear," she answered. There was nothing

more to say. She held Andrew as the afternoon dragged on. His stomach began to growl, with the coming of dusk, but he made no move to leave her lap, or ask about dinner. I cannot bear one more meal in that dining room, Jane thought, as she tightened her grip. I think I would rather starve.

She could feel Andrew jump a little when the footman rang the first bell for dinner. "Don't you wish that Mr. Butterworth would invite us to eat with him?" he asked finally.

"That would solve our problem," she told him, keeping her voice light. "Actually, Andrew, he sent a letter to your grandfather last night, inviting us to spend Christmas at his sister's house in Huddersfield."

He sat up on her lap, his eyes wide. "Please tell me that you accepted!" he demanded, reminding her forcefully of his grandfather.

She shook her head. "It probably isn't proper, my dear, so I am afraid I will have to turn him down."

"Miss Mitten!" he exclaimed, and if she had not been so miserable, Jane would have been amused by the exasperation in his voice. "This would solve our entire problem!"

I wish it were so easily solved, she thought. I wish a visit to Mr. Butterworth's would brush away years and years of suspicion and dislike and terrible storytelling. "I don't think it would help us much, Andrew." She sighed and lifted him from her lap, going to stand by the window. "I doubt that we are very high on Mr. Butterworth's list of Christmas charities right now, considering the way Lady Carruthers treated him after church today. Andrew?"

While she was talking, he had seated himself at her desk, and then arranged the paper and pen in front of him. "Oh, Andrew, we dare not write Mr. Butterworth," she said.

He wasn't listening to her, but staring in front of him. In another moment, he nodded and began to write. "Miss Mitten, you always tell me that I should persist, when faced with a dilemma," he told her as he wrote. "It's true, isn't it?"

"Well, yes, but . . . Oh, Andrew . . ."

He finished the line, then put down the pen. "Miss Mitten, you've been teaching me the truth all these years, haven't you?" he asked.

"Of course I have," she replied, stung by the implication. She smiled again, when she realized what he was doing. "I suppose this is called being hoist on my own petard, isn't it?"

He looked at her doubtfully. "I . . . I hope not, Miss Mitten!"

She laughed and hugged him. "Very well, then, write away. We'll face the dragon over dinner, and then smuggle this note to Stanton in a bottle."

His expression of doubt remained. "I . . . I had rather planned just to hand it to him, Miss Mitten," he said.

"Andrew, you have no more imagination than your father!"

He observed her with a smile that relieved her heart as nothing else could have. "Miss Mitten, this is the first time you have mentioned Father without tears in your eyes or a glum look."

"I suppose it is," she said slowly. "But own it, Andrew. There were times when he was such a . . . a . . ."

"Slowtop?" Andrew offered, his eyes lively.

"Exactly. Now do hurry or we shall be late for dinner, which will only disgrace us further."

It was an easy matter to slip the note to Stanton, and then hurriedly take their seats in the dining room before Lady Carruthers had time to look around more than once or twice at the expanse of empty chairs. She cleared her throat with a sound that startled Cecil, slumped as he was over the consommé in front of him. "For what we are about to receive, may the Lord make us truly thankful," Lady Carruthers said, and then picked up her spoon and glared at Jane.

I dare the Lord to call that grace, Jane thought. She folded her hands in her lap, unable to even contemplate the thought of eating. If I cannot eat, I can at least take her attention away from Andrew, and his various crimes and misdemeanors, she told herself. Heaven knows I have given her enough amusement at my expense to keep her occupied for an entire holiday season of meals, and off Andrew's back. But why should either of us suffer? she thought suddenly. Possibly it is time I abdicated my title of perfect poor relation.

She looked at her cousin Cecil, who was drinking his soup with that air he wore of perpetual injury. How someone so languid can sit up all night at a card table and play away his entire quarterly allowance, I cannot fathom, she thought. She glanced at Andrew, who was making himself small in his chair, as he usually did during meals. We deserve far better, even if we are a poor relation and an unwanted child.

Jane put down her spoon and took a deep breath that came from somewhere deep inside her. I am depending upon you to be right, Mr. Butterworth, she thought, as she pushed back her chair and went to Cecil's side. Willing her hand not to shake, she rested it against his forehead as he stared at her in open-mouthed surprise.

"Dear me, cousin, you are brave to have left your bed," she murmured, hoping for that right touch between concern and humility. She crossed her fingers behind her back and looked at Lady Carruthers. "Is his skin always this color?" She rested her cheek against her cousin's forehead now. "Cecil, you are so brave to come to the country. I doubt that many would have gone through such exertions to see an aging relative. I had no idea."

"There is nothing wrong with his color," Lady Carruthers snapped.

"Perhaps not," Jane said with what she hoped was serenity. "My mistake, Cecil." She picked up her spoon and calmly sipped her soup while Andrew stared at her.

It is not working, she thought in quiet desperation as she forced herself to eat. After what seemed like years, Cecil slowly rose from the table and stood looking into the mirror over the sideboard. Yes! she thought, as he touched his cheek with his fingertips. Yes!

He had difficulty moving toward the sideboard for a better look, so she rose quickly to help him. "There, there, cousin," she whispered. "Don't exert yourself if you do not feel up to it. We know how brave you have been."

To her intense delight, Cecil was trembling now, and patting his face with both hands, turning his head from side to side to catch all the light. "What do you think it is, cousin?" he asked her at last, in a voice that sounded weak to her ears.

More hypochondria than exists in small countries, she thought, praying that her lips would not start to twitch. "I am certain that Mr. Lowe could be here in an hour or so to tell you," she said, "if, indeed, you have an hour to . . . to . . ."

Lady Carruthers was on her feet by now, and grasping her son by his shoulders. "I would be extremely careful of him, Lady Carruthers," Jane murmured. "Do let me summon Mr. Lowe."

"Do that, Jane," the woman said as she helped her son back to the table. "Rest your head there, my little love, and I will tell Stanton to hurry with that dratted tisane he promised hours ago."

I am certain that tisane is on its way to Cecil from the kitchen by way of Madrid, Jane thought. She leaned close to Lady Carruthers to whisper, "I wouldn't leave Cecil alone, cousin." Cecil whimpered, and Jane bit her lip until she could go on. "I'll mention the tisane again to Stanton, and write a note for the doctor, mum. Come, Andrew, and let us search for smelling salts. Oh, Cecil, do be brave!"

Once in the hall, it was a simple matter to tell Andrew to run upstairs and pack a bag, and then to find Stanton belowstairs. When he stopped laughing, she wrote a note to Mr. Lowe, urging him to come quickly and find something seriously wrong with her cousin. "I depend upon you, sir, for you owe me a great deal," she concluded, writing fast, and then blotting the note, which she handed to the footman, who grinned and pulled on his overcoat over his livery.

"I'm sorry to do this to you, Stanton," she said as they went upstairs together. "I promise to write to Lord Denby, and can only hope that he will forgive me for deserting him, but Andrew and I are running away for the holidays."

"To Huddersfield, Miss Milton?" he asked, his smile broad.

"If Mr. Butterfield has not changed his mind, Oliver, and I do wish you would call me Jane occasionally. In fact, make it a New Year's resolution, if you would." She touched his arm. "It's long overdue, Oliver, as are a number of things around here. See you in January."

"And not a moment before, Jane."

Chapter Eight

The ease of their escape from Stover Hall for the holidays she could only credit to Mr. Lowe, who, when he arrived, took one look at Cecil, by now in bed and truly pale, and ordered total bed rest and complete quiet.

"I suggest a change of scenery for Andrew during the holidays, Lady Carruthers," he told her in all seriousness. "Cecil must have total silence, and we know how rambunctious small boys can be."

One would think you had no idea how quiet Andrew already is about this place, Jane thought, as she listened and marveled. Have a care here, Mr. Lowe, or my cousin will try to palm her responsibilities off on me. I know this from vast experience.

"I shall take Andrew to London with me, and leave Jane in charge," Lady Carruthers said. "She is such an expert with invalids."

Mr. Lowe exceeded Jane's wildest flights of imagination as he shook his head sorrowfully. "No, Lady Carruthers, this illness requires a mother's presence. Suppose, just suppose, that you were far away when Cecil here . . ."

Cecil whimpered on cue, and Jane dug deep within herself when Mr. Lowe turned away and coughed long and hard.

". . . when Cecil took a sudden turn," the good doctor concluded, when he found the means of speech again. He leaned closer to Lady Carruthers. "Madam, it is epizootic fever, and one never knows."

Jane gasped. "But . . . but Lord Denby? Is he safe here with Cecil in the house?" she asked, hoping for the proper quaver without overwhelming the situation.

The look Mr. Lowe fixed upon her suggested forcefully that he was at his outer limit. "Lord Denby must be left strictly alone, Lady Carruthers. Stanton is quite capable of relieving you of all duties on that head." Mr. Lowe rested his hand on Cecil's arm. "I'll give him a draft that will allow sleep, and return to my office and mix up powders, which you will administer every four hours until the crisis is past. Come, Jane, and let us leave these two alone."

"The . . . crisis?" Cecil asked, his eyes wide.

"No one has a carte blanche on life, Cecil," he replied. He bent over Cecil, his lips close to her cousin's ear. "I trust your affairs are in order. Come, Jane. I must prepare those powders without another moment's delay."

The hallway was too close, so the doctor took her by the arm and hurried her to the bookroom, where he sat down, rested his head on his arms, and muffled his howls of merriment against the desk.

"Epizootic fever?" Jane asked, making no attempt to disguise her skepticism.

"I believe it is a condition of horses," he managed before he had to retreat to his handkerchief again for another round of mirth.

"And these powders you are going to prepare?"

". . . will do nothing worse than turn his piss bright blue, my dear," he concluded, with another swipe at his eyes. "Will that do, or am I still in your debt?"

She nodded. "It will do, sir, but you know that you will always be a debtor."

Without a word he reached across the desk and took her hand. "I know, Jane, I know," he said, his voice soft now. He kissed her fingers, then released her hand. "Do you tire of doing everyone's dirty work? Mine, as well?"

In the morning they were ready, bags packed, when Mr. Butterworth's carriage rolled to a stop at the front entrance. "Ready, my dears?" the mill owner asked when the footman opened the door.

"Andrew, you help Reeves with my bag, there's a good lad," she said, pulling Mr. Butterworth inside. When Andrew had left the house, she leaned close to whisper, "Sir, we must wait just one minute. Carlton took a urinal upstairs a moment ago, and I must listen."

"Mr. Lowe paid me a visit last night, so I know the whole of it," he said with a grin. "You are a rascal, Miss Milton."

"I suppose I am," she agreed. "Who would have thought it?"

Mr. Butterworth's grin grew wider as they stood together in the hall. He laughed out loud when an anguished yell split the morning quiet. He laughed louder when Jane tugged on his muffler. "I cannot take you anywhere, sir," she said, pushing him toward the door.

"Take *me*? Take *me*?" he protested. "You and the doctor are the ones who have conspired to ruin Cecil's manly dignity." He offered her his arm, which she took. "Remind me never to get on your cranky side, if you have one." He helped her into the carriage.

"Everyone has a cranky side," she told him as she seated herself and made room for him to sit beside her. "Even you, I suppose, Mr. Butterworth."

"Especially me, my dear," he replied, and she was struck by

the seriousness in his voice. "Repenting at leisure is not the sole purview of gentry. Even mill owners have been known to do it."

He said nothing more to her, but directed a remark about the horses to Andrew that led to a discussion on a bit of bone and blood that Mr. Butterworth had his eye on in the spring's Newmarket trials. They returned briefly to Mr. Butterworth's home where Joe Singletary, out of breath and stuffing papers into a briefcase, joined them. Jane watched the secretary, remorse on her mind. "I fear that Andrew and I have forced you to leave a few days earlier than you would have wished," she said, helping Joe retrieve stray papers as the postilion closed the door.

"No matter, Miss Milton, no matter," the mill owner said. "This just gets Joe home a day or two sooner to his sweetie, eh, Joe?"

The secretary nodded and blushed, but made no comment. In another moment, he and Andrew continued the discussion on horses that Mr. Butterworth had begun. Jane leaned back and closed her eyes, relishing the warmth of the sun through the glass.

She must have slept then, because when she woke, her head was resting on Mr. Butterworth's thigh, and someone had covered her with a traveling blanket. The mill owner's hand was heavy against her waist, and she suspected that he slept, too. Across from her, Andrew was curled into a ball. Mr. Singletary looked up from the papers in his lap. He nodded when she mouthed, "Is he asleep?" So she closed her eyes again, content to remain where she was. Mr. Butterworth, she thought, you are a comfortable man. Such a pity that you are wasting your comfort on Jane Milton.

He knew how to choose inns for luncheon, too, because the food was hot, and the service attentive. Even Andrew noticed. "Miss Mitten, when we go anywhere with Grandfather or Lady Carruthers, we never have food this fast," he whispered, while Mr. Butterworth was busy praising a particularly fine leg of mutton and the footman, all smiles, who bore it in. "And *we* have a crest on the door, where Mr. Butterworth does not!"

She smiled at Andrew and straightened the napkin tied around his neck. "But have you ever heard Lord Denby or your aunt show such appreciation? Have they ever complimented a waiter?"

Andrew shook his head. "There is something to that, isn't

there?" he commented as he held out his plate for a slice of the mutton.

Indeed there is, she thought, as the journey continued. If Mr. Butterworth runs his mills the way he treats people, then he ought to be declared a national treasure. I could tell him, she told herself, the way he tells others. She smiled to herself. After all, Mr. Butterworth, if I embarrass you, you can only blame yourself, as you are always admonishing me to speak my mind. She leaned closer to the mill owner, who was watching Andrew read, a smile on his face.

"Mr. Butterworth, you are a remarkably kind man."

". . . Oh, I don't . . ."

"Surely you are not going to become missish, as you accuse me!"

She laughed. "Of course you are kind. Truly, sir, you are so good with people, and the wonder of it is, you mean every word of your kindness."

He continued to smile at her, but there was a wistfulness in his eyes she hadn't noticed before. "Have you ever stopped to consider that I might be following your own example?"

It was so preposterous that she laughed, then covered her mouth when Joe Singletary stirred and muttered something in his sleep. "You cannot escape a compliment so quickly, Mr. Butterworth!" she teased. "Some people are just born good, sir. The rest of us must have goodness thrust upon us by rigorous discipline!"

"Precisely my point, Miss Mitten," he murmured, then turned his attention to the scene outside the window. "And look now; it is beginning to snow."

Peaceful in her heart, she did not object to a change of subject. In his own way, I suppose Mr. Butterworth is like Lord Denby, she considered, looking at the mill owner's profile as he gazed out the window. Lord Denby's essays have done so much to reform the morals of an entire officers' corps, and Mr. Butterworth works so hard to improve the lot of the oppressed. I suppose I am more fortunate than I know, to have the acquaintance of such men.

They passed through Leeds as the afternoon sun lengthened, and she was glad when Mr. Butterworth said his home was just beyond in Rumsey, and there was no need to stop in the city. She knew they would pass down the High Street to Devon, where the workhouse stretched for two gray blocks. "There it is, sir," she murmured into the mill owner's sleeve, so Andrew would not hear. "My alma mater."

He looked for a long moment. "Snow does wonders for institutional buildings, Miss Mitten."

"I suppose it does," she agreed.

A few more blocks, and more silence, and they were in the country again. The snow was falling harder now, and she could feel the horses straining on the road. They topped a rise, and came down into Rumsey. Lights were coming on, a wink here, a wink there, and men bundled in overcoats and mufflers strode with purpose, leaning against the wind. In the distance she heard a factory whistle.

Mr. Butterworth rubbed his hands together and chuckled. "Rumsey's workers are going home to hearth and wife, and brown bread and chowder, Miss Mitten," he said. "That whistle's from Rumsey's own mill, which I intend to own, when the present proprietor beats it into the ground."

She knew it was what a mill owner would say, but she had not heard him speak like that before. "I don't understand."

"His own mismanagement and ill will toward the men, women, and little children who labor for him will close him down one day," he said, his eyes on the mill as they passed it. "Ill treatment is not a cup which can be filled forever and ever, my dear, or have you noticed?"

I have noticed, she thought, with a glance at Andrew. She didn't mean to sigh, but she did. Mr. Butterworth took her hand and held it, and she had no desire to pull away. I still need a friend, she thought, returning his slight pressure on her fingers.

After a moment's silence, he patted her knuckles and released her hand. "And now, my dears, do brace yourselves. When you accepted a mill owner's invitation home for Christmas, you agreed, in effect, to share his brown bread and chowder, did you not? Well, Andrew?"

"Yes, sir," Andrew said, his eyes serious.

"Even if it means visiting with people whose style is not precisely your own? Rubbing shoulders with hoi polloi?"

Andrew frowned, and put his finger in the book he was reading. "I don't know any pollois, Mr. Butterworth, but Miss Mitten taught me manners, if that is what worries you."

The mill owner leaned forward across the carriage and rubbed

Andrew's head. "Of course Miss Mitten taught you," he said with a laugh. "You would probably remember your manners in a teepee, eh? Or a mill owner's tenement?"

"You're quizzing me, sir," Andrew said. He came over and sat between Jane and Mr. Butterworth.

"I am, indeed, laddie. Oh dear, the horses are slowing down now. If you don't think you can bear with equanimity your first glance at your home for the few weeks, do look away," Mr. Butterworth said.

Jane smiled, relieved to hear Mr. Butterworth's lighter tone again. No matter what his home is like, it will be more pleasant than Stover Hall for Christmas, she decided. I am determined to admire what I see.

She stared out the window at the mill owner's house. Thinking it a house is only another indication of my lack of imagination, she decided finally as she closed her mouth, and wondered at her own rag manners. At least you are not drooling, or making strange sounds, Jane Milton, she scolded herself. One would think you have never seen a mansion before.

She had always thought that Mr. Butterworth's estate near Denby was a fine affair, but this house in Rumsey eclipsed it, and put Stover Hall itself in some danger, she decided, as the carriage came closer. The style was Georgian, solid red brick, with its proportions totally symmetrical and agreeable in every way to someone yearning for order in the universe. It was a home built to last, with snow on the roof now, smoke curling from all the chimneys, and a wonderful wreath gracing the door.

"Miss Mitten, you are holding my hand rather too tight," Andrew said in protest.

"Oh! I am sorry, my dear," she exclaimed, releasing his fingers without even having been aware that she had grasped them in the first place.

Mr. Butterworth sighed and nudged her shoulder. "I know it is lacking a Greek temple or two, and a maze out back, but what is a mill owner to do, Miss Mitten? Miss Mitten? Are we still on speaking terms?"

" 'Sharing your brown bread and chowder,' indeed!" she said with some feeling.

"I suppose that was a little strong," he admitted when the carriage stopped in front of the mansion and the postilions dismounted. "But are you woman enough to admit to just the tiniest fear that you were careering toward vulgarity of unimagined depths when you accepted a mill owner's invitation?"

"I am woman enough," she said simply. "It is beautiful, Mr. Butterworth."

"In a word, Miss Milton, muslin," he said. "Bolts and bolts of it, and wool, too, in the other factory. Enough wool to put a uniform on the back of every soldier in England. Muslin for children, schoolroom misses, shy damsels at come-outs, brazen opera dancers—excuse me, Andrew—and summer shirts for gentlemen."

"All this goes on in your factories?" Andrew asked.

"That and more, lad," Mr. Butterworth said.

"I want to see it."

"And so you shall, lad," he replied. "Here we are."

The mansion was as beautiful up close as it was from the distance, with the setting sun outlining all the symmetry. Lights shone from the windows, and Jane could smell the balsam from the Christmas wreath even as she stood beside the carriage. "Lovely, just lovely," she murmured, as Mr. Butterworth took her arm.

"My father built the house, and it is mine," the mill owner said, steering her through the snow that was starting to drift as the wind rose. "Because I live in Denby, my little sister Emma and her husband Richard Newton reside here with their three"—he smiled as the door opened and children came out—"their three and a half offspring. Richard handles the day-to-day operations of both mills."

You are a favorite, sir, Jane thought, as the mill owner was accosted by children. She released his arm and rested her hand on Andrew's shoulder instead as they watched as Mr. Butterworth hugged them all in turn.

Mr. Butterworth clapped his hands to get their attention. "Curtsies and bows now," he ordered. "Let me introduce Miss Jane Milton and . . . and Andrew Stover from Denby, who have consented to spend Christmas here with us." He leaned close to Andrew and whispered, "Am I guessing, or would you rather just be Andrew Stover, rather than Lord Canfield?"

Andrew grinned at him. "Much rather, Mr. Butterworth!"

"Very well, then. Jacob, this is Andrew. I expect the two of you to fetch the Christmas presents from the postilion over there and take them to my sister." He glanced down at the little girl who was tugging on his pant leg. "You, too, Lucy." He put his arm around a young girl who was almost as tall as Jane. "Miss Mitten, this is Amanda. He kissed her cheek. Amanda smiled at Jane, then turned to help Lucy, who was holding out both arms for a package far too large.

"I wonder that you want to be away from them for three weeks out of every month," Jane murmured as he took her arm again and led her up the steps. She looked around at the children. "I would rather be here."

"Would you?" he asked. She could tell he was going to say something else, but the door opened again upon a woman far gone with child. "Ah, my dear Emma. How you've grown!"

Jane smiled as the mill owner carefully hugged his sister, who kissed him and then gave him a little push. "He is a dreadful tease," the woman said to her, as she held out her hand. "He will be making jokes at my expense through this entire visit." She belied her words by standing on tiptoe to give him another kiss. "But he will tell you that is what brothers are for, Miss Milton. You *are* Miss Milton?"

"She is in very deed," Mr. Butterworth agreed. "Andrew is somewhere down there, running with the pack already. Miss Milton, this is my little—well, my not-so-little—sister Emma Newton."

The woman made a face at her brother and held out her hand to Jane. "Wretched brother! My dear Miss Milton, I trust you will not object if my Jacob takes over your charge? They appear to be somewhat the same age, and Jacob had been pining to play with boys, instead of pesky sisters."

"I have no objections whatever," Jane said, admiring the handsome woman and looking for some resemblance between her and the mill owner. She saw it in their height, and the easy way they had with each other. "Come, Andrew," she called, looking behind her. "Make yourself known to your hostess."

She admitted privately to her own pride when Andrew came up the steps, Jacob hot on his heels, and bowed neatly in front of Emma Newton. "This is my cousin Andrew Stover," she said. "Andrew, this is Mrs. Newton."

To her surprise, the smile left Emma's face. She looked at Andrew seriously, and then knelt awkwardly in front of him, until they were on eye level. She put both of her hands against his face, and then her cheek as well. "You are so welcome, my dear," she murmured. "I am so glad to meet the Latin scholar I have heard so much about."

Oh, she is wonderful with children, Jane thought, as tears came to her eyes. I am so glad Mr. Butterworth let us tag along to Rumsey and the cotton mills. She leaned close to the mill owner and he obligingly bent down so she could whisper in his ear. "It seems that Andrew and I have come up in the world, wouldn't you say? Such a lovely welcome from your sister."

"She is a lovely woman," he replied.

He seemed so scarcely to be in command of his own voice that Jane looked at him in surprise. "Mr. Butterworth, you really ought to abandon Denby and come back to live with your own relatives," she whispered.

He turned to look at her, his face so close. "I am just speaking my mind, sir," she said softly, and surprised herself further by kissing him. Oh dear, she thought as she pulled away quickly and Mr. Butterworth straightened up. Put me around a little family feeling and I get sillier than usual. *What* possessed me? "Well, you advised me to speak my mind," she reminded him. Embarrassed, she glanced at Emma Newton to see if she had noticed her own lapse in manners, but the woman was still regarding Andrew.

"You won't mind if, during your visit here, Jacob tags after you, or if Lucy gets sticky fingers on you," she was saying to Andrew.

"Oh, no, mum, I won't mind a bit," he told her earnestly.

Jane smiled and looked away. "Your sister has made a conquest," she said to Mr. Butterworth.

"She does that regularly," he replied. He took her hand and patted it in that brusque way she was familiar with. "Now, ladies and gentlemen, let us go inside. Emma, may I help you up, or should we find a block and tackle?"

Dinner with Mr. Butterworth and the Newtons was so wonderful that Jane wanted to pinch herself. I wonder if these people have even the slightest idea how lucky they are, she thought, as she enjoyed the flow of conversation around her. Mr. Butterworth nudged her every now and then to remind her to eat, but she found herself filled with satisfaction by the company she kept.

Emma and Richard Newton presided at the head and foot of the table in the breakfast room, with Amanda to supervise her little sister Lucy, and then remind her mama that they did have an actual dining room. Emma Newton had only laughed and patted her brother's arm. "Yes, Amanda, but then we would have to shout to be heard and send messages by carrier pigeon," she said. She looked around her, and then at Jane. "I like this, Miss Milton, even if we are a bit like whelks in a basket."

So do I, Jane thought, as she wondered again how Mr. Butterworth could bear to spend time away from the Newtons. I do not know that I would ever let them out of my sight, she told herself. I cannot imagine what the attraction is at Denby, and so I shall remind him.

The only crisis came when Lucy knocked her milk over while reaching for another bun. Jane could almost feel Andrew tense and suck in his breath, and then relax almost palpably when everyone in the family threw their napkins toward Amanda, who dabbed up the milk for her little sister. As though nothing had happened, Amanda continued her conversation with her father on the merits of studying Italian instead of needlework at Miss Finch's Day School.

Jane watched as Andrew leaned toward Jacob. "Aunt Carruthers would have scolded me until bedtime," he whispered.

"Why?" Jacob asked.

Andrew shook his head, as though he had never considered the matter in that light. "I really don't know."

"How fortunate that she is not here then," Jane replied, then smiled as she thought about Cecil.

"You look like the cat with the canary," Mr. Butterworth commented on her other side.

"I was merely wondering if Cecil has decided to whom to bequeath his debts," she said, "or even if he is still among the living."

"One can't be too careful with epizootic fever," the mill owner said seriously, which further tried her dignity. "Do have another bun, Miss Mitten."

"You call her Miss Mitten?" Lucy asked, looking at her uncle with big eyes.

"Yes, Lucy pet," he replied. "It is her nickname." He winked at her. "Even your old uncle can quiz pretty ladies."

"She is pretty," Lucy agreed. She looked at Jane. "What do you call my uncle?"

"Mr. Butterworth, of course," she replied, amused. "What else?"

Lucy frowned. "I should think maybe Uncle."

"He's not my uncle," Jane said.

"Then what *is* he?" Lucy persisted, with the understanding of a four-year-old.

"What, indeed?" she quizzed.

"The best friend she will ever have, Lucy," he assured her without hesitation or embarrassment. "On that note, Richard, let us shoo away your offspring, detach the females to supervise them, clear off this table, and spread out those blueprints I saw you bringing home. Are they the plans for the mill workers' quarters?"

Richard helped his wife from her chair. Mr. Butterworth blew Lucy a kiss, then swatted her with the blueprints he picked up from the sideboard. "Is it business, Uncle Scipio?" she asked with a frown.

"Most assuredly, Lucy," he told her, tapping the blueprints. "It keeps butter on your bread."

"And on other people's bread as well," Jane said, moving Lucy along. From the corner of her eye she could see Mr. Butterworth pulling back the blueprints to take a swat at her, too, so she stepped out of range, feeling only the breeze as he missed. Lucy laughed. "Uncle Scipio! You are worse than I am," she scolded.

Emma was laughing as they followed the children to the sitting room. She took Jane's hand. "I want to call you Jane, even if Scipio cannot. Or will not!"

"Jane it is, Emma," she said simply. "Now how can I best help you this evening? I don't imagine you are too comfortable these days."

"I am not," she agreed. She stopped and squeezed Jane's hand. "Do you know, that is what Scipio writes about you!"

"He writes about me?" Jane asked, surprised.

"Oh, yes. You and Andrew," she confided. "He says that you are always studying people's comfort, and that he wonders if you have a thought for yourself ever."

I have many thoughts for myself, she told herself, and none of them productive lately. "He is the one who is all kindness," she said after a pause that felt awkward to her own ears.

If it was awkward, Emma chose not to notice. "No, my dear,"

she contradicted with that serenity that Jane was finding so appealing about her. "I know my brother far better than that." She hesitated, and Jane was struck by her sudden seriousness. The moment passed, and she smiled again. "Come, Lucy, and let us impose upon Miss Mitten to give you a bath, so Mama is not forced to bend where she does not bend anymore!"

This is far more fun than soothing Cecil's crochets, Jane decided as she knelt beside the tub.

"You have the touch, Jane," Emma said as she reclined on Lucy's bed, her shoes off.

"Or at least I have not completely forgotten," Jane replied as she gave Lucy a hand up, then lifted her onto a towel. "Andrew has been in my charge since he was an infant. Here now, Lucy, do hold still so I can wrap you up." She picked up the child and sat with her close to the fire. "What beautiful golden curls you have," she told Lucy as she dried her hair.

"Uncle Scipio says I will break hearts someday," she announced, then wrinkled her nose. "I do not know what he means, and Mama won't tell me."

Jane laughed. "Then I shall not, either! Be assured that it is a fine thing for uncles to say."

Lucy sighed dramatically and threw herself back against Jane, who breathed in the fragrance of clean-washed hair and tightened the towel around the little girl. I think I could sit like this forever, she thought. "Do you ever wonder at your own good fortune?" she asked Emma.

When there was no answer, she looked around to see Emma asleep. Jane smiled and put her finger to her lips. "I think your mother is quite worn out," she told the child on her lap.

Lucy nodded and turned Jane's head until she could speak into her ear. "She is going to have a baby, you know," she confided in a breathy voice that tickled Jane's ear.

"I thought as much," Jane said. "If we are very quiet, I am certain that you can find your nightgown, and we will not even have to disturb her." She draped the towel around Lucy; to her amusement, the little girl grabbed the long end and swirled it over her shoulder. "Such a flair," she murmured, as Lucy stalked into the dressing room, one arm extended, as though she intended an oration.

"Oh, indeed," said Mr. Butterworth from the doorway. He looked over his shoulder. "Richard, come do the honors here for

Em, and Miss Mitten and I will manage your dramatic daughter."

Both men were in shirtsleeves, and Mr. Butterworth's fingers were ink-stained. "I can't leave blueprints alone," he confessed. He washed his hands in Lucy's bath water while his brother-in-law carefully picked up his wife. Emma opened her eyes long enough to blow a kiss to Jane. "Thank you, my dear," she murmured. "This is a fine start to your holiday with us." She rested her head against her husband's arm as he carried her from the room.

"Isn't there a nursemaid?" Jane asked, handing him the towel she had used on Lucy's hair.

"Oh, yes, but my little sister is far too good-hearted, and let her go home for Christmas," he said. He dried his hands. "And here you thought you were going to have peace and quiet in Rumsey, Miss Mitten. Mill owners are notorious users of people, or don't you read the penny post?"

She scooped up Lucy and whirled her around. "At least I do not have Cecil," she exclaimed. She took the towel from him. "Or even Lord Denby, although he is the dearest man."

"Could it be . . . a revolt by the perfect poor relation?" Mr. Butterworth teased.

"Possibly," she said. "During my visit I intend to deal with problems no greater than what book to read to Lucy, and how she likes her porridge. Climb up, love."

"I don't like porridge," Lucy confided as she got into bed.

"Of course you do not!" Jane sat down beside her. "Shall we dismiss your uncle?"

"First he will give me a kiss," Lucy commanded, holding up her arms to Mr. Butterworth, who sat on the bed and kissed her on the forehead with a loud smack. "Then he usually gives my mama a kiss, but you will do, Miss Mitten."

"She will, indeed," Mr. Butterworth agreed and kissed Jane's forehead with another loud smack. To her astonishment, he took her face in his hands and kissed her lips. "That's to pay you back," he said softly.

Lucy clapped her hands. "Now you may leave, Uncle Scipio."

Yes, do, Jane thought, her mind in a jumble. Give me a chance to calm down the color in my cheeks now. With real relief, she watched him blow another kiss to Lucy and then go to the door. "Good night, my dears," he said. "Jane, would you like me to hunt down the boys and subdue them?"

So I am Jane, she thought, and she could think of no objection. "If you would, sir," she replied.

Jane knew that she read to Lucy, but for the life of her, she couldn't make sense of the words. No matter; Lucy's eyes were drooping, and she closed them completely before Jane finished the chapter. "And I am certain they lived happily ever after, little one," she whispered. "That's how it is with fiction." She kissed Lucy, and left the room on tiptoe.

It was just a matter of following the sounds to locate Jacob and Andrew, but she stood for a moment outside their room, convincing herself that she was silly to make much of Mr. Butterworth's actions. Jane, he could be your uncle, she told herself, as she opened the door. No, he couldn't, she decided as she watched the boys look at each other, grab their pillows, and start toward Mr. Butterworth. He stood with his back to them, staring out the window. No, he could not be my uncle, she decided.

It was the perfect moment to close the door and retreat, but she stepped inside. "Mr. Butterworth, do beware," she said, then shut it, and leaned against it, laughing as he turned around to roar at the boys, who shrieked and dived for the bed.

"Now I am to expect you to settle down to sleep," he said, standing over them as they scrambled under the covers. "Although I cannot imagine how you will, after that kind of treatment. I never could." He glanced over his shoulder at her. "I was that young once, my dear. Can you credit it?"

"Oh, yes," she replied. "Looking at you now, your board of directors would probably say you have not aged a day!"

He laughed and sat on the bed. "Go away, Miss Mitten," he ordered her cheerfully. "If I can summon the strength to leave this room eventually, you should speak for tea in the sitting room."

She closed the door. She asked a servant in the hall where the sitting room was, and seated herself beside Amanda, who was attempting to separate a jumble of embroidery threads.

"Did Lucy get into these?" she asked.

Amanda shook her head. "I am completely to blame," she confessed as she tugged apart a green and a blue strand. "I do so dislike embroidery, and am trying so hard to convince Papa that I would rather take Italian than embroidery."

Jane reached for the threads, which Amanda gladly relinquished. "Let me try for a while. You can order tea for us and your uncle, should he emerge unscathed from Jacob's room."

"I will escape with relief," Amanda said as she leaped to her feet. She was back soon and seated herself again. "Oh, you are good at that!" she declared with some feeling. "I need some patience quickly, don't I?" she asked, to Jane's amusement.

"Immediately, my dear," she said, enjoying Amanda's laughter. "I don't think it comes like that, however."

The girl picked up a smaller clump of thread. "Is my mother all right?" she asked, her voice low. "I saw Papa carry her down the hall."

"She is tired, Amanda," Jane said. "What would you think if you and I took over the household duties for her?"

"I would like that, but I have never done it before," Amanda replied. "There, two strands!"

"Bravo! I am quite good at running a household," Jane said. "A few days of bed rest will be my Christmas gift to your mama, and I can help you run things."

Amanda nodded, then leaned close to Jane. "I think Mama is due to be confined quite soon," she whispered. "I mean, Papa is already bringing work home early, and pacing around." She giggled. "I recognize the signs!"

In a few minutes they were joined by Richard Newton. The tea tray arrived, followed shortly by Mr. Butterworth, who stood in the doorway tucking in his shirttails. He sat next to Jane and picked up a handful of thread while Amanda poured the tea in her mother's place.

"Get Andrew away from Stover, and he is quite another child," he commented, draping several untangled threads on his leg.

"Second thoughts about inviting us, Mr. Butterworth?" Jane teased.

He shook his head. "Not even one. You are the one who will be inconvenienced, Miss Mitten." He looked at his brother-in-law. "I predict that you may become quite busy here! Richard, I must be an idiot, but I was not aware that Em was so far along."

"You *have* had your head in a cupboard lately," Richard commented with a smile of his own. "I think I know why now."

My but this is a long silence, Jane thought, as quiet descended on the room.

"Yes, indeed, Richard, running two mills is a greater challenge than one, especially at long distance," he said at last. "Perhaps I should think about moving back to Rumsey permanently."

"Excellent!" Richard said, with a clap of his hands. "I must warn you that Em has her eye on the Fabersham estate, which will come vacant in six months or so. By June we could return your house to you."

I could not bear it, Jane thought suddenly. The ball of thread in her hands grew blurry. Who on earth would I turn to, when life is unbearable at Stover?

"My removal from the district would certainly fill your cousin Lady Carruthers with considerable relief, wouldn't it, Miss Milton?" the mill owner was saying to her. His tone of voice no different than it ever was, to both her chagrin and her relief.

Oh, he expects a quizzing answer, she thought, as she pressed her finger to the side of her nose to stop the tears. Something light and frivolous that I have always been incapable of, and drat him for not knowing me better, even after all these years. Please God, let me say something unexceptionable.

"I would miss you," she said simply. "There would go my only friend."

The room was still silent. Carefully Jane returned the embroidery to the basket, too irritated with herself to look anyone in the eye. That was the wrong thing, Jane, you goose, she scolded herself. Do better!

"Oh, I am silly," she said. "I blame your brother-in-law entirely. He has been advising me to speak my mind lately." She attempted what she hoped was an elaborate sigh, the kind that Lucy was so expert in delivering. She must have been successful, because Amanda laughed. "I suppose he will force me to cultivate new friends, if he moves, and so I shall. Do excuse me, please."

Chapter Nine

She spent a perfectly miserable night, the dream returning in full force to wake her in tears. She stared at her hands, holding them up to the moonlight that streamed in the window. After the first moment of terror, she knew she would find nothing on them, and this night was no different. She wiped them on the sheet anyway.

The only relief she felt was in knowing that no one in the Newton household could have heard her cry out. Amanda had apologized for the pretty room, tucked as it was next to Mr. Butterworth's office. "Mama wanted me to tell you that we do not consign all our guests to outer darkness, but she thought it might be a good, quiet place!" Amanda had told her, when the footman set down her traveling case. "Uncle Scipio says his office is the only place where Lucy cannot find him."

And so it was quiet, except that she could have sworn she heard someone in the office anyway. As she wearily wished the night away, she thought she heard various creaks and scratches. I am certain Mr. Butterworth has far better things to do at three in the morning than pore over blueprints, she told herself.

And then she was thinking about the mill owner, and wondering if this was what love felt like. Oh, I hope not, she decided at last. I am miserable.

No, it is not precisely misery, she told herself, after a moment's consideration. She gave up on sleep and seated herself on the chair in front of the cold hearth, doubling her legs under her and reaching for a blanket at the bed's foot. It is as though I am on edge for no reason. That is it. My senses all feel as though they are humming. She rested her head against the back of the chair. Mr. Butterworth has never given any indication that I am more than a friend. True, he kissed me, but he was teasing. Wasn't he?

There was one thing to do, and she did it, thinking through all the reasons that she could not be in love with Mr. Scipio Africanus Butterworth. First, there is that stupid name, she told herself, then smiled, despite her misery. But it suits him some-how, in the same way that those outrageous waistcoats do, the ones that scream out that he is not, and never will be, gentry.

Lady Carruthers is right; he does smell of the shop, she thought. What he is, and always will be, is a mill owner, a man of wealth and property with his eye on the ledger. If by some wild leap he actually married you, Jane, he would always be bringing home blueprints, or spending too long at the factory to work on the machinery, for all you know. There would never be the worry of another woman, because that is not in him. He is a man of business.

She paused, and waited for this thought to disgust her, but to her further irritation, it did not. "Trust you, Jane, to look over his shoulder at the blueprints and offer your opinions!" she accused herself.

Well, then, if his mill owner status does not repel you as it should, she told herself, begin with the essential difficulty: He is too old for you. She sighed and wrapped the blanket tighter about her shoulders, listening for the mice next door. Except that he is enthusiastic, and he has not put on too many pounds to ren-der him fit only for an invalid's chair at Bath.

The thought of Mr. Butterworth, busy as he was, even ap-proaching Bath to drink the water made her laugh. She covered her mouth with her hand when the mice became silent. Oh, I hope they do not come in here now to forage, she thought, pulling her feet in closer to her body. No, we cannot argue that his years have rendered Mr. Butterworth fit for the boneyard, she conceded.

The thought made her smile. Good, Jane; you are moving in the right direction now, she congratulated herself. Toss this into the pot until your cup runneth over: He is already talking about buying another mill, and moving back here to oversee them more closely, and you announced to him in a burst of inanity that you were looking for a husband who would devote much at-tention to you. He would never have the time.

It was easy to think, but even as the notion passed through her brain, she knew in her heart that he would always find the time for her, if he loved her. Jane, this is an organized man, used to juggling numerous enterprises, she reminded herself. He would make every moment count with you. Face it, Jane; you cannot think of a single reason why Mr. Butterworth is not the best idea you ever had.

This is not working, she thought, as she threw off the blanket that was suddenly stifling her. She went to the window and dragged open the draperies, letting the colder air wrap around her neck and shoulders like fingers on her windpipe. She closed her eyes in utter despair and forced her mind into calmness.

Maybe it was the cold air that did it, or the deliberate wrench of her thoughts. As she stood at the window, her irritation with herself turned to sorrow. You have no objections to marriage to Mr. Butterworth, but oh, my dear, he has far too many against you to ever consider a proposal.

It was a splash of icy water on her mind, one that made her shiver and get back into bed. He knows better than anyone *your* status, never mind his own. He knows that you are an old maid every other man has overlooked, you are too thin because you forget to eat, and you are cowed by your relatives to such an extent that he must brace you by telling you to speak your mind. You have no clever repartee. Beyond a little native cheery temperament that not even Lady Carruthers could harrow out of you, you have nothing to recommend you except a capacity for hard work on behalf of others. Servants are paid for that.

Her thoughts were so harsh that she blinked in surprise, then sank lower in the bed, until she had enveloped herself into a tight ball. She cried then, sobs that she muffled as best she could, and which finally sent her to sleep. When she woke, she was herself again.

Over breakfast, Mr. Butterworth proposed a visit to the mill, which Andrew seconded almost before the suggestion was entirely out of his mouth. "It is crass commerce, Andrew," he warned. "The sort of thing your relatives—Miss Mitten included—should steer you far away from."

"Of course I want to see it," Andrew insisted. He looked at Jacob, as though seeking encouragement. "Jacob tells me there is machinery, and lots of it. I *have* to see that!"

Mr. Butterworth laughed with such heartiness that Jane felt an absurd urge to join in. "Andrew, you are a child after my own heart!" he declared finally. "Noisy machinery, eh? And you *must* see it?"

"I, too," Jane spoke up. She dabbed the porridge from Lucy's face and lifted her from her chair. "That is, if you can wait for a little while until Amanda and I discuss household management belowstairs, now that your sister has agreed to rest in bed."

Mr. Butterworth wiped his eyes and beamed at Amanda. "My dear niece, did you ever think your Uncle Scipio was so clever? A useful house guest has to be the eighth wonder of the world." He touched Andrew's arm when the boy passed his chair. "You, my young friend, will do as your . . . Jacob says and find some cotton wadding for your ears. It is all noise and movement in my factory." He nodded to Jane. "As for you, Miss Mitten, manage away! I will visit with Emma and assure her that we are in excellent hands."

Oh, my hands *are* excellent, Jane thought; I contemplate them half the night. "Very well, sir," she said, getting up from the table. "Come, my dear, and let us discuss menus."

Mr. Butterworth surprised her by rising, too, then putting his hand firmly on her shoulder until she had no choice but to sit again. "Go ahead, Amanda," he instructed, "and take Lucy with you. Miss Mitten sometimes forgets to eat, although I cannot imagine such a thing."

Embarrassed, she looked at her plate to see it still full of bacon, eggs, and toast. "Now, how did that get there?" she murmured as she picked up her fork. Mr. Butterworth sat beside her this time, and she felt a sudden flash of anger. "I know how busy you are, Mr. Butterworth. I *will* eat," she informed him.

"And I *will* watch," he replied, obviously unruffled by her clipped words.

He is only being kind, she thought, as she ate and he finished perusing the morning newspaper, with the occasional glance in her direction. She put down her fork finally and he folded the paper. "A little more, Jane?" he coaxed.

"Very well, sir! If you will finish the bacon, I will finish the eggs."

"And the toast?"

She tried not to frown, but could not help herself. "You are a trial, Mr. B," she told him finally, when he continued to regard her.

" 'Mr. B,' " was his only comment. "I like that."

She sighed and bit into the toast, then smiled at his own overdramatic sigh. "Miss Mitten, it is only toast. Not a penance!" She knew she should have been uncomfortable when he moved closer and draped his arm across the back of her chair, but she reminded herself that he was filching bacon from her plate. And it should have surprised her when he finally put his arm around her shoulders and gave her arm a squeeze.

"Did you have a bad night, Jane?" he asked quietly.

She didn't mean to shiver at his words, and she hoped he did not notice. "I . . . a strange bed is always difficult the first night," she said, wondering why she was whispering and then wondering why she allowed him to rest his cheek against hers and keep it there.

"Maybe we should talk, my dear," he said finally, when she made no comment, nor any movement away from him.

I hope Mr. Butterworth's cologne is found in heaven, she thought, forgetful of the rest of her toast. I could breathe it forever. "I will remind you that I *have* been speaking my mind, sir," she told him.

"Not enough, Jane, not enough," he said, his voice low, as he rose from the table. "Ah, Lucy! Did you think I was planning to keep her all to myself this entire day? Miss Mitten, to the kitchen, please. It is where we Butterworths send all our house guests!"

Don't think about him, she told herself as she sat belowstairs with Amanda, the cook, and the butler, discussing the week's menus. He is solicitous of everyone's welfare; you know that from your years of acquaintance. If I am the perfect poor relation, then he is the perfect host. Still, I wonder if he would understand, she thought, as the cook explained to Amanda the merits of lady fingers and bonbons in the same course, preceded by a sultana roll with claret sauce.

"What do you think, Miss Milton?" Amanda asked.

"I promised I would never tell," she said, then put her hand to her mouth.

Amanda laughed. "You are such a tease, especially when I crave your advice!"

"I think it is an excellent combination, my dear," she replied automatically. She thought a moment, and wished she had been paying attention. "Heavens, but isn't that rather a heavy-duty course for family dinner?"

"Miss Milton, we are planning the Board of Directors banquet for this Friday night!" she exclaimed. "Don't you remember? Mama wanted to call it off, but Uncle Scipio says you are a prime organizer. Say it is all right, Miss Milton, or I will worry in earnest."

Mind yourself, Jane, she ordered herself. Kingdoms have probably fallen through half this much inattention. "My dear, fifteen is not a year too young to give a dinner for a Board of Directors," she said firmly. "I will be there to help you every moment of the way."

"Miss Mitten, my uncle is right," Amanda said, her glance so warm that Jane could almost feel it. "He has told us in so many letters that you are a treasure." She looked at the cook. "That will be our menu."

I am no treasure, Jane thought. I am a keeper of secrets and I am weary with it. She rose from the table. "I believe your uncle is waiting for us upstairs. Mrs. Hinchcliff, you are a wonderful cook, and we repose all our confidence in you."

"My uncle does that, too, Miss Mitten," Amanda confided after they left the kitchen. She giggled. "He calls compliments the 'First Rule of Management'! Mama laughs at him, but we always have the best service."

"He is completely right," Jane agreed. "Amanda, that is a lovely ribbon in your hair!"

"And you have such beautiful eyes, Miss Mitten!" Amanda teased in turn.

They were still laughing when they reached the foyer. Andrew and Jacob fidgeted in the entrance, but Mr. Butterworth had assumed his lately typical pose of staring out the window with his hands behind his back. He must have heard them because he turned around with a smile of his own. "General merriment belowstairs, eh?" he asked. "If I were a cynic, I could not live in this disjointed house!"

"Uncle Scipio, you could never be a cynic," Amanda said. "Here is Miss Mitten, and I will go to the nursery to watch Lucy. Mama is well?"

"She is fine, niece." Mr. Butterworth held out his arm to Jane. "Come, my dear Miss Mitten, and you can take the final plunge into the shop." He looked around elaborately. "We will never tell Lady Carruthers our dreadful secret."

She didn't mean to pull away from him when he said that, but she could not help herself. Mr. Butterworth took a long look at her, but she knew it was beyond her just then to hide the bleakness in her eyes. I simply must sleep tonight, she thought in desperation as he took her cloak from the butler and put it around her shoulders without making further comment.

The carriage took them quickly to Huddersfield, Mr. Butterworth keeping up the conversation with Andrew and not forcing any participation from her. She was grateful for his command of the situation. She even dozed a little, too exhausted to stay awake, even though what he was telling them about spinning cotton was fascinating in its detail.

She woke up when the carriage stopped, hopeful that no one had noticed her lapse, except that she was leaning against Mr. Butterworth, and his arm was around her, and around Andrew on his other side. "It is water-powered, Andrew," he was saying. "You see how the mill sits directly next to the river?"

"And there is the waterwheel," Andrew said.

"Precisely. In fact, there are two. We use the river and send it on its way. Clever of us, eh, Miss Mitten? We used to give the cotton fibers to workers in their homes to spin by hand. Now machines do it." He clapped both their shoulders. "My dears, you are looking at the modern age."

When the carriage stopped, Mr. Butterworth took Jacob's hand. "You two rascals stop in the office. Mr. Singletary will show us around." The boys were gone with a bound, not even waiting for the steps to be lowered, and slamming the door behind them. Jane rested her head against the cushion and closed her eyes. "Forgive my inattention," she murmured.

"Done, madam," he said, and gave her shoulder another squeeze. He wouldn't look at her then, but at the floor. "Miss Milton, how long have we known each other?"

"Years and years, sir," she replied.

"How many more years must we know each other before you will trust me totally?"

It didn't sound like a question requiring an answer, so she did nothing beyond lean her cheek against his arm, and then straighten up. He looked at her. She must have been far too tired, because she thought she saw something in them even beyond their usual kindness. "I don't know, Mr. Butterworth," she said frankly, when she wanted to knock his hand away from the carriage door where it rested and talk until she was empty. "But now there are little boys probably driving Joe to distraction, so we must follow."

He opened the door and helped her from the carriage.

"Breathe deep, my dear," he said, his voice normal again. "I know that some are experimenting with generators which will be powered by coal. When that is perfected, we will not require clean rivers to run our mills. This valley will stink and everything will turn black."

"It sounds daunting, sir," she said.

"It is," he agreed, as they crossed the footbridge. "The machinery will turn faster and we will make more cotton cloth, and far more money, but something will be gone." He pointed to a line of row houses in imminent state of collapse. "Those blueprints last night? Richard and I are tearing down this slum to build better workers' quarters." He pointed to the end of the row. "There will sit a school for the mill workers' children."

"Why are you doing this?" she asked as he opened the door to the factory for her. She grimaced at the noise inside, and he closed the door again and leaned against the outside wall.

"Let us just say that I have pulled too many children from the machinery, Miss Milton, and I have listened to the gospel preached by Robert Owen. Workers—adult workers—can be treated well, and they will still produce." He pointed across the valley. "That mill over there and that one beyond it use children as young as five to crawl under the equipment and straighten tangles in the warp and woof. I cannot do it. We start no child younger than twelve here. I know this makes me the laughingstock of other mill owners, but I do not give a damn, Miss Milton. It is that simple."

"Robert Owen and his socialism," she murmured.

"You read the penny post," he said as he opened the door again. "Bravo, Miss Milton. Mostly we are ignored by the gentry, who would not soil themselves with commerce." He leaned close to whisper in her ear. "May I tell you a secret?"

I have far too many of my own, she thought. "Of course," she said, speaking up because the machinery was loud.

"The Lord Denbys of the country who choose not to notice what is happening in England are going to dwindle and blow away like chaff. And the wonder of it is, they will be clueless."

"Sir, you are a radical!"

"Guilty as charged," he said promptly, then grinned. "Miss Milton, what would I *do* without your plain speaking?"

She was content to follow Andrew and Jacob, who were held in check by the admirable Joe Singletary, and watch the mill owner, when she hoped he wasn't aware. Besides being noisy with the clack of looms, the mill was warm. In a few minutes, Mr. Butterworth had removed his coat, and carried it draped over one shoulder. In a few minutes more, he had handed it to her and rolled up his sleeves. She watched, amused, as he walked behind one of the looms, squatted there, and gestured for a wrench. In another moment, he was deep in the machinery. She was smiling when Richard came up beside her.

"My brother-in-law has forgotten more about running a cotton mill than I will ever know," he said, admiration evident in his voice. "He knows the business from the seed to the bolt in the warehouse."

"How on earth did he acquire an education like that?" she asked, speaking up to be heard.

He shrugged. "I have never been given leave to talk about that." Mr. Butterworth called to him; in a moment they were both involved under the silent loom.

So you have secrets, too, Mr. Butterworth? she reflected. Thoughtfully, she smoothed down his coat and continued after the boys. The clacking behind her started up again, and Mr. Butterworth soon joined her, wiping his hands on a totally inadequate fabric scrap. "Sir, I understand why you have never taken the time to acquire a wife," she told him, standing on tiptoe to get close to his ear, in the noisy room.

"Oh, you do?" he asked, bending down to oblige her.

"You are far too much trouble for any woman," she said with a smile. "If you came home to my house wearing a year's supply of grease, I would change the locks!"

"No you wouldn't, Miss Mitten," he said, then winked at her and strolled ahead to talk to Joe Singletary.

"No, I probably would not," she said in a normal voice, knowing that nothing could be heard over the machinery. "I probably would not."

She nearly bumped into the little troupe of spectators, who had stopped before another loom, also silent. "Miss Milton, do you see that wrench behind you?" Mr. Butterworth asked.

She did, laughed, and brought it to him.

"Well-trained already," he commented as he took it from her. "Andrew, are you interested in . . ."

"Oh, I am!" he exclaimed, and handed his jacket to Jane.

Boys and toys, she thought, watching them together under the loom. She held her breath when Andrew crawled inside the loom, then let it out slowly, knowing that Mr. Butterworth would never be careless with a child.

"He has an aptitude that you must work hard to stifle now," Richard was saying to her. "Andrew has a good wrist with that wrench."

"And who would ever have known it?" she said.

"Scipio has an eye for these things."

"Indeed he does," she agreed. "I continue to wonder that he lives in Denby instead of here, where he is obviously so at home."

"It is not such a mystery," was all Richard said. In another moment, a clerk from the office called him away.

Well it is to me, Jane thought. She applauded when Andrew, under Mr. Butterworth's direction, started the loom in motion again. She waited for them to rejoin her, but when Mr. Butterworth launched into what looked like a pantomime of the loom operation, she continued by herself, admiring the magnitude of the operation, and the graceful way the workers, men and women, moved in and out among the looms. Someone was always ready with another large spool of thread to attach in time to keep the weaving regular. The motion and the sound thrilled her, and she was not amazed at the interest of small boys, when it captured her, too. I wonder if Mr. Butterworth requires a teacher at his mill school, she thought, as she watched one of the younger workers direct the fabric around a bolt as it came off the loom. Andrew will be away at school next year, and I will need employment of my own.

"It has a hypnotic effect, hasn't it?" Mr. Butterworth said when he and the boys rejoined her.

She nodded, knowing the difficulty of being heard, and continued her stroll through the factory, noting that Mr. Butterworth's waistcoat by now was hanging open and one of the buttons looked ready to come off. No woman would wish the management of this mill owner, she told herself.

"You look as though you are having a pleasant thought," he said in her ear.

She nodded, in perfect charity with him. "It is completely at your expense," she said, speaking up to be heard.

"My blushes, Jane," he said in return.

"No, sir, actually, it is the grease there on your collar and that

smudge by your nose," she said, taking a corner of his already
deckled neckcloth to dab at his face. "You are worse than ten little boys."

"Far worse," he agreed. "And do you know . . ."

Know what, she never knew. Out of the corner of her eye she
watched Richard hurrying toward them, pulling on his own coat.
He took her arm. "Miss Milton, I have a message from home
that tells me they have sent for the doctor." He looked at Mr.
Butterworth. "You, sir, are in charge of two boys. I am taking
Miss Milton back to Rumsey. Emma needs her far more than
you do, at the moment."

"Unlikely," Mr. Butterworth said quickly, and then to her surprise, blushed. "Especially if you ask me to manage these two
hell-born heathens. So Emma has chosen this moment to increase the population?"

They were all hurrying toward the main office now. "I don't
know that it is a matter of choice," Jane said, when she could be
heard better. She handed Mr. Butterworth's coat to him in the
office, then tugged off the button on his waistcoat, and put it in
the watch pocket. "I will sew it on later with double thread."

He smiled at her. "Better hurry along now. I will take the boys
shopping." He took her hand, bowed elaborately over it, and
kissed her fingers, while Andrew and Jacob laughed. "Miss Mitten, you are the year's most put-upon guest. Other company is
treated to good food, pleasant surroundings, a ball here, an as-
sembly there. We Butterworths send you to the kitchens, drag
you to factories, and now expect you to attend our confine-
ments." He covered her hand with his other one. "And the wonder of it is, I don't believe you mind a bit. Is that your secret, my
dear?"

Standing there in the mill office with the owner holding her
hand, and Richard impatient to be off, it occurred to Jane that
Mr. Butterworth had hit upon something she had never really
considered before. She squeezed his hand. "If that is so, sir, then
you must stop calling me the perfect poor relation," she said, her
voice soft. "Maybe there are some of us who do things out of
other motivations."

"Love, Miss Milton?" he asked.

"Yes, I believe so, sir." She looked him in the eye. "I suppose
that is one of my secrets."

To her surprise, he hugged her, then released her just as

quickly. "I would have all your secrets for Christmas, my dear," he said.

"That would be a terrible present," she said before she thought. Oh, Jane, do lighten this! She looked at her dress. "And now you have gotten grease on me, as well!"

"It washes off," he said, following her to Richard's carriage, where he waited impatiently. "Everything washes off, Jane."

Does it? she asked herself, as the door closed and the carriage started. Does it?

Chapter Ten

Jane was certain that Richard Newton broke records on the drive from Huddersfield to Rumsey, but she was prudent enough not to comment. Not that a comment would have registered, anyway. Richard spent the entire drive leaning forward in the carriage, his elbows resting on his knees, staring at something fascinating on the floorboards that she could not see. He only acknowledged her as the carriage slowed to take the turn into the lane before the Butterworth mansion.

He looked at her and managed a smile. "I suppose you are wondering why a veteran of these matters should be so anxious, Miss Milton," he began.

"I don't wonder at all," she replied. "I would wonder more if you *weren't* up in the trees."

"I care for her so much," he said simply, and then tore from the carriage before it even came to a stop.

She was left to descend by herself, relieved to see another carriage in front of the house. Thank goodness the doctor is here, she thought. Mr. Butterworth may have sung my praises to his family, but I do not know that my talents as a house guest extend as far as assisting in childbirth.

As it was, she found herself seated cross-legged in the nursery, entertaining Lucy with stories while Amanda fretted and stewed and paced the floor enough for both of them. As Jane watched Amanda, she thought of the hours before Andrew's birth, when she had done that very thing. When the little girl finally rested her head against Jane's leg and closed her eyes, she thought of Blair in Ireland during Lucinda's confinement and delivery, and her own anxiety that he was not there.

"Blame the Irish," he had told her a month later when he returned from garrison duty in Dublin to see his son. And so she had, even as she wondered why he had not moved heaven and earth to be present when Lucinda needed him the most.

Sitting in the nursery with the winter sun weakly warm on her face, she couldn't help rehearsing in her mind Blair's reaction to his son. Almost as though he knew Andrew wasn't really his, she thought suddenly, and then startled herself so much that she sat upright and woke Lucy.

"I'm sorry, my dear," she said, and patted Lucy's back until the child curled up against her and resumed her nap. Jane, what are you thinking? she asked herself. You *know,* even if no one else will consider it, that Andrew is Blair's son. And yet. She closed her eyes, too, remembering Lucinda's terrible death, Blair's obvious sorrow, and then his return to Ireland, where he stayed until the army sent him to the Peninsula. And then it was only short furloughs home—a Christmas here, an Easter there—all the way up to Waterloo.

Perhaps that is how the Stovers were raised, she thought, excusing them, and then saw in her mind Emma Newton so pregnant, and still getting down on her knees to look into Andrew's face and touch him as a mother would, and all on their first meeting only yesterday. Oh, Blair, she thought, did *you* believe the rumors, too? Or are members of the peerage just less generous with their affections than mill owners and their wives, those people you hold in such disdain?

"Oh, I do not understand," she said out loud, then looked at Amanda, who was making her circuit in front of the window. ". . . I do not understand how these matters can take so long," she amended, when Amanda stopped. And I do not understand why after all these years I am becoming suspicious, as well, she considered, as shame warmed her face, along with the afternoon sun.

She was spared the unpleasantry of further introspection by Richard's appearance in the doorway, his normally cheerful face accessorized by a huge smile. "Amanda, you have another sister," he said, when she hurried to him. He winked at Jane.

"Emma is fine and already apologizing to you for her continuing neglect of a perfectly good house guest."

Jane laughed, and woke Lucy with the news. "I knew it would be this way," the girl told her father as he held her on his lap. "Mama couldn't really mean to have another pesky boy!"

Mr. Butterworth soon returned to the house with Andrew and his nephew, declaring that the boys had eaten enough cream cakes at the Bell and Clapper to bring the cook out to watch. "I thought we would have to find her a chair and burn some feathers under her nose when she saw it was only two rather small boys," he said, handing his overcoat to the butler. "Tell me, Miss Mitten: am I an aunt or an uncle this time?"

After dinner, which no one ate except Mr. Butterworth, they were allowed into Emma's chamber for a glimpse at the latest Newton, a dark-haired daughter with solemn eyes. When the baby crossed her eyes, Lucy looked at her mother, who was watching her with a smile of her own. "She's not really finished out yet, is she, Mama?"

Emma laughed, and snuggled her smallest production tighter between her armpit and her breast. "Spoken like a mill owner's daughter! Lucy, she will improve vastly in a matter of days." She touched Lucy's face. "I assure you that she will hang straight on the bolt." She looked at Jane, more apology in her eyes. "And now my husband tells me that you have all decided among yourselves to divide up the night so that I will get some rest. Oh, Jane! What must you think of us!"

"I think you are all wonderful," she said promptly. "Now let me put her in her cradle." Carefully, she picked up the baby, who made mewing sounds and pulled herself into a tighter bundle as Jane held her close. "I suggest we all leave Emma in peace."

She carried the baby to the small nursery that adjoined the dressing room and smiled at her own reluctance to put her in the cradle. "Do let me hold her, Miss Mitten, or I will think you a tyrant," the mill owner insisted, reaching for his niece. Jane placed the baby in his arms, and he carried the child to his shoulder, where she settled her head against his neck as though she belonged there. "They certainly do meld into one, don't they?" he commented.

"Particularly if the person holding the baby seems to know

what he is doing, Mr. Butterworth," she said. "You are an excellent uncle."

"I wonder if I would be an excellent father," he said, his voice soft, as he put his niece in her cradle.

"It is certainly high time you considered such a step," she said, her own heart sinking, "especially if you are contemplating a move back to your estate."

"You don't think I am too old?" he asked, as he straightened up.

I wish you would not ask me, she thought, hoping that her complexion was not turning as rosy as it felt. He seemed to realize that it was an impertinent question, and he turned again to regard his niece. "Lady Carruthers is right," he said finally, not looking at her. "A gentleman would never ask a question like that. She would say that only a mill owner would be so crass. I suppose it is so."

It took all her will not to stare at him, because he sounded so upset. Poor Mr. Butterworth, she thought suddenly. And poor me, when you leave Denby. "I think it is a wonderful idea for you to return here, marry, and have a family of your own," she said, hoping that she was not sounding as wistful as she felt.

"You'll miss me then?" he asked.

"I will miss you," she assured him, the pleasure of the baby replaced by a dreariness that made her tired all of a sudden. "Yes, I am certain of it," she said, turning away because she did not trust herself to look at him. "Please excuse me."

After Andrew and Jacob were reconciled to bed, if not to sleep, she sat dry-eyed in her room, unable to focus on the book in her hands. I wish I had not come here, she thought, and put the book down. People in unhappy households should remain in them, Jane, she told herself. That way, they would never know what they are missing.

She knew she would stay awake until it was her turn to return to the nursery, but she woke hours later to murmured words and a steady pressure on her shoulder. For one terrible moment as she struggled to get up, she was back in Denby. "I cannot face it," she said, her voice loud to her ears in the quiet of the room, panicky even.

"I can understand that," Mr. Butterworth was saying. "Pound for pound, babies are a fearsome lot, indeed. I wonder that anyone tolerates them." He chuckled. "It's all right to open your eyes, my dear."

She did, steeling herself as she always did, and then sighing with relief. "Oh, Mr. Butterworth, it is you!" she exclaimed, clutching his arm.

He sat on the edge of her chair, and did not remove his hand from her shoulder. "Who were you expecting?" he asked, when she released him.

"I'm not sure," she said before she thought. "Oh! Excuse me, sir. You must think me an idiot."

"Never have yet," he commented cheerfully. "My dear, it is your turn in the nursery." He helped her to her feet, and before she could stop him, tucked a loose curl under her cap. "I will escort you, Miss Mitten."

"You needn't . . ."

". . . for there is no telling what dangers lurk below."

He was never a man to argue with, she decided, as he walked her down the flight of stairs and into the baby nursery. Her heart lightened for a moment, as she gazed at the baby. "She has been sleeping all this time?"

He nodded, and put his hand on her shoulder to pull her closer as he whispered, "I suppose she is exhausted from the rigors of making her first appearance." He gave Jane's shoulder a little shake. "Which means that she will wake up on *your* watch, I am certain. My good luck continues! You need merely change her nappy and carry her to her mother, while I retire to my bed for a peaceful night. My felicitations, Miss Milton!"

He left the room, closing the door behind him quietly, and she stood there as her stomach tightened into a sour ball and her fingernails dug into her palms. I cannot do this, she thought in panic. I can do anything for everyone, but I cannot do this. You have to, she told herself, but the terror would not stop this time. She took a deep breath, and then another, waiting for her usual good sense to take over, but it did not. Two more quick breaths, and she was light-headed. I must fetch Mr. Butterworth back, she thought. I will give him any excuse.

She wrenched open the door, ready to run after him, then looked across the hall, and blinked her eyes in amazement. He sat there watching her, calm and composed as though he were double-checking invoices at his desk. "Ah, my dear, have you decided that babies are cute, but slow company?" he said, patting the space beside him on the settee. "Do join me."

She shook her head, unable to stop staring at him, and gulping in air until she felt her knees start to buckle. Mr. Butterworth was at her side immediately, his voice as calm as ever, as he put his arm firmly around her waist and made her walk on rubbery legs to the settee, where he sat her down.

"Just one deep breath, Jane," he commanded, in a voice far from his usual complacent tone. "Hold it a moment, then take another."

She did as he said, struggling against the little points of light that flickered around the edge of her vision. When she released that breath and finally took another, they went away. When she started to shiver, Mr. Butterworth let go of her and removed his coat, which he draped over her shoulders. "I need to tell my brother-in-law to be less stingy with coal at night," he murmured as he put his arm around her again.

She shook her head and tugged his coat tight about her shoulders until the shivers passed. In another moment she relaxed and leaned against the settee back, and Mr. Butterworth released his grip on her. "Thank you," she murmured. "I don't know what happened to me." It didn't sound convincing to her ears. She knew without looking that the mill owner would not be so easily led off the trail, but she was struck by another thought. "Mr. Butterworth, why were you sitting there?"

"Why, indeed?" he whispered back, sitting a little sideways so he could see her better. "My dear Miss Milton, in the spirit of *bon ami* that appears to be a particular province of Christmas, I thought I would be the first person in the history of the world to do something kind for *you*."

"I'm quite all right now," she assured him, unable to summon enough courage to look him in the eyes. "Really I am."

He did not answer her for a long moment, but gently took hold of her chin and forced her to look at him. Her eyes welled with tears, but he would not allow her to turn away. "Jane, may I tell you that the single most frightening moment of my life was when I shook you awake upstairs and you opened your eyes."

"Oh. I couldn't . . . the light . . . mistaken," she mumbled. She pushed his hand away from her face, unable to look at him. "I am quite fine now."

"Jane, pay attention!" he said, his voice not loud, but sharp.

"There was such a look in your eyes that I thought I was looking at someone who was staring into hell." He shifted on the settee. "I must admit that just thinking about it now makes *me* shiver."

She could think of nothing to say, so she focused her gaze on his waistcoat, a garment so colorful that its hues were still visible, even in the hall that was lit only by a sconce on the table. When her tears started to fall, he gave her his handkerchief. In another moment, his arm was around her shoulder.

He let her sob into the handkerchief, then turn her face into his chest to muffle the sound. "I don't pretend to know what is going through your mind, my dear," he said finally, his voice low but conversational again, "but I am curious about one thing: Is it that you are afraid to go to sleep, or afraid to wake up?"

"It is both, sir," she admitted, and felt the breath go out of him.

"My God, Jane," he said, "my God." He put his other arm around her until she was almost dissolved into him. She cried again, wishing that she did not sound so useless, but unable to remedy the matter.

Mr. Butterworth held a corner of the handkerchief to his eyes, then returned it to her. "The matter is this then? If you go to sleep, something will happen to that baby. And if you wake up, you will be too late."

It sounded absurd as he said it, but she nodded. "I cannot stay in there, Mr. Butterworth. I should never have agreed to but . . ."

". . . but it is always expected of you, isn't it?"

She nodded. "I suppose I could learn to say no."

"I don't think you can, my dear Miss Milton. It's not in you to say no."

She sighed. "Then I am foolish, just as Lady Carruthers says."

She didn't think he could hold her any tighter, but he did. "No, my dear, you are not foolish! You are just more kind than nine-tenths of the population." He gave her a sudden hug that made her gasp for breath, then released her. "And I don't know that I would ever want you to change. Perhaps I have been in the world too long, but there is something so refreshing about goodness." He smiled at her. "This is certainly no reflection on my own life, is it?"

It was her turn to feel surprise. "Mr. Butterworth, you are everything that is kind, so how can you . . ."

But he wasn't paying attention to her. "My dear, I think my newest niece is tuning up. Can you hear her?"

She could, and was unable to suppress her sigh of relief. She rose to her feet, but Mr. Butterworth did not release her hand. "Sir, I think I can manage now," she told him.

"I daresay you can," he stated, rising with her, but letting go of her hand. "My brother informed me last night that the nurse-maid has been summoned and will be here today, thus ending any need for family—and house guest—vigils."

He followed her to the nursery and watched as she changed the baby. "Considering that it has been . . . oh, what . . . ? twelve years since Andrew was small, you're quite good at that, Miss Mitten," he whispered. He held out his arms for his niece, red-faced now and waving her fists. "Or does a woman not forget?"

"I am certain that is it, Mr. Butterworth," she replied, grateful for ordinary conversation again as she tidied up. "Now if you will hand her over, I will take her to her mother, and you can re-tire for what remains of this night."

"You'll be all right?" he asked, as he returned his niece to her. "I had rather thought to remain here. Perhaps we could talk."

There must have been a thousand reasons she could give him why that would not be a good idea, each more logical than the one before, but she could not think of one. "You would not like what you hear, Mr. Butterworth," Jane said, and then from nowhere, "I am not what I seem."

"Who of us is, ma'am?" he answered. To her eyes and ears, his equanimity appeared as unruffled as if she had just told him that violets were purple. "I am a good listener, though."

"And a busy man," she replied. "I doubt that Richard will be much use to you at the mills for the next few days! Good night, Mr. Butterworth."

She wondered in the next few days if her dismissal had been too abrupt. No doubt he was busy, dividing his time between the woolen mill in Huddersfield and the new cotton mill where Andrew and Jacob hurried every morning to watch the slum being torn down to make way for new housing. The boys—a stranger would have thought them friends for years—were filled with reports each evening at dinner, but Mr. Butterworth was conspicuous by his absence.

Emma, absorbed in her new daughter, only laughed when Jane expressed her worry about her brother overworking himself. "It is what he enjoys the most, my dear," she said, easing herself into a comfortable position as the baby—named Olivia Rose by Amanda and Lucy, after considerable discussion—began to nurse. "Give him a problem, and he can hardly wait to solve it. Olivia, do have a care! They are attached to me, after all!"

Jane smiled as she watched the nursing mother. Obviously he has decided that he does not relish my problems, she thought, as the baby settled down to long, steady pulls. I cannot blame him; I do not relish them, either.

She knew that he came home at night because she heard him talking to Richard, and laughing at this or that, as the two of them sat in the breakfast room and rehashed the day. He came into the boys' room one night as she was reading the nightly chapter of *The Children of New Forest,* and stood leaning against the door frame until she finished. "Well read, Miss Milton," he declared. "You could probably make a factory invoice interesting, suspenseful, even."

How does he do that, she thought, dispensing compliments as easily as some people breathe? He came closer; she wished he would put his hand on her shoulder in that careless way of his, but he did not.

"Andrew and Jacob, come with me to the woolen mill tomorrow," he told the boys, sitting on their bed. "Christmas is nearly upon us and I have dismissed the workers so we can break down the machinery and make a few improvements before we begin work again."

"Dirty work, sir?" Andrew asked, even as he looked at Jane for permission.

"Oh, yes. The worst kind. Jacob's mother will cringe when we come home."

"Mr. Butterworth, are you remembering that tomorrow night is the Board of Directors dinner here?"

"How could I forget, with so many females to remind me?" he replied cheerfully. "Amanda is wandering around in a distracted fashion, mumbling to herself about ironing tablecloths and polishing silver." He laughed. "She is usually more concerned with slippers and matching ribbons. And I suppose my sister is just calmly watching it all."

"Oh, yes," Jane agreed, relieved at his light touch. "She tells me that nothing could be better for Amanda than to be overworked."

"And you, Miss Mitten?" he asked. "Does all this rushing about, settling cooks' quarrels, and wrangling with fishmongers give you a sound night's sleep?"

"She could hardly finish this chapter, Mr. Butterworth," Andrew confided, as she looked away from him in embarrassment.

"Very good!" he announced, and gave each boy a resounding smack of a kiss. "Tomorrow morning, seven o'clock sharp, gentlemen!" he told them as he pulled up the covers and pinched out the candle.

"The boys will not be underfoot tomorrow," he told her as they left the room. "What a good fellow I am."

"You are indeed, sir," she said. "I am sleeping well, so you needn't concern yourself about me."

He widened his eyes and stepped back as though she had struck him, and she could not help but laugh. "That is better, my dear," he told her. "Dependable, competent, useful Miss Milton!"

She did not know if he was aware that his words had a slight edge to them. She may have been mistaken, because he seemed his usual, expansive self. "I . . . I try to be, sir," she said, not sure how to answer him.

He stopped in the hall and turned to face her, so she had no choice but to stop, too. "Probably this is academic, Miss Milton, but what happens to you after the Board of Directors' dinner is over, and you are less busy, or when the reunion for Lord Denby finishes this spring, or when Andrew goes away to school in the fall?"

She could not answer him.

"Of course it is not my business," he continued. "Perhaps if I were a gentleman, I would be attuned to the niceties of the situation, but, Miss Milton, I am not a gentleman."

He bowed and walked away, and she could only stand there and watch him go, more alone than she had ever felt in her life. "Mr. Butterworth," she called after him.

He turned to look at her, his eyes hopeful. "Yes, my dear? You know how I advise you to speak your mind."

"You would not like me very much, if I did," she said softly, not even sure if he could hear her, because they stood so far apart.

He opened his mouth to reply, but Amanda bounded into the hall, the picture of distraction. "Uncle Scipio, I am in desperate need of Miss Milton," she exclaimed, breathless.

"Everyone is in desperate need of Miss Milton," he said with a half smile that went nowhere near his eyes, as far as Jane could see. "Well, look behind you. We tend to carry on long-distance conversations, so it is no wonder you missed her."

"Amanda, whatever is the matter?" Jane said, with a last glance at Mr. Butterworth, who stood watching them both before he turned on his heel and took the stairs two at a time.

Amanda hurried to her side, holding out her hands. "Miss Milton, our cook is not speaking to our housekeeper and the scullery maid is throwing out spots!" She dabbed at her eyes. "Don't you think this is the wrong time to get sick? What are we to do?"

"There is never a good time to get sick, Amanda," she said, striving for soothing tones when she wanted to stamp her feet in frustration. "Let us see to her first, and then rehearse a little kitchen diplomacy for Cook. Courage, Amanda! Things are seldom as bad as they seem."

There is never a good time for anything, she told herself as she followed the girl belowstairs. Life is all interruption and commotion, untidy in the extreme, with enough loose ends to trip up a trout. She took Amanda's arm at the foot of the stairs, and was rewarded with a glance of combined relief and gratitude.

"Miss Milton, are you ever at a loss?" she whispered as they entered the servants hall.

"All the time, my dear," she replied.

Amanda smiled and Jane could almost see her relax. "Miss Milton, you are so good at restoring my peace of mind!"

Too bad I cannot do the same thing for myself, she thought, as the housekeeper bore down on them and the cook, her arms folded, took up a defensive position in front of the unlit stove. Jane took a deep breath and flashed what she hoped was a confident smile. "Amanda, you need merely to listen to Cook, and nod whenever she pauses, and I will deal with the housekeeper."

An hour later, a truce had been declared in the servants hall.

With a flourish, Cook lit the stove again and was soon heard humming over the vegetable soup and looking about for a sieve, while the housekeeper returned to her knitting by the fireplace. The scullery maid—who confessed to eating strawberries meant for the fifth course, even though she knew strawberries gave her hives—was sent to bed with an all-purpose dose of both tonic and an admonition from the butler.

"Miss Milton, I have been thinking lately that it would be great fun to marry and run my own household, but now I think I will not rush it," Amanda told Jane as they climbed the stairs.

Jane smiled and kissed her good night. She could think of nothing except her own bed, but as she passed the Newtons' chamber, she noticed a light on. She knocked on the door.

Emma was just handing Olivia Rose to the nursemaid. She patted the bed and Jane sat. "Richard and Scipio were last sighted heading for the breakfast room with more blueprints," Emma said. "I hear that you and Manda have been quelling domestic disturbances." She reached for Jane's hand. "And tomorrow is the Board of Directors dinner, and then there is Christmas." She put her hands together in a prayerful gesture. "If I am very good, perhaps I can talk Richard into carrying me downstairs to the sitting room after dinner. I know these directors' wives, and I can spare you that much!"

"I am certain you can talk him into anything," Jane said. "You must excuse me, but my pillow has been calling to me for some time now, possibly ever since your housekeeper told me for the fourteenth time—I counted—'I does wot I can, but Cook is haggravatin,'" she mimicked.

Emma laughed and clapped her hands. "After this circus, Stover Hall will seem like a haven to you, won't it?"

"I will miss you all," she said simply. "Good night, my dear."

"Good night to you," Emma replied. "Just think, Jane. After tomorrow night, you will be quite at your leisure, with nothing more to occupy your mind beyond whether you prefer white meat or dark! Won't that be a relief?"

It is my greatest nightmare, she thought, as she nodded, smiled, and left the room.

Chapter Eleven

Jane had not planned to attend the Board of Directors' dinner, but the matter was decided for her by Amanda and Emma, and seconded by Mr. Butterworth that morning. "I cannot manage if you are not there to prop me up," Amanda claimed, overriding Jane's own attempt to assist belowstairs by keeping Cook and housekeeper far apart. "How am I to know what goes on in the dining room?" Emma asked. "Richard will only grunt about it, Amanda will never see what you will see, and Scipio will be far too technical. I insist, Jane, I simply insist. Am I not right, Scipio?"

"Of course, my dear sister," Mr. Butterworth replied promptly. "Jane, Jane! Never discommode a lactating female! Do you want Olivia to have a prune face tonight, if my sister is unhappy?"

It was so outrageous that she could only blush, and allow herself to be led by the mill owner to Emma's ample wardrobe. "You have no excuse of nothing to wear," Emma called from her bed. "There are times when I have a waist, and when I do, I think we are much the same size."

"Except that Miss Milton will need to take a quick hem, considering that she is not a Long Meg, like those of Butterworth origin. Ah, this is the dress I like the most," he said, gesturing to a pale blue sarcenet in the clothespress. "I gave it to Emma for Christmas last year. Wouldn't you say I have excellent taste?"

She would. She stood still while Mr. Butterworth held it up to her. "I don't know that I possess enough"—she hunted for a word that would not turn her face even more red than it felt already—"enough amplitude to do it justice, sir."

"You do, Miss Milton, you do," he assured her, then winced when she looked at him. "If looks could slaughter . . ."

"You know, you are difficult to argue with," she said, moving away from him.

"Yes, I am," he agreed, all complacence. "Em, can we borrow that cobwebby looking shawl with the silver threads? It won't keep you warm, but in the ten years since we first met, I have never known you to be ill. Here it is, my dear."

With a wink and a bow, he left her, with the promise to return before the afternoon was too far advanced, and to keep Andrew out of the machine oil at the factory. Shaking her head, Jane came out of the dressing room with the dress over her arm. "Do you know, Emma, I thought I knew your brother," she said. "Outside of a certain fondness for waistcoats that make me blink, I thought he was a normal fellow."

"No, he is not," Emma replied.

"Perhaps it's just as well that he never married," Jane mused. "He would come home with oil on his clothes, and ink stains up to his elbows from improving upon blueprints. That is, *when* he remembered to come home! Oh, Emma, I am depending upon him to be here this evening."

"He will be here," Emma assured her.

Between calming Amanda's fears and setting her to work supervising the laying of the table in the dining room, Jane hemmed the dress and watched the clock. Two o'clock came and went, and she found herself pacing in front of the window. It was nearly three when the carriage returned from Huddersfield. Well, that is a relief, she thought, hurrying down the stairs. The butler was busy with the silverware so she opened the door and gasped at what stood before her. Words failed her. I do not know that there is enough soap and water in Yorkshire to make a dent, she thought.

"Any chimneys need cleaning?" Mr. Butterworth asked, and the boys giggled. "Pots to mend? Barns to muck out?"

"Don't try me, Mr. Butterworth," she told him, wondering for a moment which of the boys was Andrew. Douse them in grease and I defy any mother to know, she thought. And what identical smiles! Even yours, Mr. Butterworth. How good that I am a patient woman.

They looked so pleased with themselves that she could only sigh. "I trust you got all the parts reassembled and there is nothing left over," she said.

Andrew nodded, his eyes bright in his oil-streaked face. "Mr. Butterworth added another cog and more belting and he says that it will spin even faster."

The mill owner shrugged. "What can I do, Miss Mitten? Nieces are a notorious expense, and I must assist Richard in keeping Olivia in dolls and sweets. Go on, boys, and I'll catch up." He watched them dart past her into the house. "That is, I will follow them if you let me inside, Miss Milton," he teased.

"I should not," she told him as she still barred the door. "Emma said you would be clean and ready to greet the guests."

"Then she is doomed to disappointment," he said, with no evidence of remorse. "Come here, my dear, and let me introduce some of our guests right now."

Not until he mentioned guests did she notice that another carriage had pulled up behind the Newton vehicle. "Please tell me that you met them on the road," she began.

"Oh, no! We've been enjoying a remarkable afternoon at the woolen mill," he said. "I would take your arm, but I do not think it is a good idea. Miss Milton, may I present Robert Owen and Jeremy Bentham? Gentlemen, this is Miss Milton, that excellent teacher I was telling you about."

I have heard of these men, she thought. Oh, don't stare, Jane. And close your mouth. Her mind in a muddle, she watched as the two men descended from their carriage. "Mr. Robert Owen?" she repeated, even as she mentally kicked herself for sounding like an Almack's miss with more hair than wit.

"It seems that you have heard of me," he said, and she promptly decided that she loved the Welsh lilt to his speech.

"I have, sir!" she exclaimed. "Every time my kinsman Lord Denby reads of you in the newspaper, he gives it a good rattle and calls you a damned scoundrel." Oh, my Lord, what did I just say? she asked herself, putting her hand to her mouth. "I mean . . ."

To her incredible relief, the factory owner threw back his head and laughed. "No, Miss Milton, do not improve upon the text!" he exclaimed when he could talk. "It's a high compliment, wouldn't you agree, Jeremy?" And over his shoulder to Mr. Butterworth, "You were right; she *is* an original, Scipio."

All right, Jane, she told herself as she held out her hand to him, the least you say, the better. Oh, dear, I have offended him, she thought, when he did not extend his hand.

"Miss Milton, better that you should shake Jeremy Bentham's hand twice instead of mine once," he was saying, when she gathered up her heart enough to listen. "I'm guilty of playing with the machinery, too."

She shook Jeremy Bentham's hand and glared at Mr. Butterworth. "You were on your best behavior, sir, and now you have led a member of the Board of Directors astray," she scolded.

"No, my dear, he is blameless," Mr. Bentham said. "Rob and I arrived at the factory first, and there was all this lovely machinery broken down and ready to reassemble. He could not restrain himself, and I am too old to either restrain or argue with a Welshman."

He was still holding her hand when it dawned on Jane who he was. "Jeremy Bentham!" she exclaimed. "Oh, my!"

"Guilty as charged, Miss Milton," he declared in turn, and released her hand. "What? You are amazed that an antiquarian such as I is still able to function under his own sail?"

"I do not know *what* I am, sir, except amazed at the company I am keeping," she said frankly.

He twinkled his eyes at her, looking far younger than his obvious years. "The Damned Scoundrel and the Anti-Christ, too, eh?"

When in Rome, she thought, and plunged ahead. "I must tell you, sir, that Lord Denby gets *really* out of trim when he reads that your utopian factories actually make money."

"Un-English, ain't it, ma'am?" Robert Owen said. He nodded to her and bowed to Mr. Butterworth. "We will return for dinner with most of the grease removed, my dear. Scipio, I advise you to put *her* on the board! Plain speaking is refreshing in a female. Good day, Miss Milton."

"Plain speaking will be my ruin, Mr. B," she said as she watched the carriage continue back down the lane.

"No, Miss Mitten, it will not." He came close to her and draped his arm over her shoulder in a manner so brotherlike that she thought of Blair with a pang. "I had no idea that Mr. Bentham was coming, but Robert apparently thought he might be interested to see what we are doing here in Huddersfield. Do you know that I keep a copy of his book *A Fragment on Government* on my bedside table?"

"To impress the upstairs maid?" she teased, and laughed when he gave her neck a tweak. "And look, sir! You have smeared grease on me!"

He released his hold on her. "It's what you deserve, Miss Mitten. Now the servants will talk about you!" He clapped his hands then. "Well, hurry along now, my dear, and don't make me dawdle. You are keeping me from my tin tub, or at least a wire brush."

Grease was harder to remove than Jane thought, and her neck was rosy before Emma pronounced her fit for society and turned her over to her own dresser. "Upshaw, under no circumstances is Miss Milton to wear a lace cap tonight," she said, as she covered herself discreetly and burped Olivia.

"Emma! I am nearly thirty," Jane protested.

"You are still unmarried and your hair is beautiful," Emma replied serenely. "Well done, Olivia! You sound like your Uncle Scipio after a large meal." She held her daughter away from her and looked into her eyes. "Olivia, at least I can depend upon you not to unbutton your top breeches button like your dear papa. No cap, Jane, or . . . or I will give sour milk!"

"Tyrant!" Jane declared as she blew a kiss to Emma and left the room.

An hour later, Jane could only smile at her reflection and then remember Mr. Butterworth's secret weapon. "Lucy would say I am finished out, and I have you to thank, Upshaw," she said to the dresser.

The dresser stepped back for another look, and then re-arranged a tendril by her ear that needed no improvement. "I think you should burn all your caps," the woman said. "Surely they weren't your idea, Miss Milton."

No, they were Lady Carruthers' idea, Jane thought, as the dresser left the room. She rested her hands in her lap and frowned at her reflection. I have been listening to her for years, and I wonder why? When Andrew goes away to school next year, there is no reason why I could not find a teaching position somewhere else. True, I will miss Lord Denby, but he is determined to die, and I am weary of death.

"Jane?"

She focused into the mirror and saw Mr. Butterworth standing in the doorway, dressed for dinner and looking far more elegant than she remembered from other functions at Denby. "Is that a new rig out?" she asked.

"Heavens, no," he replied. "You know how I hate to dress up for functions. You've seen this any number of times at those gatherings in Denby where my mill owner presence is not a hiss and a byword."

"Radical tonight, are we?" she murmured. "And what, sir, are you doing standing in my door?"

"I knocked and called your name, but there you were, swooning over your face in the mirror and totally oblivious. May I come in? I know it's improper but . . ."

" '. . . I am just a mill owner,' " she chimed in with him, and then laughed. "Of course you may come in! What you saw was not someone dreamy-eyed, but rather Jane Milton in all her calculation, sir."

"And?" he prompted, seating himself beside her dressing table.

"I am tired of the crochets of old men who think they have a foot in the grave, and a cousin who delves into rumor and who schemes better than Lady Macbeth, and her son with nothing on his mind but his wardrobe."

The mill owner smiled at her. "And all this from a new hair arrangement?" he asked.

"Perhaps," she considered. "I am not so old, sir, that I cannot make my way in the world."

"No, my dear, you are not."

She waited for him to laugh, but he gazed at her reflection in the mirror instead, as though unable to look at her directly. I am being rude, she thought suddenly. "Mr. Butterworth, I do not mean to imply . . ."

". . . that I am old? Well, I am not, Miss Milton," he said. "I will be forty-five next year, and most days, the years do sit lightly on me."

She turned to face him. "They have been good years, have they not, sir? When I think of all that you have accomplished, and the influence you are even now exerting . . ."

"That accounts for ten years only, madam," he interrupted, and the anger in his voice made her shiver, even more because it seemed to be directed inward. "Even a jackass like Cecil would call that a poor return on investment."

She put her hand on his arm. "Mr. Butterworth, I do not understand you."

"No, you do not, my dear Miss Mitten." As she watched in consternation, he made a visible effort to collect his emotions. He patted her hand. "Ah! Put it down to nerves, dear lady. If *the* Jeremy Bentham likes what we are doing here and comes onto the board, that will be worth the addition of ten or twelve ordinary mortals."

He sat back in the chair and was silent a long minute. She knew his habits and did not interrupt his thoughts, but tucked in a stray hairpin, and wondered if a little lavender behind her ears would not war with the fish course that she and Amanda were in high hopes about. "I must go downstairs," she said, rising from the dressing table. "Amanda will be in a stew, and here I sit."

"Listening to an old man rave," he finished for her.

"Never that," she said firmly. "You are not old and you do not rave."

"And you are invariably kind." He reached inside his coat and pulled out a slim box. "Would you *kindly* wear this necklace tonight? It belonged to my mother, and would look especially fine against that blue fabric."

She opened the box and smiled to see a sapphire on a silver chain. "It's beautiful and I will borrow it happily," she said.

He took the necklace from the box and put it around her neck, fiddling a moment with the clasp. "I have larger sapphires that he gave her later—it was his favorite jewel—but this little stone was the first gift from his first quarter profits on his first mill. A self-made man right out of a pig farm in the Yorkshire Dales, ma'am." He rested his hands on her shoulders. "Even the other factory owners would sniff when he walked through the Exchange, but by God, Jane, he could spin straw into gold, and he bought *their* mills."

She touched the necklace. I wonder if I could ever express in words what you mean to me, she thought. I wish I were even remotely close to your league, even as you tell me of pig farms. "I'll take good care of it tonight," she assured him.

"Well, give me a hug for luck, Miss Mitten. I feel the need of it."

She did as he said. "And I thought you were so confident," she spoke into his waistcoat, her arms tight around him.

"Maybe we don't know each other as well as we think we do," he replied, resting his chin on her head a moment, until he must have realized what he was doing to her coiffure. "Oh, do excuse me. If I ruin Upshaw's efforts, she will smite me, and Jane, I am afraid of *her*!"

Maybe we don't know each other, she thought, as she laughed

and backed away to tinker with her hair again. You would be appalled if I ever actually did speak my mind.

It was a sobering thought, and it claimed her attention, even as she met the other guests in the sitting room before the butler summoned them to dinner. She had her own surprise to see Lord Ware among the company of businessmen. I have not seen you since Blair's funeral, she thought. Do we *all* keep strange company? He came immediately to her side and bowed.

"Miss Milton! This is a rare pleasure," he said to her, drawing her a little aside. "I stopped to see Lord Denby on my way here, and he told me of all the response you have received to your invitations. And reluctantly admitted that you and Andrew had been abducted by the mill owner for Christmas."

"I would hardly call it that. Is Lord Denby doing well?" she asked, her conscience suddenly smitten. "I wrote him one letter when I arrived, but since then, things here have been at sixes and sevens."

Lord Ware nodded. "He complained of some ill usage by your abandonment, but he did own that his sister was fully occupied with Cecil, who seems to have contracted an unusual disease"— he leaned closer and whispered in her ear—"that I thought only afflicted horses! Miss Milton, who would have thought that under your calm demeanor lurks a dreadful rascal?"

"Who indeed?" she replied, and stood on tiptoe to speak softly to him. "Lord Ware, I had no idea *you* were one of those fiery socialists who gets involved with commerce, and a board member, as well."

He looked around him. "I am not alone in that, Miss Milton. You would be surprised, I think, to know how many do what I am doing. I know a wave of the future when it smacks me in the face. Others of our class are even so forward-thinking as to be involved in canal ventures." He laughed softly. "But I am no friend of travel by water—I get seasick in a hip tub!—so I have chosen instead to inject an occasional shilling into scabby textile commerce."

Jane touched his arm. "You cannot lightly quiz your way through this, my lord," she teased in turn. "You are a radical for actually wishing to help factory workers instead of merely exploit them."

"My dear Miss Milton, I own to a conscience," he admitted. "I would wish that more of our class did. Which reminds me:

Stanton told me that you invited Edward Bingham to the reunion."

Now why should Edward Bingham remind you of a conscience? she asked herself. If I knew you better, I would ask. "The man from Connecticut?" she asked. "I did invite him, but we doubt that he will attend, and it *is* a very long way, my lord."

"In more ways than you know, my dear," he murmured. "Let us say, if he turns up, I will be astounded."

She laughed. "Now you will tell me that my dear Lord Denby has secrets. Excuse my skepticism!"

She thought he would laugh, but he only nodded, then bowed and rejoined the circle of men engaged in fervent conversation that seemed to involve much waving about of arms, and head nodding. When the butler announced dinner, she watched him make his stately progress toward the dining room and wondered to herself if she knew anyone without a secret. I still repose all my confidence in Mr. Butterworth, she thought, as she watched him coming toward her, Amanda clinging to his arm. His melancholy tonight I will assign to a case of nerves. How refreshing that he is mortal.

"Miss Milton, may I take the two of you down to dinner?" he asked. "Amanda here is clutching me like a leech in pond water, and I am depending upon you to give us both countenance, considering that you look so fine."

"If I did not know how frequently you dispense compliments to every Tom, Dick, and Harry, I would blush," she whispered.

He turned to Amanda. "It appears she does not take me seriously, niece."

I would like to, she thought, I would like to. "Come, Amanda," she said. "Let us go forward, girding our loins and hoping that the venison is this year's, and that no one drops the aspic between the kitchen and the table!"

Much later she stood with Amanda at the entrance while Mr. Butterworth and Richard saw the guests to their carriages. She smiled when Amanda took her hand and held it as they stood close together. "Success, my dear," she said. "Your father and uncle look satisfied enough for twenty mill owners. I hope you have an extravagant Christmas list, because they will be in a generous mood!"

Amanda sighed and gave Jane's hand a squeeze. "This is reward enough. Thank you," she said simply. "Uncle Scipio tells me that your sole aim in life is to go about making the rest of us look better."

Some of us don't even need my help, if help it is, she thought, as she watched Mr. Butterworth saying good night to his guests. If mill workers in Huddersfield sleep better at night, and with stomachs more full, it is because of this man. And he compliments me?

"Miss Milton, have you a moment?"

She turned around in surprise to see Lord Ware shrugging himself into his overcoat. "I always have a moment for you, my lord," she replied as she helped him and then walked with him to the door.

Lord Ware nodded to the mill owners, but would not relinquish his hold on her when Mr. Butterworth offered to help him to his carriage. "Miss Milton is far prettier," he said, "and you would think me in queer stirrups indeed if I kissed you on the cheek, Mr. Butterworth!" he declared.

The mill owner just bowed. "I never argue with eccentricity, Lord Ware. Mind you do not catch a chill, Miss Milton, or we would not be able to continue our exploitation of you!"

"A good man," he commented as he allowed her to help him to his carriage. "Step inside a moment, my dear, for there is something you should know."

She did as he asked, allowed him to hand her in, speak briefly to his coachman, and then close the door on them.

"Lord Denby is not well?" she asked, leaning forward and whispering for no good reason that she could think of, considering that they were alone in the carriage. "I will return immediately, if I must, sir."

He shook his head, and then took hold of her hand. "My dear, are you aware that Lady Denby is spreading rumors?" he asked.

"I have been aware for years that she is determined to discredit Andrew," she replied. "It is all so pointless!"

He shook his head again, this time with even more emphasis. "I have heard those rumors, too, my dear. I was not referring to them."

"Then I suppose I do not know to what you are referring, my lord," she said, when he was silent for a long moment.

"She is saying things about you," he stated finally.

"Me!" she exclaimed, drawing back from him. "Oh dear! Did she actually look up epizootic fever in a book or something?"

"I wish it were so harmless," he replied, as if the words were being pulled from him with pincers.

"Then tell me, my lord," she said. "I have apologized to her for so many misdemeanors through the years that my skin is as thick as an elephant's. What is another apology?"

He shook his head. "It is not simple." He leaned closer, taking both her hands in his. "Miss Milton, she seems to think that you know more about Lord Canfield's death than you ever told anyone."

Oh, I do, she thought. Much, much more.

"I told her she was imagining things, and that Blair was so close to death for so long that any suspicions would be unthinkable," he continued.

"Unthinkable," she echoed, hoping that her voice did not sound as hollow as it seemed to her ears.

"Precisely," he said, releasing her hands and sitting back to appraise her. "It is common knowledge to most of us that she wants Cecil to inherit the title and estates."

"And that I am Andrew's only champion at Denby," she said. "She must mean to drive me away, so he has no one left."

She waited in silence, but Lord Ware said nothing more. "Will I see you again before the reunion?" she said finally.

"No, my dear. After tomorrow's meeting at the factory, I am ordered home by Lady Ware, who, for some unaccountable reason, chooses not to spend Christmas alone." He opened the door for her, and helped her down. "I wanted you to know, Miss Milton. I value your good sense."

"Thank you for that, my lord," she murmured, and stood in the driveway until his carriage left. I wonder why it is so hard to do the right thing? she asked herself.

Lord Ware was the last guest to depart. She stood a long time in the driveway, her mind full of disquiet, watching the snow begin to fall. A flake here and a flake there, she thought. It seems like nothing, but by morning there will be such a pile of it. Her eyes filled with tears. A word here, a look there, and Andrew is dismissed from what is rightfully his. A word here, a whisper there, and I am undone. "There is this one difference, Jane Milton," she murmured out loud. "The accusations against Andrew are without basis. But somehow she knows."

"Knows what?"

Jane jumped, then put out her hand to steady herself. "Mr.

Butterworth, was I talking to myself again?" she asked, striving for a light tone.

He took her by the arm. "Yes, indeed, and standing here in the cold!" He hurried her up the steps and back into the entrance hall, shutting the door behind him and locking it. "Heavy of eyes but light of heart, Amanda has taken herself off to bed. My brother-in-law is probably describing scenes of triumph to my sister, and you and I are left with time on our hands. Jane, what is the matter?"

He tacked the question onto the end of a string of lighthearted comments, and it took her a moment for the sudden serious tone of his voice to register in her mind.

"It is nothing that a good night's sleep will not cure," she said, wincing in spite of herself.

"And how long since your last good night's sleep, Miss Mitten?" he asked softly, following her up the stairs. "A week? A month? Six months? Since Lord Canfield died? Or has it been so long that you can't remember?"

"You are impertinent," she said, even as she amazed herself with her own rudeness.

"Oh, I am," he agreed, taking her by the hand and making her sit with him on the top of the steps. "We're that way, you know, those of my class. We wade right into a problem. My betters call that crass, but do you know, Jane, I sleep nights. And when I wake up, I don't come leaping up out of a chair as though I had seen a ghost!"

"You startled me!" she said. "That was all it was."

He got to his feet quickly. "You're a liar, Miss Milton, and I am tired. Good night."

Her mind numb, Jane pulled up her knees and rested her forehead on them as the mill owner stalked away. In a few moments, she heard his door slam, the sound carrying in the quiet corridor. In a moment, another door opened, and Richard stuck his head out. Jane made herself small on the stairs, grateful for the shadow. "Your brother is in a pelter about something," she heard him say. "I thought he was over those."

She sat very still for the better part of an hour, leaning her head against the railing, wondering what to do with herself. She was tired right down to the soles of her feet, but it wasn't the kind of tired that had sent her to peaceful-enough slumber the last few nights. It was the familiar exhaustion that seemed to come from her heart, and not from a body weary with the day's business and needing the rejuvenation that a night's rest would bring.

How odd this is, Jane, she thought. You cannot bear to close your eyes, but when you finally sleep, you dread waking up. You work so hard—so hard!—every day to please everyone, and you cannot please yourself. You dread Lady Carruthers, but you dread yourself even more. You are your own worst enemy; you cannot trust yourself enough to close your own eyes, and that is a sad reflection. Now I have done the impossible, she thought, as she stood up, feeling older than the oldest woman living. I have made Mr. Butterworth angry. Shame on me.

After a look in at Andrew and Jacob, to tug the covers up higher around them and stand a moment by the window watching the snow fall, she went to her own room. She returned the sapphire to its case, touching the stone and marveling to herself that it retained the warmth of her body. But I do not feel warm, she thought. How can this be?

She undressed, draping Emma's lovely gown over the chair and arranging the soft folds of the shawl on top. A pin here and a pin there, and her hair came undone as well, settling around her shoulders in a familiar way that calmed her mind a little. Another moment and she was buttoning her nightgown. "Now I lay me down to sleep," she whispered, unable to finish the little verse. The Lord will not want to keep my soul.

"If he should die before I wake." She stared into the darkness that wasn't dark enough to suit her, hardly daring to think what forms the room would take on when she opened her eyes into the terror that always came first, just before it turned into morning.

Chapter Twelve

It was the same dream as always, with the sounds that were impossible to ignore, but ones which had not the power to wake her until the book in her lap slid to the floor and landed with a splash at her feet.

She was awake then, and out of her chair, and staring into the wide eyes of a man drowning in his own blood. With a cry of her own, she reached for his neck to stop the gush, but he was just out of her grasp. She tried again; even though her arm stretched longer and longer in her dream, he was farther away. She reached again, crying for help. There was Mr. Lowe as always, standing on the other side of the bed and shaking his head at her. "I told you it would be like this. Weren't you listening?" She pleaded with him to help her, and then began to cry when he turned around and left the room after a wink and a thumbs-up sign.

"Don't leave me!" she cried. "Oh, please, not this time!"

"I wouldn't dream of it, Jane. Move over."

Fogged with sleep, drugged by her dream, she slid over, and then gasped when she opened her eyes. "Mr. Butterworth?" she managed to say, even as she made no objection when he gathered her into his arms and pulled the blankets around both of them.

"The very same. A little more casually dressed perhaps, but then, I have never been a fashion plate, dear Jane."

She shivered and let him pull her so close that she felt like part of him. "You shouldn't be here," she said, even as she clasped her hands tighter around his back.

"I disagree," he said. "I can't think of a single other place where I should be, more than right here. Your feet are cold!"

Still she shivered. "Turn around, my dear," said the mill owner finally. "Like spoons. Perfect," he said in her ear as he clasped his hands over her stomach and pulled her against him. "I defy you to be cold now. I am certain that I have sufficient avoir dupois for both of us."

Too weary to argue, Jane put her hands over his and pillowed her head on his arm. She had the vaguest memory of being clasped like this by her father years ago, before he left them. "You won't leave?" she asked, caught in that memory that flared up like a struck match, and then snuffed out. "I mean . . ."

"No, I won't," he said, resting his cheek against her hair. "Go to sleep, Jane."

Disinclined to argue, she did as he said, relaxing with a sigh. "Won't the maid be surprised when she comes in to start the fire?" she asked, as she gave up the struggle to keep her eyes open.

"My dear Jane, it is only three in the morning," the mill owner replied, his own voice drowsy. "None of the Newtons' servants are that ambitious. Just turn your worries over to me for a while."

"Can't . . . you have . . . big meeting today," she managed.

"Hush."

She slept then, unable to do anything else, because she was tired and warm, and the beating of the mill owner's heart was steady against her back. *His arm will grow numb if I lean on it like this,* was her last thought before she surrendered herself to sleep.

He was gone when she woke up, and the room was bright with that peculiar light of sun reflecting off snow. *I wonder what time it is,* she thought, as she sat up and looked around the room. The maid had already lit the fire, and the room was warm enough to tell her that she hadn't done it recently. And there was a can of water with a towel over it, everything as orderly and tidy as though nothing was different about this day.

Jane stretched and put her hands behind her head, relishing the pleasure of waking so peacefully. *How long has it been that I have bounded awake, and practically on my feet?* she asked herself as she let herself be absorbed into the mattress again. "Jane, you have had a good night's sleep," she announced to herself.

She closed her eyes, and when she opened them again, she could tell that the sun was much higher overhead. Still she remained where she was, breathing deep of Christmas smells that had a way of drifting up several flights of stairs, no matter whose house. *Gingerbread,* she thought, *and something with cinnamon.* She sat up and glanced at the empty pillow beside her own, almost ready to believe that she had dreamed Mr. Butterworth's presence in her bed last night. She frowned; there was no indent in the pillow. *I am balmy, indeed,* she thought, doubtful until she took a careful look at her own pillow. She leaned over to sniff it, and was rewarded with the faintest fragrance from the cologne that the mill owner liked. *He was that close,* she mused, her mind quiet and at peace. *No wonder I slept so well; there wasn't room in my bed for a nightmare.*

She dressed thoughtfully, after a glance at the clock to confirm the fact that her stomach was growling for a reason. *Here it is the noon hour, and I am actually hungry,* she acknowledged, with a feeling of surprise. *Will wonders never cease?*

The house was silent, and she had no qualms about encountering the mill owner in the breakfast room. It is not that I am shy about any of this, she told herself as she opened the door. "Well, yes it is," she murmured, her hand poised on the doorknob. "I do not very often allow men into my bed in the wee hours of the morning." She paused and leaned her forehead against the paneling of the door. Thank God he was there, she thought. Is there not to be an end to what I owe this kind man?

She opened the door, agreeably surprised to see Emma seated at the table, buttering a muffin. "My dear, shouldn't you be in bed?" Jane asked, as she smiled at the footman and allowed him to seat her.

"I am tired of being in bed," Emma announced. "Thank you; that will do." When the door closed, she leaned toward Jane. "My dear, I find myself at that condition which Richard delicately refers to as my mother wolf phase: if it moves, I will eat it. No sudden motions, Jane!"

Jane laughed and took a muffin from the basket, as Emma poured her some tea. "You are kindness itself to allow me to sleep so late," she said. "I suppose I should apologize for being such a slug, and on Christmas Eve, too, but I would be a hypocrite if I did."

Emma nodded. "Amanda only just woke up a short time ago. Scipio and Richard assured me that the two of you had worked hard enough over last night's dinner to allow for a late morning." She touched Jane's hand. "Thank you again for helping my darling negotiate the fearsome shoals of a dinner party! Scipio assures me that you are happiest when you are busiest, but I cannot help think that this holiday has been rather more work than pleasure for you."

"I have never enjoyed one more," she said. "Your brother certainly has my measure. Has he always been such a judge of character?"

She knew it was a joking question, so she was not prepared for Emma's expression. The woman held the muffin in midair, a look of such sadness on her face that Jane could feel her own heart sinking. "Emma?" she whispered.

She might as well have said nothing. The woman stared at her, seeming to contemplate a distance far beyond the little stretch of table that separated them. "Everyone's character except his own," she said, her voice low, the words coming spontaneously to Jane's ear. "Why, *why* are people hardest on themselves?"

It wasn't a question to answer, because Jane couldn't be sure Emma was aware she was asking one. As she watched, Emma sighed and her eyes focused again, this time on the muffin she still held. Jane slowly let out her breath, wondering what glimpse she had seen of Mr. Butterworth that only a sister, and a loving one at that, was privy to.

And then Emma was Emma again. "What were you saying, my dear?" she asked, as she dabbed marmalade on the muffin. "I seem to be woolgathering, and this is hardly the season for it."

"Nothing at all," Jane said, striving for calm again, when her mind was suddenly so full of questions. None of this is my business, she told herself. I am in no one's confidence. "Actually, I was hoping that you would give me a task before I turn into a total vegetable and end up as tonight's table arrangement."

Emma laughed, and Jane let her breath out slowly. "Nothing could be easier," she said, and pointed to a box on the sideboard. "Scipio brought that dreadful thing in here this morning and asked me to put you to work when you woke up."

"Dreadful?" Jane asked.

"Oh, it is full of invoices and receipts that need to be divided between the two mills. Usually the task is Richard's but he was busy this week, wringing his hands and then pacing up and down!" Emma said, then sighed. "Jane, never, never arrange your amusements so that a baby falls due on Christmas."

"I wouldn't dream of it," Jane teased, "considering that I do not have the means to produce such an event!" She picked up the box and returned with it to the table. "Just separate them? Oh, I see. Each mill has a different name. Emma?" She looked at Emma, who was gazing into the distance again. "My dear?"

"You heard her, didn't you?" Emma asked, her hand going to her breast. "No? Jane, I do believe Olivia is awake. Give me a hand up, please. If I hurry, I won't leave a trail of milk all down the hall. Happy Christmas, indeed!"

Jane smiled to herself as she finished her luncheon, returned the dishes to the sideboard, and took the papers from the box. This will not keep me busy enough, Mr. Butterworth, she thought, as she sorted the invoices and bills of lading into separate piles on the table. It was mindless work, however, and just the sort of thing to keep her brain empty of anxiety. She welcomed it, sitting there in the breakfast room with the sun beginning its afternoon slant through the house, and winter birds chattering around a suet ball.

She was halfway down the pile when she picked up a folded sheet with her name on it. The handwriting was Mr. Butterworth's and she opened the note, spreading it out before her on the invoices, knowing almost before she read a word what it would say, and for the first time in months, not dreading it.

"My dear Miss Mitten," she read, her lips moving but no sound coming out. *"I do believe that earlier this week in a moment of fun, you told me that you wanted a red cloak for Christmas. I told you that in return, I wanted all your secrets. Do you know now that I am perfectly serious?"*

"You do not know what you are asking," she murmured, as she put down the note. "You have no idea."

" 'Let us talk tonight, Miss Milton,' " she continued, reading out loud now. " 'Be so kind, please. If you do not find a way to a good night's sleep, then I do not think I will, either. And what use have I for a red cloak? Scipio.' "

She read the note again, then folded it and tucked it up her sleeve. She sat perfectly still in the quiet room, thinking to herself that she should remove the mousetraps that she and Amanda had placed in Mr. Butterworth's office. Those were never mice, were they, sir? she thought. I have been keeping you awake, have I not? And you want this burden? She sat in silence until the footman surprised her an hour later, bringing in a new tablecloth to lay for dinner.

Not wishing to face the mill owner yet, she carried the box upstairs to his office and placed it on his desk with the invoices for each mill labeled separately. She sat in his chair, smiling to herself as she started to straighten the papers on his desk, then thought better of it. I am certain there is a system here, she imagined, and I would only disrupt it. She sat still, oddly at peace with herself, as she looked at the miniatures on his desk. Emma as a young woman was easy enough to identify, and there were a much-younger Jacob and Amanda. "No Lucy, sir," she said out loud. "You are getting behind, what with Olivia to account for now."

Behind the others and turned sideways was a gilt-edged frame which should have contained a miniature. She picked it up, wondering at an empty frame on his desk, and turned it over. "To my darling, Scipio," she read out loud. "Love forever."

She held the frame in her hand for a long moment, then returned it to its position behind the other miniatures. Secrets, secrets, we all have secrets, she told herself. Poor Mr. Butterworth. Did a lovely lady change her mind? She could not have been so bright, if she threw you over for another. She looked at the empty frame again, then left the office on tiptoe, even though the hallway was empty. Why do we always leave so much unsaid?

They opened presents after dinner that night, grouped around Emma in her bed while Olivia, her belly full, slumbered on her mother's knees. Mr. Butterworth, full of apology for missing dinner, came in with his overcoat still on, bringing in the cold air with him. Jane was almost too shy to smile at him, but she did anyway, finding a small satisfaction that he looked slightly at odds himself.

It was a very small exchange of gifts, which relieved Jane of any embarrassment over having nothing to give. Before she could even stammer a single apology, Emma took her hand in a firm clasp. "Jane, what would Richard and I have done without you this week?" she said simply. "I cannot fathom a finer gift from you than yourself."

"See there, Jane?" Mr. Butterworth said as he took off his overcoat. "Once in a while, virtue *is* its own reward." He sat on the foot of the bed and put his arm around Andrew. "In this age of cynicism, laddie, who would have thought it?" He hugged Andrew, and Jane smiled as they grinned at each other.

She glanced at Emma, and noticed tears in her eyes as she watched her brother. "Emma, we are surely wearing you down to a nub," she said.

Emma shook her head. "What is that to me, my dear?" she said. "I am happy."

It was said so simply that Jane felt her own eyes filling with tears. I am, too, she thought. Here I am, ready to confess the worst story imaginable to a kind man, and I am happy about it. Lady Carruthers is right; I am a perfect ninny.

"We are almost waist deep in sensibility," Mr. Butterworth was saying to Andrew. "Here, lad, have a gift from me. You'll probably have to hide it when you return to Stover Hall, but I trust you are sufficiently resourceful."

Andrew unwrapped the package and pulled out a wrench. Everyone laughed as he stared at it, his eyes wide. "Mr. Butterworth! It is not a *child's* wrench!" he declared.

"Lord, no," said the mill owner, with a wink at Jane. "In future if you ever tire of being a marquis, I can find something for you to do in Huddersfield."

"I would like that more," Andrew said quietly as he rested the wrench in his lap, then ran his finger the length of it.

Oh dear, Jane thought, as Emma blew her nose and picked up Olivia to hide her tears. This will never do. "I am certain we are tiring you, Emma," she said. "What would you say that we adjourn and leave you and Richard in peace?"

"Not yet," the mill owner insisted. "Buck up, Em! Jane Milton, this is for you." Over her protests, he handed her a large package still cold from the outdoors. "Oh, why must women object when someone gives them a little something, Richard?"

"It's part of their charm, Scipio," his brother-in-law replied, as he sat closer to Emma, who was crying in earnest now. "My heart, what *is* the matter?"

"I am happy! I told you!" Emma sobbed. She wiped her eyes. "Jane, do open it before I simply drown Olivia."

If I do not open it, the matter will end here, Jane thought as she looked at the box in her lap. I know what it is, and I know what I owe for it. I can tease and say that ladies don't accept gifts beyond flowers and books, or I can give the man the terrible gift he wants in exchange. "Are you certain, Mr. Butterworth?" she asked, her voice low.

"Positive," he said. "Open it."

With Lucy to help, she took the ribbon off the box, then held her breath as she shook out a red cloak from the tissue that surrounded it.

"Red?" Emma said dubiously. "Scipio?"

"It's dark enough red, so no one will doubt that she's a complete lady. Try it on, Jane."

She did as he said, enjoying the warmth of the wool, and the weight of it on her shoulders. "Not exactly a cloak for a poor relation," she said.

"Far from it," Mr. Butterworth agreed.

Lucy tugged at her uncle's coat and he obliged her by sitting down again and taking her on his lap. "Why did you give her a red cloak, Uncle Scipio?" she asked.

He hugged her and smiled at Jane over Lucy's head. "No reason, Lucy. The material caught my eye."

"Uncle Scipio, you would never go in a cloth warehouse," Amanda began, then laughed when everyone else did. "You know! As a customer!"

"My dear niece, what I do sometimes even surprises me. What do you think, Jane?"

Lucy pulled away far enough to look up at him. "Mama says that we always have reasons for everything we do. And she is Miss Mitten, not Jane."

"Such a literal thing you are," he said. "Well, let us say I gave it to Miss Mitten because I . . . I like the way she takes care of Andrew! Will that satisfy you?"

"Lucy, you are a mystery," Richard murmured, shaking his head. "Come now, all of you. Did I not hear your uncle say that he was taking you to midnight church tonight? Go get ready."

"Ah, the mill owner's voice," Mr. Butterworth said as the children hurried from the room. "When did I promise midnight church, Richard, eh?" He looked at Jane. "Will it do?"

She nodded, too shy to speak. She draped the cloak carefully over her arm, smoothing down the fabric. "What have I done?" she asked.

"Found the perfect color for a cloak," Emma said, dabbing at her eyes and then putting the sleeping infant back across her knees. "It is amazing what that shade does to your skin, my dear."

Jane looked up from the fabric, and then realized that she had spoken aloud. "I'll wear it to church tonight," she said.

"Jane, you needn't go! I was only sending out Scipio on that errand of mercy. You know, wear out the children so they will sleep tonight and then open their other gifts in the morning," Richard said.

"No. I will go, too," Jane said. She returned Mr. Butterworth's faint smile, and hurried from the room. What better place than a church for the confession I must make tonight, she thought, even if there is no absolution.

She was composed and calm when he knocked softly on her door an hour later, the cloak warm about her shoulders and her bonnet precisely right.

"That *is* a beautiful color," he said, looking at her from head to toe. "And I was right about the length." He offered her his arm and she took it. "I took the fabric to Em's dressmaker and had her children stand next to me until I found the child whose head came just right below my shoulder, the way you do."

"You're an observant man then," she replied, for want of anything better to say.

"I had better be," he murmured. "And here are our charges! Courage, Miss Milton. I never blush for Andrew's manners, thanks to his upbringing." He gestured toward his nieces and nephew, standing by the front door. "And I can threaten these with half rations!"

She smiled at him. "I am certain that your threats terrify no one, Mr. Butterworth."

"Not lately," he agreed. "I'm getting soft."

She mulled that in her mind, content to walk in silence beside the mill owner who, obliging as always, matched his stride to hers. The children hurried on ahead, Andrew and Jacob holding Lucy's hand, while Amanda walked behind them, as if undecided whether she belonged with the children or the adults. The mill owner finally called to her and offered her his other arm, which she accepted.

"Amanda, you're growing up too fast," he said as they walked together toward the small church Jane had noticed on their drives to and from the mill. "I suppose I will be buying fabric for a wedding dress, in a couple of years."

"I am only fifteen, Uncle," she protested.

"Time passes, love, until it is gone and we are old before we know it," he said in a tone so final to Jane's ears that Amanda said nothing more.

He was silent through the midnight service, and Jane wondered if he was regretting his gift and what it meant. I cannot blame him, she thought, as she followed him back from the altar and knelt beside him again. It *is* a daunting thing to realize that at some point in our lives, we must stand alone. She looked at him. But surely you have already discovered this, Mr. Butterworth, she thought. I learned it, too, but you must know.

She shivered as they knelt together, then moved closer to him as the children came back to kneel beside them. "What, Miss Mitten?" he whispered to her. "Are you cold? I had thought that cloak warm enough for Arctic winters."

He seemed to know she would not answer him, and returned his gaze to his own hands clasped in front of him. In another moment he closed his eyes. Impulsively, Jane leaned toward him. "Pray for me, Mr. Butterworth," she whispered back. He nodded, and remained on his knees until the priest called on the congregation to rise.

She had second and third thoughts as the mass ended, and wondered what Mr. Butterworth would think if she bolted from the church and packed her bags for Stover Hall. She could claim that Lord Denby needed her, or that Lady Carruthers was at her wit's end with Cecil, and be gone by morning. A glance at Andrew, who stood outside stamping his feet and chatting with Jacob, calmed her. He would never forgive me for snatching him from his new friends, she thought. I will simply have to carry through with what Mr. Butterworth demands, even though I lose his friendship in the bargain. For someone who is such an observer rather than a partaker of events, I lead a complicated life. Who would have thought it?

She wondered if Mr. Butterworth suspected her own vacillation. He clung rather tighter to her arm, once he had successfully navigated the shoals of best wishes to the priest, and Christmas greetings to numerous parishioners. She smiled and curtsied through any number of introductions, making no effort to free herself from his grasp. "I promise not to bolt," she whispered, then stood on tiptoe to whisper in his ear. "You shan't lose a return on your investment."

With a smile he released her arm. "Miss Mitten, if I did not know you were a step or two higher than I on the social rung, I could accuse you of keeping an eye on that bottom line, yourself."

"I am no bookkeeper, sir," she protested.

"And so I remind myself," he murmured, then turned his attention to the elderly gentleman who had shared their pew. "Mr. Walthorpe! Promise me that you will have the very best Christmas ever!"

"Mama thinks that Uncle Scipio can charm roses off wallpaper," Amanda told her as she joined the children.

"I suppose he can," Jane replied, watching Lucy stamp her feet and turn in circles. "Lucy, are you cold?"

When Lucy nodded, Jane glanced at the mill owner, who appeared in no hurry to leave the church. Second thoughts of your own, sir? she thought. She turned to Amanda. "My dear, you and the children can go ahead. I will wait here for your uncle."

She stood where she was in the snow beside the chapel doors, the cloak warm around her shoulders. Snow was falling, and in the brief light from the lanterns, she watched the flakes fall against the dark material, burst with their own unique glory, and then melt into nothing. *And so do we all, on a grander cosmic scale,* she thought, watching the patterns so distinct and ephemeral—snowflake philosophy on early Christmas morning. *If it is true that animals talk to one another in this hour of Our Lord's birth, then I suppose I can gather some wisdom about me to keep me warm through the rest of life.* She frowned. *If only I can keep my friend, as well.*

She stared off into the beauty of the night, watching the snow all around her until she felt isolated even from the church, which was almost close enough to touch. The children were gone from her sight now, but through the peculiarity of atmosphere, she could still hear them laughing and talking. *Andrew, I wish I could just leave you here with Richard and Emma,* she thought. *Then I would take the mail coach to New Lanark in Scotland and tell Mr. Robert Owen that I would be happy to teach in his school for the children of mill workers. Lady Carruthers could tell everyone who would listen in Denby that she knew nothing good would ever come of me. I would never again have to devise reasons to avoid walking past the door to Blair's room, or drop what I was doing to listen to that fribble Cecil and his complaints. Lord Denby could die in peace, without me there to devise plans for reunions.*

"I would also never see you again," she whispered as she turned to regard the mill owner, engaged now in conversation with the priest. Tears came to her eyes and she brushed them away. *That would be the worst of all,* she decided.

As she watched, the mill owner gestured to her to join him. She hesitated, and he wasted not a moment in coming down the few steps to take her hand and tuck her arm in his. "Miss Milton, Father Nichols says that we are welcome to stay in the church and chat."

I hardly imagine my confessions can be classified as chat, she thought, but she nodded to the priest, and allowed the mill owner to lead her back inside the church. She sat where he indicated, pulled the red cloak tighter about her shoulders, and rested her feet on the prayer bench to keep them off the cold stone floor.

Mr. Butterworth sat beside her and put his arm around her shoulders to pull her closer. He said nothing, but stared at the altar in front of them, a half smile on his face. *Almost as though you are enjoying this,* she thought in surprise. With a sigh, she nestled closer to him and rested her head in that comforting place between his armpit and his chest that she had discovered last night—was it just last night?—in her own bed.

The chapel was so silent that she could hear the faint ticking of Mr. Butterworth's watch in his vest pocket. The pleasant sound, so prosaic, calmed her heart. She relaxed finally, and closed her eyes when the mill owner removed her bonnet and then rested his chin on top of her head.

He did not prod; he did not pry. She couldn't have told anyone how much time passed, or even that it passed at all, except that the watch ticked so steadily. *Where do I begin?* she asked herself. "Hold my hand," she said, not even opening her eyes as he covered her tightly knotted hands with his own. She took a deep breath.

"Mr. Butterworth, what would you say if I told you I killed Blair?"

Chapter Thirteen

She held her breath then, waiting for him to flinch and draw away from her, but he did not. Instead, he kissed the top of her head, then rested his chin there again. "I suppose anyone's instant reply would be to deny that such a thing was possible, and then change the subject with a vengeance," he told her finally. "But I do not know that anything is impossible, even from the most improbable sources, Jane."

It was not the answer she expected, and she pulled away from him to look at his face. "What are you saying?" she asked.

"I suppose I am suggesting that I am pretty hard to shock." He chuckled and pulled her closer to him again. "Why don't you just tell me what happened, instead of wasting one more minute blaming yourself?"

"The blame *is* mine," she insisted.

"I suppose it is, if you like that kind of torture." He shrugged. "And if we do not see eye to eye on the matter, what then, my dear?"

She did not know what to say to the mill owner's matter-of-fact comment. As she sat there, he put his hand between her clenched fists until she felt herself relax, and then twined his fingers into hers. "Perhaps you can answer a question of mine," he said, after another long silence passed.

She nodded, and he squeezed her hand. "My dear, when Blair was brought back from Belgium, were you aware that Andrew began to visit me?"

"No!" she said in surprise. "He never said . . ." She stopped, remembering that first month when she knew that nothing would ever be right again.

"Perhaps you can begin there," the mill owner suggested. "I found Andrew playing at the lake—well, more like just sitting there. He said that no one would let him see his father, and that you seldom left his room." He paused, and then brought her hand up to his lips. "What did they make you do, Jane?" he asked, his lips against her fingers.

"They made me take care of him!" she burst out, her words so loud and ugly that she winced at the sound of them in the quiet nave. " 'Let Jane do it!' " she said in perfect imitation of Lady Carruthers. "And Mr. Lowe was so happy to agree with her!"

Mr. Butterworth did flinch then. "My God, Jane," he said. "The *doctor*? The whole neighborhood knew that Lord Canfield was seriously wounded but . . . what was wrong?"

"Everything," she replied, pulling her hands away to dab at her eyes. "Mr. Butterworth, he had been shot in the neck and the wound simply refused to heal." She leaned forward to pound on the pew in front of her and stopped only when her hand began to ache. "It would not heal!" She grasped the front of his overcoat and stared into his eyes, which did not waver from her face. "Mr. Lowe said a musket ball had grazed his subclavian artery. In fact, it was still there under his collarbone. Blair could rub along for a week or even two weeks, and then that horrible wound would open and he would bleed. We never knew when it would happen."

She was silent then, and dropped her hands from his coat, embarrassed with herself. She leaned closer until her forehead rested against his chest. The mill owner pulled her close, his arms around her. "Let me guess," he said finally, his voice muffled by her hair. "You were all afraid to let Andrew see him, for fear that he would begin to hemorrhage suddenly, and terrify the boy."

"That was it," she told him. "Blair made Stanton and me swear that no one would know how bad it was . . . or would become, I suppose. He was adamant, and we obliged him."

"He wanted to spare everyone?"

She nodded, too weary to speak. "It was a horrible sight," she said finally. "Mr. Lowe showed me how to staunch the bleeding with styptic and then press the heel of my hand just so against his neck until the wound clotted." She started to cry. "It took so long and my arm would get so tired. Oh, Mr. Butterworth, you can't imagine!"

"No, I can't," he murmured, pulling her onto his lap, and wrapping his overcoat around both of them. "Here I thought I could, but I can't. For the love of God, why didn't Lowe do this instead of you?" He gave her his handkerchief and she sobbed into it. "Jane, he was the physician!"

She cried until she was almost nauseated with her tears. Mr. Butterworth held her close and rocked back and forth with her as though she were Lucy or Olivia. She was helpless to do anything except cry until his handkerchief was a useless, soggy ball. "Just a moment, my dear," he said, pulling her away enough to undo his neckcloth. "We may have finally discovered a use for these silly things. Here." She took his neckcloth and wiped her face, then dabbed at his shirtfront. "Oh, never mind that, Jane," he said, holding her close again. "I know from our years of acquaintance that you are one to excuse all kinds of chicanery, but unless you can give me a reason for Mr. Lowe to continue drawing breath, I'm going to call him out."

She stared at him, her eyes wide. "You would never!" she exclaimed.

"Miss Mitten, you underestimate this particular mill owner," he replied grimly. "There are things about *me* that you would never believe. Come now, and give me a good reason for Lowe's existence. I will settle for one."

You are serious, she thought, regarding the mill owner. With only the light of the perpetual flame behind the altar, and what moonlight filtered through the windows, she could barely see his face, but his words were so clipped and unfamiliar. "I can forgive him, Mr. Butterworth," she said, after a moment's contemplation of his face. "Blair was one of his best friends. Mr. Lowe could not bear to watch him die."

The mill owner sighed and tightened his grip around her. "Jane, I believe you would find excuse for Judas Iscariot himself. So Mr. Lowe couldn't watch his friend die, but it was all right for you to bear the brunt?"

"You know that I do all the tasks no one else wants at Stover," she said simply.

"You were forced to bear all this yourself," said the mill owner, amazement unmistakable in his voice.

"Stanton and I took turns caring for him. Not even the servants were allowed in the room to help. Even Lord Denby had no idea of the total complication because that was Blair's wish."

"A damned selfish wish," Mr. Butterworth said grimly. "I wonder that you are not angry with him still."

She released his lapels and stared at him. "Do you know, I think I am sometimes. I shouldn't be, of course," she added in a rush.

"Of course you should be," he insisted. "Say what you like about Lord Canfield, but I will contend that he treated you as poorly as the rest." The mill owner was silent then.

"I can forgive."

She felt her face go red as his silence continued. I am an idiot, she thought, too shy to look at him now. She rested her head against his chest again, drawing comfort from the steady beat of his heart. "Go ahead and say it," she told him finally. "I am the most silly, compliant woman you ever met."

She was rewarded with a chuckle that she felt more than she heard, and then he gripped her even tighter. "No, Jane Milton," he said, his voice so soft. "What you are is braver than most men, and more forgiving than most saints." He sighed. "No wonder you have never married. You put us all to shame."

"The shame is mine, sir," she replied, shaking her head. "I told you that I killed Blair."

"I think I understand, my dear Miss Mitten. In those—what was it: six or seven months?—did you actually leave the room once and Blair died? Was that how it was?"

"No. I fell asleep," she said quietly, pressing her fingers hard against the bridge of her nose so she would not cry. Without a word he took her hand away and she fell against him, sobbing.

"Oh, my dear," he crooned, rocking with her again. "Oh, my dear."

Her face pressed against his neckcloth, Jane cried until she was certain there were no tears left. It was a storm of tears, a rage of tears that startled her by their very intensity, even as they were muffled within the mill owner's overcoat as he held her close.

"Did no one allow you to cry?" he asked, his lips close to her ear, when she rested against him, exhausted.

"There was no time for my tears," she said, and shook her head. "Lord Denby was in ruin, and Andrew . . . I know that I failed him then."

"He spent time with me, my dear," Mr. Butterworth said. "He was so certain that Lord Canfield was refusing to see him because he wasn't his real father."

"Oh, no!" she exclaimed. "Stanton and I said nothing to him because of that awful promise." She sat up. "That was the wrong thing, wasn't it?"

"You can undo it," the mill owner assured her. "Just tell him the nature of the wound, and how much Lord Canfield wanted to shield him." He put his hand on her neck and pulled her back to rest against him again. "Andrew will keep, Jane. You are not through yet, are you? Do you fear to go to sleep because of what happened?"

She nodded. "I know it is perfectly nonsensical, but I will do almost anything to keep from falling asleep, no matter how tired I am." She hesitated, and Mr. Butterworth peered at her expectantly. "I wish that were all," she said finally, the words pulled from her like cockleburs from tangled hair. *Must I tell you more?* she pleaded silently. *I cannot bear it. It is a pity that you are so intelligent, sir. I think you will figure it out.*

To her dismay, she was right. After a moment's reflection, he spoke slowly, almost as hesitant as she, and her heart sank. "God bless you, Jane," he said, his voice low. "It's not so much the falling asleep as the waking up, is it, my dear? Blair wasn't dead."

She shook her head and he drew his overcoat tighter about them both when she began to shiver. "He was bleeding to death before your eyes, wasn't he?" Mr. Butterworth asked gently.

She nodded, unable to find the words to convey the full horror. "It was . . . was like a fountain," she managed to say finally, irritated with herself because she couldn't stop trembling. "Mr. Lowe had warned me that the end would come that way when— not if—the artery burst, but not in my worst moment did I imagine it would be so terrible."

"Damn Mr. Lowe," Mr. Butterworth muttered. "Jane, did you try to stop it?"

She nodded again. "I must have packed a pound of alum against that artery, but nothing worked. I tried so hard," she pleaded with him, "really I did!"

"Jane, I know you did," Mr. Butterworth said. "Was Blair . . . was he . . . conscious?"

"Yes." She felt the tears rising again. "He couldn't speak, but he was begging me with his eyes to do something. I *had* to do something!" She took a deep breath, and then another quicker breath until her head felt light. "I put the heel of my hand against his neck and just held it there."

She winced as Mr. Butterworth sucked in his breath and sat back then. "My God," he breathed. "Jane, are you telling me that as long as you held your hand there, he would live?"

I knew I would repulse you, she thought in agony. "Yes," she said, and it was the barest whisper. "I did not know what to do, Mr. Butterworth. I was so afraid. God forgive me." She knew her voice was low, but the words seemed to carry on the cold air and circle around in the nave until she was weary with the sound of them.

"I sat that way for at least an hour," she continued, even though the mill owner had said nothing to urge any more of the story from her. "Through my negligence, he had bled open the artery entirely." She sighed, got up from Mr. Butterworth's lap, folded his damp neckcloth, and set it beside him on the pew. He did not move, but she knew his eyes were on her. "Mr. Butterworth, I told him I loved him, and took my hand away. Good night, sir. I will take the mailcoach back to Denby tomorrow. Forgive me for burdening you. I knew it would be more than you wanted."

She turned to go, but quicker than sight Mr. Butterworth grabbed her hand and pulled her back down beside him. "What did you do? Faint? Scream? Run from the room?"

Shocked, she stared at him and tried to pull her hand away,

but he would not allow it. "Of course not, Mr. Butterworth! I held his hand until he died. Why would you think . . ." She sighed. "Mr. Butterworth, you know it was never in me to run away."

"Of course it was not," he replied, and then touched her face with the back of his hand. "I just wanted you to realize it."

She leaned forward then to rest her chin on her palms and stare at the outline of the altar. A great wave of exhaustion poured over her and she closed her eyes. "He was going to die, wasn't he?" she asked.

"Most certainly."

"There wasn't anything I could have done."

"No." He rested his hand on her back. "You were given the impossible task."

"I wish I could have done better, sir," she confessed.

He rose and pulled her up, too, then stood contemplating the altar with her. "My dear, you bore it all with uncommon grace," he said at last, and she was touched by his words, which seemed to come out of him with such effort. "I wish that you would tell Andrew the full nature of his . . . of Lord Canfield's wounds."

Jane shook her head. "I swore to Blair that I would spare him that much, and I must keep my word. Mr. Butterworth, he is too young for such details."

"I contend that he is not," the mill owner replied, "but it is not my business, is it?"

"I think not," she replied gently. "I made a promise. Leave Andrew to me, sir, and I will do my best."

"My every dependence is on that, my dear," he said.

It sounded so formal to her ears, so strange that she looked at him, and found, to her surprise, a man looking supremely uncomfortable. How odd this is, she thought. "You needn't worry about Andrew and me, sir, especially when you have so many concerns that pull you in such different directions," she said, suddenly unsure of herself. After a moment's hesitation, she rested her hand on his arm. "Especially do not worry about me."

"Not even a little?" he asked with his old familiar tone.

"Not even a little," she assured him. "I have already forgiven them all."

"That is the wonder of it, my dear. I believe you mean it."

Oh, I do, she thought. She paused, then stood on tiptoe to kiss his cheek. "I suppose it remains for me to forgive myself, aren't you telling me?"

He smiled. "I was never known for my subtlety, Miss Mitten."

"Just your kindness, then," she murmured. He flinched, and she looked at him in surprise.

"Not even that," he said. "Miss Mitten, I . . . I have my own regrets."

Standing there in the cold chapel, Jane realized with a start that he had never said anything so personal to her before. It has always been about others, hasn't it, sir? she asked herself, wanting to speak out loud, but deciding against it when a wintry look crossed his face. You have an empty picture frame on your desk, and your own troubles which you will not share. I think you are a kind man, but you only deny it. I have no claim on you that entitles me to pry.

She held out her hand to the mill owner and he took it. "Thank you, Mr. Butterworth, for hearing me out. It really wasn't much of a Christmas present, was it?"

"It was what I asked for," he said as he shook her hand.

"Perhaps someday you will speak as candidly to me," she said simply. Her words sounded so bold to her ears that she blushed, and then was grateful for the darkness.

"You are too young for that," he said quickly, and she knew he regretted his words the instant they were spoken because he turned his head away.

"And you are not so old, Mr. Butterworth," she replied, wondering at her own temerity. I suppose if animals talk to each other on the night of Christ's birth, than even timid women can speak their mind, she told herself. "Go ahead, sir," she said. "I believe I will remain here a while longer and make some attempt to reacquaint myself with the Almighty."

He offered no objection, and even seemed relieved, in Jane's estimation, to face a solitary walk home. "Don't stay away too long, my dear," he said. "Soon my nieces and nephew will be waking to see what else is theirs this day, and your approbation will be required in the sitting room, no matter how bloodshot your eyes."

"I shan't be long, sir," she said quietly. "Thank you again."

Her mind at peace, she listened to the mill owner walk from the church. She did not hear his footsteps in the snow, and wondered for the longest moment if he was going to return to the chapel. "I wish you would, sir," she whispered. "Tell me what is troubling *you*." She was on the verge of going outside herself when she heard the crunch of footsteps on dry snow. The sound brought tears to her eyes, and she felt an absurd desire to rush after him. And what would you say to him, Jane? she asked herself. For some reason he has not minded your messy troubles, but he has given you no leave to examine his own.

"Ah well, some other time, Mr. B," she said. She wrapped her new cloak tighter around her shoulders again and sat in the pew closest to the altar. "I have done endless penance, Father," she said out loud, "and now I have confessed in the presence of a very good man. Help me, Lord, to forgive myself."

Sitting by herself in the chapel, she wasn't aware of the passage of time. It rested lightly on her shoulders as she thought through the year past as though it had happened to someone else, then quietly closed the door on it. I must think of Andrew, she told herself, and find some way to shield him from Lady Carruthers, who ought to be his friend, but who is not. I know that the reunion will work wonders for Lord Denby; a man cannot mourn forever. When Andrew is safely in school somewhere, and everyone else is taken care of, I will leave. She held her breath, waiting for fear to set in, but there was no fear this time. "Thank you for that, Mr. Butterworth," she murmured, "among the many things I have to thank you for."

The night was absolutely still as she started back to the mill owner's home. The snow must have stopped hours ago, because she could see Mr. Butterworth's footprints in the snow. She followed them, stopping once, her eyes filling with tears, when she noticed them turn and start back in the direction of the church. "Dear Mr. Butterworth," she whispered. "Is there no one to listen to you? Oh, sir, I would listen, if you would ask me."

She waited, felt foolish for doing so, and hurried the rest of the way. Soon she was in the lane, where she walked slower, allowing herself for a small moment to pretend that it was hers. I wonder what the spring flowers are like here, she thought. I would plant lilacs all along the front of the house and open all the windows. And if the blossoms blow into the house, what of it?

She hurried up the few steps to the front door and then stared down at the stoop. Someone had obviously sat there in the snow and the cold. Her heart pounding, she sat down carefully beside the space where the mill owner must have waited for her. "Mr. Butterworth," she said, "I think I love you."

Her own voice sounded loud to her ears, so she looked around quickly, and then touched the spot next to her. "Actually, Mr. Butterworth, I am certain that I love you." After a moment's reflection that had nothing to do with the Almighty, Jane went into the house and up the stairs, sure of herself in the dark.

The door to her room was open, the bedcovers turned back, a fire in the hearth, small but glowing warm with coals that winked in the darkness. Thoughtfully she removed her cloak and draped it over the back of the chair, then went to the door and listened. In a moment she heard the chair creak in Mr. Butterworth's office. *Now I am to sleep and you are to be vigilant, sir?* she thought. *I only told you my troubles; I never expected you to* assume *them.* "Go to bed, Mr. Butterworth," she whispered, then closed her door just loud enough so that he would know she was back.

With nothing more on her mind than the perplexity that seemed to be—she was discovering—an unexpected byproduct of love, she lay down to sleep. As she was closing her eyes, it occurred to her that her mind was on nothing but the mill owner. Drowsy now, with no tension beyond a tingling in her toes because she had sat too long on the stoop, she heard the door to the office open and then close.

I wish you would come in here, she thought, then waited to feel the blush of shame that she would even think something like that. Nothing. Her face felt the same as always, and there was no rush of heat to her bosom. *I have become so matter-of-fact,* she thought, as his steps receded down the hall. *All I am feeling right now is disappointment. Oh, this is a new Miss Mitten, indeed. I wonder if I will like her?*

She woke by degrees in the morning, lying peacefully on her back and listening to doors opening and closing, and children running down the hall. In another moment she heard Richard laughing, and then Emma's calm voice over Olivia's mewing cry. She lay where she was, observing that she had not started awake, bolt upright with all her nerves on edge. She lay there, her body relaxed, her mind in that disengaged somnolence she had almost forgotten.

With a yawn that seemed to swell up from her toes, she turned onto her side. The fire was out, so she knew the maid had not yet arrived, but something was different. She sat up and leaned on her elbow, looking around the room. The cloak she had placed over the chair was at the foot of her bed now, and the chair had been pulled up closer to the fireplace, almost as though someone had sat there and propped his feet on the coal fender.

I must be mistaken, she thought, as she got out of bed. She sat in the chair, closed her eyes, and breathed in the faintest odor of the mill owner's cologne. She could not be sure, but the chair even seemed to be warm. Just when I imagine that nothing on earth can surprise me, she thought, allowing the notion to drift, unfinished, through her mind. She was still sitting there when Lucy burst into the room, Amanda close behind, and tugged at her arm.

"Miss Mitten, we are supposed to be in the sitting room now, and here you are, just . . . just sitting!" the child said, as Amanda laughed.

"Let me get dressed, my dear," Jane said. "I will join you."

Lucy stomped her foot. "That is *not* the way we do it here!" she insisted, as Jane tried hard not to laugh.

"What I am supposed to do, then?" she asked.

"Find a robe and slippers, Miss Milton," said the mill owner from the doorway. "If Lucy is not happy, then no one is happy on Christmas morning, or so I have discovered."

"Very well, sir," she said quietly. "I would never disregard a summons." While he stood in the doorway, she went to the dressing room, wishing all the while that her nightgown was not the most-washed and worn piece of flannel in the district. The robe is not much better, she thought in dismay as she put it on and belted the waist. I never met a shabbier woman than Jane Milton at—she glanced at the clock—seven of the clock in the morning. And why did I not think to bring slippers here? Barefoot I will be, then.

"Miss Milton! I cannot wait much longer!"

Mr. Butterworth laughed and leaned himself away from the door frame. "Lucy, you have all the manners of a road mender! Amanda, be a good niece and take this bundle of impatience back to the sitting room. Lucy, I will have her there as quick as I can."

Amanda nodded, then pointed at the mill owner. "Uncle Scipio, you are already dressed! That is not one of the rules." She peered closer. "Well, you have no neckcloth, and you are wrinkled, so I suppose I should not object."

"Good of you, Amanda. Now get Lucy to the sitting room."

Oh, Amanda, he is already dressed because he never undressed last night, Jane thought in dismay. For all I know his neckcloth is still at the church, and probably a frozen lump. He sat beside my bed half the night, ready in case I should wake in a nightmare. I doubt there is a woman alive who deserves such attention. I am certain I do not.

Andrew stuck his head in the doorway. "Miss Mitten, Happy Christmas!"

"And to you, my dear. Have you seen my hairbrush?" she asked as she looked at her dressing table.

"It is right in front of you. Sit down, Jane," the mill owner said, indicating the dressing table stool. "A couple of quick strokes will do it, and I am, as ever, the soul of efficiency. It is a virtue bred into those of us who must toil for a living."

She made no objection as he brushed her hair, enjoying instead the steady pull of the brush, done with more firmness than she ever managed. In a moment her hair was crackling.

"Nice color," he said as he set down the brush.

"It is just black, Mr. Butterworth!"

"It is interesting," he told her. "Sort of un-English. Now, where is a ribbon?"

"I don't use ribbons," she said, feeling a little flame in her cheeks.

"You should." He went next door to his office and returned with a length of package twine. "Here, now. Lucy hasn't time to wait for you to poke pins here and there! Jane, were you never four?"

She laughed and turned to look at him as he tried to tie her hair back. "Of course I was four!"

"Hold still!"

Smiling, she did as he said, taking care not to move as he gathered her hair in his hands and tied a bow low on the back of her neck. "There!" he exclaimed, and rested his hands on her shoulders. "I pronounce you entirely . . ."

". . . adequate," she finished, enjoying the sound of his laughter.

"No, no," he declared, not letting go of her shoulders. "I had in mind, uh . . ."

". . . Suitable? Satisfactory? Unexceptionable?" she teased.

"No, actually. Quite, quite lovely," he said, his voice low. He rested his cheek next to hers for the briefest moment. "Especially dressed in flannel that I think used to be blue. Miss Milton, you are all amazement at seven in the morning."

And you are all amazement any time of the day or night, she thought. She looked at him in the mirror, and he gazed back, his glance as unwavering as hers. "Mr. Butterworth, I wish you would . . ." She stopped. What do you wish, Jane? That he would stand back? Move closer? Touch you again? Kiss you? Oh, Jane, lighten the moment, she thought. That is, if you want to.

She decided that she did not, but Mr. Butterworth stepped back and indicated the door. "If we do not hurry, your stock—which had been recently soaring among the infantry—will sink to new lows on 'Change, my dear lady."

Now it is "my dear lady," she thought as she allowed the mill owner to take her hand and hurry her along to the sitting room. I believe there is enough complexity in this man to fill a medium-sized room.

It was a relief to smile to the assembled Newtons, wish them Happy Christmas, tuck her bare feet under her, and watch the children open presents. Mr. Butterworth settled himself in an armchair and promptly fell asleep. Jane managed to intercept Lucy and prevent her from climbing on her sleeping uncle. "We should never have sent Scipio to midnight Mass," was Richard's only comment as he helped his younger daughter arrange a sofa and wing chair in her Christmas dollhouse.

Emma sat beside Jane and opened her gown to nurse Olivia. "Scipio did not think you would object if Richard bought Andrew the same gifts we had arranged for Jacob."

"It was so kind of you," she said, pressing her little finger against Olivia's hand and enjoying the strength of the infant's grasp. "This has been quite the most wonderful Christmas."

"For me, as well," Emma said. She looked at her sleeping brother. "And for Scipio, I think." She hesitated. "Jane, he is not a happy man, for all that he would like everyone to think otherwise."

Jane nodded. "He keeps himself quite busy, tending to other's welfare, doesn't he? I know that Andrew and I have been grateful recipients of his many kindnesses."

"The busier he is, the better he likes it," Emma stated. "We have introduced him to any number of ladies from his own class and background, and he is the soul of courtesy, but nothing ever comes of it." She sighed, and raised Olivia to her shoulder to pat her back. "In fact, a few years ago, he told me not to bother anymore. Excellent, Olivia! And so I have not." She placed the baby against her other breast, tickling her cheek with the nipple until the baby began to suck again. "I tell him there must be someone in the world for him, and he just laughs and changes the subject. Ah, me."

She fell silent then, watching her baby nurse. Jane looked at Andrew, who was playing jackstraws with Jacob. With a pang, she remembered last Christmas at Denby, spent seated beside Blair, ever watchful of him. When she emerged from the sickroom long enough to ask Andrew how the day had gone for him, he had only shrugged, mumbled something that she hadn't the energy to ask him to repeat, and vanished into his book again. This is far better, she told herself, as Emma coaxed a burp from the sleeping baby.

"Hold her, my dear?" she asked, handing the baby to Jane. "We do have our family rituals."

Jane watched as Amanda handed a sprig of mistletoe to her mother. Carefully, Emma knelt beside her husband, who was rearranging the servants quarters of the dollhouse, and held it over his head. With a growl that made Lucy shriek and then clap her hands, Richard grabbed his wife and kissed her soundly. Mr. Butterworth sat bolt upright, blinking his eyes in surprise. He laughed when Amanda held the mistletoe over his head and kissed him. "That's for the bonnet, Uncle Scipio," she said.

"And not because I am irresistible?" he teased, grabbing Lucy as she tried to run by. He kissed her while she struggled, then whispered in her ear. In another moment, she was holding the bedraggled bit of greenery over Jane's head.

Andrew leaped up from his game of jackstraws and kissed her cheek. Her arms went around him and she held him close. "This is the best Christmas ever," he told her. "I only wish . . ."

". . . that your father were here?" she said softly.

He looked at her in surprise. "Well, yes, that, too, but I was thinking how nice it would be to have a Christmas just as good next year."

"We will," she declared, releasing him. "I know we will."

"Not if we are at Stover," he said, his face serious again.

And that is food for thought, she told herself as she settled Olivia against her legs. She watched, delighted, as the baby stretched, then drew herself into a ball again. "She is so economical," Jane said.

"She is used to a confined space," Mr. Butterworth said as he perched on the end of the sofa. "Em, just think: In fifteen years she will be making demands on everyone and wheedling any number of commodities out of her old Uncle Scipio."

"Dear brother, you are the easiest mark alive," Emma said, as she let Richard help her up from the floor. "Come now and let us find the breakfast room. Cook has promised us cinnamon buns and no porridge, Lucy, in honor of the day. Jane?"

Jane shook her head and placed her hand gently on Olivia's belly. "Let me just stay here and relish the moment, Emma." It may not come again, she thought, as the woman blew her a kiss and left the room. In a few days we must leave, and I do not know that I will ever see these dear people again.

"I will bring you something to eat," Mr. Butterworth. He held up his hand when she opened her mouth to protest. "And I will sit here until you eat it."

Just as you sit beside me to make sure that I am sleeping peacefully, she thought. "I am a dreadful lot of trouble to you, Mr. Butterworth," she said.

"How odd this is then, because I haven't noticed," he said. He got up from the arm of the sofa, and squatted by the dollhouse with easy grace. "Lucy is an engine of destruction," he murmured, looking around the dollhouse. "Ah! Here it is." Carefully he extracted what remained of the mistletoe from the miniature trellis with its wax roses, and held it over her head. "I never got a turn, Miss Milton. Happy Christmas."

She turned her head to offer him her cheek, but he put his other hand under her chin and sat beside her on the sofa, careful not to disturb Olivia as he gently turned her face toward him. He leaned toward her and she closed her eyes, reaching up to pull him closer as he kissed her. "Merry Christmas. Happy New Year," he murmured, his lips against hers, then kissed her again. "And while we are at it, let us not forget Shrove Tuesday, Ash Wednesday, and Easter in the spring," punctuating each holiday with a kiss that left her restless and wishing that she had relinquished Olivia to her cradle.

"I could never forget the holidays!" she murmured as he pressed his hand against the warm skin of her shoulder, under her nightgown and robe.

Olivia chose that moment to move about and utter the little squeaks that Jane knew were her prelude to a cry that would bring Emma from the breakfast room. She took her hand from his neck to pat the baby, and the moment was over. The mill owner sat back on the sofa, an expression on his face that she had never seen before. He took her hand, raised it to his lips, kissed it, and placed it back on Olivia, who was crying in earnest now.

With a sigh that she was certain could be heard in the next shire, Mr. Butterworth scooped the baby from her lap. "I believe I owe you an apology, Miss Milton," he said, then smiled at her. "I mean, if I was planning to review the ecclesiastical year, I should at least have found a more respectable piece of mistletoe. What must you think of me?"

If ever a woman had an invitation to speak her mind, I am certain this is it, Jane told herself. She stood up, surprised at how unstable her knees seemed. "I think you . . ."

She stopped as Emma hurried into the room to claim the squalling infant from her brother. "Olivia, what will they think of you?" she chided, holding her daughter close. "Jane, could you find her blanket? There is a chill in this room."

"I hadn't noticed," Jane said. She found the blanket next to the box holding the new bonnet that Amanda had received from her uncle. When she turned around, Mr. Butterworth was gone.

Chapter Fourteen

If Mr. Butterworth did not perform a vanishing act, then he came as close to it as a man not an illusionist possibly could, Jane decided. After breakfast, he disappeared into his office and did not come out of it until nearly noon.

When she wondered out loud to Emma why he had taken himself off, Emily merely shrugged. "That is Scipio's way," she explained. "He sees the day as a time for children, and as he has none, off he goes to console himself with double entries."

Emma did admit to some surprise later in the morning when Andrew burst into the room where they were bathing Olivia with the breathless announcement that he and Mr. Butterworth were driving to Leeds. "This is odd, indeed," she murmured to Jane as she wrapped a bathing towel around the wriggling infant.

"May I inquire the purpose of this expedition?" Jane asked with a smile.

Andrew shook his head. "Mr. Butterworth said it is an absolute secret," he said. "Please say that I may! He said we would take Christmas dinner at his favorite inn in Leeds."

"Of course you may," Jane said, puzzled. Mr. Butterworth, you are a curious man, she thought, hoping that her face did not brighten in color from the thought of his mistletoe kisses. Olivia, you are the only witness to his enthusiasm, she told herself, looking at the baby in Emma's arms. How grateful I am that you are too young to tattle on my own enjoyment of the moment.

"Dear me, this means they will be going to the Bell and Clapper," Emma said, after Andrew waved good-bye and darted off, banging the door behind him. She took a smaller towel and dried Olivia's hair. "Scipio is combining business with secrecy, I suppose. I wonder what he intends? He will eat far too much and require a serious dose of bicarbonate of soda when they return. And he will have heard the latest mill workers' gossip and likely hired a man or two." She worked a curl of Olivia's hair around her finger. "I hope you do not mind that Andrew keeps low company!"

"I only wish I could think up an excuse to keep Andrew here in such company," Jane said frankly.

"Do you?" Emma asked.

"My dear, you have been a tonic to both of us." And that is all I will say on the matter, she thought, or my face will grow even redder than Olivia's is right now. She kissed the baby and started for the door. "Emma, you would not object if Amanda and I checked in on the Christmas goose and decked the hall while Olivia dines?"

Emma gave her a grateful look. "You know I have no shame when it comes to using my Christmas guest for all she is worth!" She made herself comfortable in the armchair, her hand on her buttons. "After dinner I give the servants a half day off. For supper we Newtons generally ferret around in the pantry. Richard will attempt an omelet, I imagine. If Scipio is in fit shape after doing duty at the Bell and Clapper, he will toast cheese." She watched Olivia begin to nurse. "This is all dreadfully common to you, isn't it?"

Jane blew her a kiss from the doorway. "I prefer to think of it as wonderfully kind to your servants. Supper in the kitchen is probably far more fun than listening to Lady Carruthers begin her annual review of all my shortcomings, and then admonish Andrew to be grateful for every bone she throws him." She frowned. "I suppose I should not say that."

"Sometimes things are easier to bear when they are spoken of," was Emma's quiet reply. "Is it so dreadful there, my dear?"

Jane nodded. "It is, and the wonder of it is that I never realized how unpleasant my Christmases have been because all I had to measure Stover Hall against was the workhouse. But now that I know you Newtons, it will be hard duty, indeed." She came back into the room and leaned against the door. "I am beginning to think that when your brother suggested that I speak my mind occasionally, I took him more truly at his word than either of us realized."

Emma looked down at Olivia for a long moment, and when she looked up, Jane was dismayed to see tears in her eyes. "Jane, if you could only convince my brother to speak his mind now!"

"I doubt he needs advice from me," she replied, after a long pause. "He certainly hasn't ever asked for any."

Emma was equally slow to respond. "Asking and needing are only distant relations, Jane. And then there is wanting . . ." Her voice trailed away.

Andrew and the mill owner did not return until after dark, when Richard was concentrating on the omelet and Amanda was placing out the silverware on the servants' table. Without a word, Emma handed the slumbering Olivia to Jane and prepared her brother a cup of water and soda, which he accepted and downed without a pause. Nodding to them all, he left the room. Just after the door closed behind him, they heard a loud belch. Andrew stared, wide-eyed, then turned away, his shoulders shaking.

"My dear brother," Emma said to no one in particular.

"Amanda, get a platter for your father. Richard, don't you dare try to flip that omelet!"

Mr. Butterworth did not reappear for the rest of the evening, but none of the Newtons seemed to think it strange. "Jane, as much as I wish he would change, Scipio is used to the solitary life," was all Emma said as they sat in the parlor. "When he tires of our company, he turns to his blueprints."

And he must also regret planting kiss after kiss on Jane Milton, Jane thought, as she nodded and continued to organize Amanda's embroidery thread. I shall have to think up an excuse to leave. This is his house; he needn't have to skulk around in it to avoid an embarrassment he would probably just as soon forget.

After reading to Andrew and Jacob, she took that thought to bed with her, deriving no pleasure from it. She sat for a long moment at the dressing table, contemplating her own serious expression. "Jane Milton," she told her reflection, "you will return to Stover Hall and remove that horrid funeral wreath from the door. You could also stop wearing drab funeral colors, except that is all you own." She sighed, picked up her hairbrush, then set it down again, thinking of the mill owner and how good her hair felt that morning when he brushed it. It occurred to her when she closed her eyes that for the first time in months, she was not dreading sleep. "Thank you for that, Mr. Butterworth," she murmured.

She thought she slept well that night, but in the morning the armchair was close to the bed, with the footstool about as far away as a tall man could comfortably rest his feet. She lay in bed, her mind in a perfect jumble. He is watching over me, she thought, touched to her soul by his late-night solicitude, and also knowing somehow that he would not want her to make any comment on it.

There was nothing she needed to say, anyway. Each morning he was gone to the mills early, not returning until late at night, when there was no time to exchange conversation beyond the commonplace, in the company of his relatives. Night after night she sat in the parlor with all the others, chatting about nonsensicals when she wanted to say so much more.

She knew she should leave, but even the hint of such a thing brought more tears to Emma's eyes, and turned Andrew quiet. Lord Denby was no help, either. By letter he assured her that he and Stanton were soldiering on quite well, what with Cecil making a slow recovery and Lady Carruthers practically chained to his side by Mr. Lowe. "Make of it what you will, Jane, but I have never seen my sister so solicitous over anyone's welfare to such an extreme," he wrote her. "She has no time to meddle with me, and I am as grateful as a man can be." He made no inquiry after Andrew; she expected none.

Any attempt on her part to end the visit seemed to come up against overshadowing events. One night during supper she had worked up her nerve to announce their departure, when Richard and Scipio, late as usual, burst in with the announcement that yes, indeed, Jeremy Bentham had agreed to serve on the board of their mills. She was reluctant to disturb the good feeling of the occasion by the damper of her own resolve to quit the place. "Or perhaps I am still far too easily cowed," she announced to her mirror that night.

Admit it, Jane, she thought the next morning, after another night of peaceful sleep and the now-expected sight of the chair and footstool pulled close to the bed, you are in need of Mr. Butterworth's solicitude, even if he will say nothing, and you have not the courage to press the matter. She thought each night that she would will herself to stay awake and tell him that he needn't ruin his own hours of sleep anymore, but she was unable to follow through with her good intentions. She kept busy enough in the Newton household to make it impossible for her to wake up in the middle of the night, where before, phantoms had been sufficient to send her gasping and staring into the dark. "Face it, Jane," she told herself. "You do not wish to free yourself from a kind man's solicitude."

Somehow they continued their visit in Rumsey far beyond New Year's Day and well into January. Her feeble arguments about Andrew's education turned moot when room was found for him to attend the vicar's school with Jacob. Emma came down with a slight cold and insisted that she would trust Olivia to no one but Jane. "Olivia, these are the flimsiest of reasons to keep me here," Jane announced to the baby one morning as she prepared to bathe her. "I would suspect your dear mother of some conspiracy, except that I cannot imagine what would be its purpose. Oh, bother it."

Again she resolved to announce their departure, and again the attempt was pushed into the background by the news this time that Mr. Butterworth's prediction about the mill in Rumsey had proved accurate: The owners wanted to sell. Amid the general rejoicing—which Andrew joined into with as much enthusiasm as the Newtons, much to her surprise—she knew she couldn't say anything.

Except that I must, she told herself the next morning as she pulled the armchair back to its usual place and repositioned the footstool. Andrew and I cannot become indefinite guests, as much as we would wish it. Lady Carruthers would call that rag manners, and for once, I would have to agree with her. She went into the breakfast room, hoping to find it unoccupied. She was not disappointed, and ate her breakfast in silence, doing her best to think up a plausible reason to leave, and coming up with nothing.

She was dabbing crumbs from her lips and thinking about one last cup of tea when the butler came in carrying a letter. She took it; the frank was Lord Denby, and her heart plummeted, as it always did. She stared at the note a moment, then took a deep breath and opened it.

To her surprise, it was from Stanton. She spread out the letter on the table, began to read, then shook her head. "Steel yourself for catastrophe, Miss Milton," she read. "The ornamental plaster on the ceiling in Cecil's room right over the bed gave way last night and he went into impressive hysterics. Lady Carruthers joined him, and Lord Denby has no peace anymore."

"Oh, dear," she said under her breath. "I wonder if we can blame the servants for this."

"Lord Denby swears the old place is falling down," she read. "He has taken to his bed again, mainly because his sister is on a rampage and Cecil is certain that he is near death. Actually, he received no damage, except that he has a bump on his head and appears—to my mind—no more addled than usual. But who can tell? I am sorry to ruin your holiday, but we need you here, Jane. Yours respectfully, Oliver Stanton."

Jane leaned back in her chair. Stanton has provided the perfect excuse, she thought. I wonder why I am not filled with relief? "All holidays end, Jane," she told herself firmly as she left the breakfast room and went in search of the footman. "It is time to return to wary diplomacy."

The coachman took her to the mill, driving slowly past the row of tenements that was only a pile of rubble now. She had seen the blueprints during many an evening in the parlor. By summer most of the block would be rebuilt and inhabited once more. She leaned forward for a better look at the corner that would house the new school. Mr. Butterworth had asked for her opinion on the design, and she had offered suggestions. The mill workers' children would be educated there until the age of twelve, and then allowed to choose between work in the factory or apprenticeship elsewhere. Staring at the leveled block, and contemplating the good things to come, it occurred to her that she had fewer choices than one of Mr. Butterworth's mill children.

I will have to change that, she thought, as the carriage slowed before the mill and then stopped. She could see her reflection in the carriage glass. I will have to change myself.

She located Richard in the mill office, intent upon the ledgers before him, and showed him the letter. He gestured toward the door that led to the mill floor. "Scipio is roaming the floor," he said. "I can send someone to look for him."

Jane shook her head, not wishing to distract him from his business. "I can find him, and tell him that Andrew and I must leave."

"We wish you did not have to go," Richard said, as she left the office.

Not as much as I wish it, she thought. She had been to the mill several times since that first visit, and she looked around with pleasure at the motion and color. Where first she had seen only confusion, now she admired the economy of movement and the rhythm of the looms and the workers who fed them. The women, uniformed and tidy, smiled shyly as she passed. She noted with appreciation that their hair was confined under close-fitting caps, and their sleeves were narrow. The floors were smooth and even. There was nothing to catch on machinery or trip them, bringing sudden maiming or death. It is so simple to do the right thing, she thought. How ironic that virtue is often a last resort, in business and in life.

As she walked through the noisy mill, a whistle sounded. The looms slowed but did not stop as some of the workers left their positions to rest or seek the necessary. She found Mr. Butterworth seated on an upturned wooden spool, his shirtsleeves rolled up, and one brace broken from its mooring. I believe he is worse than a small boy, she thought with a smile as she noticed the grease on his long fingers and a corresponding smudge near his ear.

When he saw her, he rose and excused himself from the knot of workers seated nearby and came to her. She noticed his eyes on the letter in her hand. "I suppose that is bad news from Denby, which announces that you must return to mediate, or expedite, or placate," he commented.

She handed him the letter, noting his frown as he read. "And what are you supposed to do, Miss Milton?" he asked as he handed back the letter. "Coddle Cecil into rational behavior, assure Lord Denby that he is not dying, and let Lady Carruthers trample up and down your spine? Repair that drafty old heap singlehandedly and offset years of neglect?"

She could not help but notice the irritation in his words. "I suppose that is it, sir," she replied, stung by the tone of his voice.

"Hold on, Jane, I didn't mean . . ." He stopped and ran his hand across his forehead, leaving another greasy trail. "There . . . there is so much to do here."

I could not stay angry with you for a moment, sir, she thought, especially when you are right. She said nothing, but took a handkerchief from her reticule and wiped the grease from his face, "I know how busy you are, sir. We have had a wonderful visit, Mr. Butterworth, but everything must end, mustn't it?"

"I suppose it must," he agreed, after a long moment staring at the looms. "I . . . I . . . have my own suggestion for you, Miss Milton."

He hesitated, and she felt her heart beat harder in her breast. Tell me that you love me, and ask me to marry you, she thought, wanting so much to hear the words that she felt that she had spoken them. "And it is . . ." she suggested, when he said nothing.

He opened his mouth to speak, and she waited, holding her breath. The whistle blew once more to signal a return to work, and it was as though someone suddenly drenched him in cold water. He blinked his eyes, then shook his head. "I am going to New Lanark at the end of the week to confer with Robert Owen. Shall I suggest to him that you are interested in a teaching position in his mill this fall when Andrew is away at school?"

That was it. Don't cry, Jane, she ordered herself. You've been so good at concealing your feelings all these years that you could give lessons. You may not have much of a spine, but you do have a little pride left. "I think that is an excellent idea, Mr.

Butterworth," she said, striving for the right tone and succeeding, at least to her ears.

"I'm certain you will like New Lanark."

"I'm certain I will," she agreed. Still, sir, it is a pity that we are not of the same class, she thought. I am so far below yours that I was an idiot to think you would want me as a wife. Let us pray that I will not prove so stupid again. Offer your hand, now, Jane, she told herself. Smile again and thank him for the visit. She extended her hand to the mill owner and he shook it. "Thank you again, Mr. Butterworth, for a most pleasant visit. I intend to ask Emma if she would wish to correspond with me." Pause now, Jane, and if you think you can say any more without tears, ask the question you are most interested in. "Mr. Butterworth, with this third mill you will be so busy. Shall we see you at Denby again?"

There, I have asked it, she thought. My dearest Mr. Butterworth, I do not like that look in your eyes. She folded the letter and put it in her reticule, willing her hands not to shake.

"I will be there from time to time, my dear," he replied. "Joe Singletary will return with you and continue Andrew's lessons."

"You needn't go to that trouble," she assured him.

"It's no trouble. I have some business concerns in the area that he can wrap up for me. By the time Andrew is ready to leave for school, I am certain he will have organized matters to my satisfaction . . ." He hesitated.

". . . and sold the house?" she asked.

"Yes."

Well there it is, she thought. I told him my sordid story and he was kind enough to see that I have slept well since, but there is nothing more to it. Anything I have been dreaming of was probably my own imagination. I am on my own once again.

But he was still holding her hand. Mr. Butterworth, you are getting absentminded, she thought, as she managed a smile in his general direction and gently pulled her hand away. "I hope we hear from you occasionally, sir. I—that is, Andrew and I—will be disappointed if we do not."

"You will hear from me, Miss Milton," he said. "I will want to know about the reunion."

Reunion? What reunion? she thought wildly. Oh, yes, the reunion I have contrived to put heart back into Lord Denby, when all the time I have been losing mine. She closed her eyes against the pain of that thought.

He took her hand again. "Miss Milton?"

"I am fine," she replied. "This is certainly a noisy place, isn't it?"

"No place for a lady," he said. "Good day, Miss Milton. I'll try to get home in time to say good-bye to Andrew."

"He would appreciate that, I am certain," she replied, removing her fingers from his grasp one more time.

She started when the whistle blew again and the looms picked up speed. She turned to go, but Mr. Butterworth took her by the arm and spoke into her ear so he could be heard. "Tell Lord Denby for me that I will send him a repairman for those odd jobs around the place that he requires. Can't have the entire ceiling falling in on Cecil, now, can we?"

It was a feeble joke for him, but she grasped at it with relief and nodded. "We would all appreciate someone with remodeling skills," she said, her lips close to his ear now. What would you do if I kissed you right now? she thought. No worry, Mr. Butterworth; I won't. But what would you do?

"Do you know, sir, I nearly gave you up for Lent several years ago?" she said suddenly, not even giving herself time to think.

He laughed, as she had hoped he would. "You can't be serious, Miss Milton," he said, not relinquishing his grip on her arm.

"I found that I really couldn't face Stover Hall without your good cheer, sir, so I did not." That is plainspoken enough, she thought, and far more than I ever intended to say.

"Miss Milton," he began, and he suddenly looked so uncomfortable that she regretted her words.

"Never mind, Mr. Butterworth," she said, stepping away from him and raising her voice to be heard. "I shall give up hot chocolate this year, as I usually do. Good day, sir, and thank you again for everything."

She felt in control of herself again, and able to watch with equanimity as he turned away to answer a question from a worker. She stepped farther away and watched as they conferred, knowing that she should leave, but wanting one long last look at him to remember. "I will love you until I die," she said, her voice loud and her words distinct, safe in the knowledge that he would never hear them over the thrum of the machinery.

To her horror, he turned around quickly and stared at her.

What have I done? she asked herself in panic, and then felt relief flood over her when he appeared to be looking over her shoulder at another worker, who was shouting something. Thank God for that, she thought. She managed a weak smile, and left the mill floor.

She broke the news of their departure to Andrew that afternoon, and was not surprised at his tears. Cry for both of us, she thought, as he rested his head on her lap and she patted his back.

"Can we return someday?" he asked finally, drying his eyes with his fingers.

"I imagine that Jacob will invite you back," she said. "But whether Lady Carruthers will allow it . . ." She shook her head. "No! If the Newtons invite you back, by all means, you will go, no matter what Lady Carruthers says." And I will continue my role as chief distractor, she thought. Mr. Butterworth's interest in me never went beyond a little mistletoe, and his own extreme good nature, and I have no other prospects.

Dinner was a melancholy meal, with no one eating much, and the children coming up with all the reasons why they should remain at least another month. Even patient Emma finally reached her limit and told Lucy to hush, please, before they all went into dithers. "We will invite them again when the crisis at Stover Hall is past," Richard promised, when Lucy puckered up, and Jacob frowned.

Which crisis? Jane asked herself wearily as she prepared for bed. There will always be a commotion simmering somewhere. She sat in the armchair, which smelled so pleasantly of Mr. Butterworth's lively cologne and the pomade he used on his hair. Lord Denby hovers on the brink of who-knows-what, and Lady Carruthers is so determined to see that Cecil becomes the next Lord Denby. It is all too much. I doubt that even Stanton could contrive anything successful out of all this.

She climbed in bed and lay there for the longest time, unable to sleep. Her nerves on edge, she heard Mr. Butterworth's familiar footsteps walk past her door and then pause outside his office. She closed her eyes and turned her face to the wall when he went inside and shut the door.

Still sleep would not come, not with the mill owner in the next room. Jane thought of the empty miniature frame and felt tears prickle her eyes finally. Mr. Butterworth, your sister wishes that you would speak your mind, but that empty frame tells me more than words ever could, she reflected. Surely I am enough of an adult to know that I cannot defeat an empty frame with the words "Love forever" on it.

She closed her eyes then, worn out with speculation, but she was still awake hours later when her door opened and Mr. Butterworth came in. Lying so still, and attempting to breathe deep and even so he would think she slept, Jane watched as he quietly moved the chair and sat down beside her, close enough to touch. With a sigh of his own, he stretched out in the chair and propped up his feet on the stool. To her surprise, he promptly fell asleep, his own breathing relaxed and deep.

She lay there in amazement, wondering for the first time who was comforting whom.

Chapter Fifteen

Rain was falling when they left the mill owner's house in Rumsey, the dreariest kind of rain because it seemed to fall in gray streaks from gray skies. Jane did not even need to glance at Andrew to know that the color matched his mood, too. After a long moment spent staring out the window, he burrowed into his book and kept his head down. He sniffed and swallowed several times, which she carefully overlooked. Joe Singletary attempted a little conversation, but not even horses could interest Andrew this time. When Joe looked at Jane and shrugged, she shook her head. The secretary subsided into his own corner, content to keep his own counsel.

At least until Leeds, when he leaned over and whispered to Andrew. The boy closed his book and turned his attention to the window again, with little glances at her. She was on the verge of hoping out loud that no one needed to stop in Leeds when the carriage slowed at the corner right before the workhouse and turned away from the main road.

"I am certain this is not the right way," Jane said to the secretary. "Do tell the coachman to turn back onto the High Street."

To her surprise, Andrew pulled himself out of his leave-taking melancholy. "It is a surprise, Miss Mitten," he said as the carriage moved slowly between the dismal workhouse buildings on either side of the road and then with a jingle of harness, turned into the pauper's cemetery.

If this is a joke, it is a bad one, she thought, wondering if Andrew and the secretary had taken leave of their senses. "It is not as though we need an additional dose of melancholy, Mr. Singletary," she murmured.

"Leave-taking is hard, isn't it, ma'am?" he said, sounding far too cheerful to suit her.

She remembered then that Mr. Butterworth had promised to take her to the cemetery to her mother's grave. "Oh, I think we can do this some other time," she said, trying again.

No one is listening to me, she thought, as the carriage continued down a smaller row, and then stopped. With a smile, Mr. Singletary got himself from the carriage, and held his hand out for her. "Well, since we are here . . ." she murmured under her breath.

Andrew took her hand as she opened her umbrella for both of them and started down the row. She paused, frowning. She thought Mama's grave was over by that scraggly tree, but something was different. "I think we are on the wrong row, Andrew," she said, and started to turn back. "I disremember a regular grave marker in the row."

He squeezed her hand. "Miss Mitten, do you recall when Mr. Butterworth and I went to Leeds on Christmas Day?"

Despite her own discomfort, she smiled at him. "When Mr. Butterworth required bicarbonate of soda?" *And I was kissed so thoroughly by him,* she thought. *I will never forget it, even though I am certain that I should.*

"And there was a surprise?" he added.

"I remember," she said. "You were quite secretive." She stopped and looked about. "This is the right row, except for that tombstone." Unwilling to leave the path, she leaned closer, trying to peer through the curtain of rain. "Someone's fortunes must have improved enough to afford a real grave marker. I do not suppose that happens often."

"Maybe it is your fortune, Miss Mitten," Andrew said. He took her hand and tugged her from the path.

She took a step and then stopped again, suddenly unmindful of the rain and the cold and the gray of the institutional buildings that seemed to loom like vultures over the little path in the cemetery. "Mother," she said simply, and hurried past Andrew to the tombstone.

She knew the marker had not been in place long because there were none of the pits and scourings of time, or the streaks of grime from poorly drawing chimneys. She came closer, heedless now of the soggy earth, to kneel in front of the beautiful stone. "Oh, Andrew," she said, scarcely breathing as she slowly reached out with her finger and traced her mother's name on the marker.

"I mentioned it once, and he remembered," she said, staring at the stone in wonder. "I do not know what to make of such a man, Andrew."

"He thought you would like it," Andrew said. He stood beside her, his hand resting on her shoulder. "I told him to have a rose carved into the stone, like on Mama's grave." He bent to whisper into her ear. "Mr. Butterworth looked quite serious when I mentioned Mama's grave, but I assured him it did not bother me. I mean, I never knew her."

"We know he is a kind man, my dear." Jane stood up, her eyes still on the delicate tracery, so out of place among the stark crosses with their numbers and nothing more. "Madeleine Mariah Stover Milton, 1768 to 1795," she whispered. She kissed Andrew. "Such a short life! And was it your idea to have these words carved there, too?"

He looked where she pointed. " 'Beloved Mother,' " he read. "No. Mr. Butterworth insisted upon that." He looked up at her, his face anxious suddenly. "Will it do, Miss Mitten?"

She nodded, for a moment unable to find words for the mill owner's curious generosity. "How can I ever repay him?" she asked finally.

"I told him you would say that."

"My dear, you have no idea what these cost," she replied, bending to touch the stone again, running her hand over the curve of it. "Unless I can marry a rich widower—which I don't see happening, do you?—I cannot possibly repay him for this."

Andrew shrugged. "I told him you would object, and he said what he always says, when he can't seem to think of anything else," he told her. " 'Just tell Miss Mitten that I appreciate the care she is taking of you.' And then he looked at me over his spectacles, as though it was all a great joke."

"What will we ever do with him, Andrew?" she asked.

"I don't know that there is anything we *can* do with him, Miss Mitten," the boy replied.

Of that I am certain, she thought. She smiled at Andrew and felt her own spirits rise, despite the rain, and the place, and her own collection of megrims. "We will send him a letter of thanks, and I shall assure him that I will continue to take good care of you."

Andrew laughed, and she could not help but join in. She hugged him there in the rain, the umbrella on its side, then slogged back to the carriage, where Joe Singletary waited. They rode on in silence again, but it was a different kind of quiet. She gazed out the window, content with herself and happy to be with Andrew. Mr. Butterworth, I remain so deep in debt to you, she thought without a pang. I would have wished for a different ending to the story of you and me, but I can manage.

While the sight of Stover Hall did not precisely warm her heart as it came into view that late evening, she found herself viewing it with less dread and more hope. And there was Stanton at the door, his smile not a butler's smile, but that of a friend.

"Miss Milton, welcome home," he said, helping her from the carriage. "Andrew, supper is waiting for you in the breakfast room."

She looked at him in surprise. "We are far too late for supper, Stanton. How did you know that we would be arriving today, and at this time?" she inquired, taking his arm to negotiate the steps. "I did not write you." She sensed his hesitation in the way his arm tensed under her hand, but the steps were icy.

"Have a care now, Miss Milton," he cautioned her. "I knew my letter would bring you soon; that is all." He leaned closer. "I have every assurance that Mr. Lowe has convinced Lady Carruthers to take Cecil back to London. Who knows when the entire ceiling in that room might give way?"

"Who, indeed?" she asked. "You continue to be England's most valuable butler."

He held up his hands, as though to acquit himself. "Miss Milton, collapsing ceilings are beyond my purview! Possibly this comes under the realm of divine intervention."

"And who would have thought the Almighty to have a sense of humor?" she said with a smile of her own. In perfect charity with the butler, she nodded to him and went into the breakfast room.

Andrew had already excused himself and she was just beginning a bowl of rice pudding when she heard familiar steps in the hall. She winced in spite of her resolve. Steady, Jane, she told herself, taking a deep breath to calm the sudden turmoil in her stomach. Mr. Butterworth claims that she only upsets you because you allow it.

She eyed Lady Carruthers warily when her cousin entered the room, but managed a pleasant-enough smile. At least it must have been pleasant, because Lady Carruthers glared back.

"How kind of you to honor us with your presence again," the woman snapped.

"Why, yes, cousin, Andrew and I did have a nice visit in Rumsey," Jane said, striving for serenity she did not feel. "We hope your holiday was as pleasant, considering that you were able to devote your entire time to your son. I trust his maintenance was not too onerous for you, and that he is much recovered." Oh, but I have a malicious streak, Jane decided as she watched Lady Carruthers. What can she say, without appearing to be an unfeeling parent?

"He is better, thank you, and we are returning to London tomorrow," she said, after a long moment of bristling silence. "Mr. Lowe feels it would be better."

"I trust you will be sufficiently comfortable in Cecil's chambers," Jane said. And stay away from Stover Hall a long, long time, she thought.

Lady Carruthers flashed a triumphant smile at her. "My brother has given me leave to move Cecil into the family house in town! He even speaks of deeding it to Cecil, particularly since my dear one's landlord is so unfeeling about overdue rent."

Oh, Cecil, you are worming your way into Lord Denby's estate aren't you? Jane thought with dismay. But I will be dipped in honey and lowered onto an anthill before I give my odious cousin even the slightest hint that it bothers me. "Indeed, Lady Carruthers, landlords who must toil for a living do like to be paid. I am certain it is a weakness of the lower classes."

"You would know about that, Jane," Lady Carruthers replied, "considering your own low connections of the past month."

"Yes, I would," she answered back without hesitation, enjoying the look of surprise on her cousin's face when she did not stammer, or look away, or shrink into her chair. "And do you know, cousin, I've discovered that the smell of the shop is the smell of money earned honestly by hardworking people, who never stoop to wheedling their way into fortunes they never earned. Good night, Lady Carruthers."

"I gave you no leave to go from this room!" Lady Carruthers declared, rising in all her awfulness.

"No, you did not," Jane said in calm agreement as her heart pounded in her breast. "And for the life of me, I cannot imagine why I thought I needed your permission all these years." She paused in the doorway. "Andrew will be returning to Mr. Butterworth's estate tomorrow for Latin lessons."

"You cannot do that without my permission!" Lady Carruthers was shouting now, her face red.

"I can and will," Jane said quietly. "And you have *my* permission to spread around the district any rumors about me that you choose. If you think for a moment that I care, you are mistaken."

She left the room with what she hoped was a certain flare, but was grateful only that her dress did not catch in the door, or she did not stumble over the threshold. Stanton stood in the hallway, his expression inscrutable, as long as she did not look at his eyes. He shook his head. "Poor woman," he murmured. "Our chimneys have been drawing poorly for a month and more. Too much tepid water and lukewarm tea seem to have taken a toll upon the less stable among us."

Jane covered her mouth with her hand to quiet her laughter. "Stanton, do have a little charity!"

He nodded his head in complete agreement. "Of course, miss, there will be hot water and instant service now. My only . . . regret is that this might send Lady Carruthers even higher in the boughs to sense for even a moment that conditions have improved because *you* have returned."

"Oh, do you think so?" Jane asked in mock amazement, her eyes wide. "I don't know what to say to that."

"Say to what, Miss Milton?" the butler asked in studied surprise.

With a laugh, she nodded to Stanton and took herself upstairs, stopping in Andrew's room to quietly take the book from the sleeping boy's chest, kiss him, and snuff the candles. She stood a moment looking down at him, knowing how acutely she would miss him when he left for school in the fall. We have only this spring and summer, she thought, as she closed the door.

It was late, and she hesitated before Lord Denby's door. She thought she could detect a light, so she opened it quietly.

"The wanderer has returned," she said softly. She perched herself upon the edge of Lord Denby's bed and took his hand in hers. He squeezed it, but to her dismay, there was little strength in his fingers.

"Oh ho, miss," he said, opening his eyes. "We were beginning to wonder if you had decided to throw over the peerage for the petty genteels and mushrooms of Huddersfield."

"I was tempted," she replied, putting a laugh in her voice so he would think she was joking. "And what does Stanton do but write to me that the ceiling fell on Cecil, and I knew I had to hurry home to see that spectacle."

Lord Denby raised up on one elbow and gestured to her to lean closer. "Aren't they gone yet?" he asked in a whisper. "I know Agnes is my sister, but who among us is entitled to choose his relatives? And Cecil?" He lay back down again, as if the very subject exhausted him. "He is as useful as tits on a boar, and what is worse, I despair of any improvement."

His words hung in the air like a bad smell. I could labor mightily to change the subject, Jane thought. I used to do that. I could try to cajole him into better humor, but that never earned me more than a sour look. "He will always be Cecil," she said. "Thank God that he is not your heir, Lord Denby."

He gave her a long look, but for once did not challenge her. When she tried to add another pillow behind his head, Lord Denby waved her off. "Can I get you anything, my lord?" she asked.

Lord Denby said nothing and she began to wonder how long he would be irritated with her. "It was a long month," he said finally, making no attempt to hide his ill-usage. "You were unfeeling to abandon me to my sister and nephew."

"I suppose I was," Jane agreed, with enough equanimity to make him scowl at her. "Christmas is a time for families, my lord, and I thought you would be content enough here with your closest relatives."

She waited for another scowl, but Lord Denby merely sighed and closed his eyes. "I think we have not been a family for a long time, Jane," he said finally, when she had almost thought him sleeping. "Have we ever been a family?"

"I . . . I don't know the answer to that, sir," she said quietly, touched by the sadness in his voice.

He watched her face and she said nothing. "You're different somehow, Jane," he said at last.

"I stood up to your sister in the breakfast room," she told him. "She will likely be in here in the morning with all kinds of tales to tell, and I am sorry for that, but I am quite weary with attempting to find her good side."

"That is blunt enough," he commented. "Did Butterworth return with you? I am hoping for some cribbage tomorrow."

She shook her head, then crossed her fingers so that she would speak calmly. "Mr. Butterworth has purchased another mill and he told me that it would keep him away from our district. I do not believe that we will see him this spring."

"No cribbage?" he repeated, and the disappointment in his voice smote her like a fist to her back.

No cribbage, she thought, and no more kindnesses, or bits of wisdom delivered in his salty Yorkshire way. "I'm sorry, sir," she said. "He will be selling his estate, and has left Mr. Singletary here to make the arrangements." She rose to go, simply because she found that she could no longer sit still and discuss the mill owner. "Sir, you must look about this as good fortune indeed. It is your opportunity to buy the property and have the lake at last."

If she thought the idea would please him, she was mistaken. "That will be tame, indeed, my dear," he murmured.

More than tame, she thought. It will be devastating. She went to the door, then stopped on impulse, hurried back to Lord Denby's bed, and kissed his forehead. "Good night, sir," she said softly.

She knew she had startled him, but she was not prepared for the sudden tears in his eyes. He took her hand. "Do you know, Jane, since that book came out, I have been reconsidering my life," he said, the words coming from him with some difficulty. "I do not like what I see."

"Then you are alone in that opinion," she replied quickly.

He shook his head. "I fear not, my dear. There are some who wish me ill, of this I am certain."

She sat on his bed again and took his hand, but could think of nothing to say. Andrew does not wish you ill, she thought, but could you actually *be* his grandfather? Cecil does not count. "I think, rather, that many are in your debt, my lord," she said finally. "You have served as such an example to the officer corps throughout your career."

"Jane, would you recognize a hypocrite if you saw him?" he asked.

"Oh, sir," she said, and kissed his hand. "I wish you would tell me what is troubling you."

Watching the indecision cross his face, she almost thought he would. Mr. Butterworth, the only way I can repay you for your unexampled kindnesses is to do the same for someone else, she decided, as she sat by Lord Denby and held his hand. "Please, sir."

But the moment was gone. He sighed and took his hand from her loose grasp. "It is not a pleasant tale, and surely not for a lady," he replied. "Good night, my dear. Let us hope for better things tomorrow."

I wonder if there is anyone in this house without a secret, Jane thought as she snuffed the candles, remained there a moment in the darkness, and then left Lord Denby's chamber. She stood in the hall, nerving herself, and then started down the stairs.

Stanton stood at the bottom of them, looking up at her. "Oh, I do not mean to keep you up," she said with contrition. "It must be nearly midnight, Stanton."

"And then some, Miss Milton," he answered. "You know that a good butler never retires until all his charges are safely to bed."

"I should know it," she said, content to stand next to him. Thank goodness this man has no subterfuge or secrets, she thought. "Since you insist on being so useful, even at this ridiculous hour, I have one more thing to do tonight," she said. "Stanton, would you help me remove the wreath from the front door?"

The words were harder to get out than she would have thought. She swallowed several times, and then could only look away and close her eyes. "I have resolved . . ." she began, and could not finish.

The butler put his hand on her arm, which should have startled her, but somehow did not. "You are certain?" he asked.

After another hesitation, she nodded. "I promised Mr. Butterworth that I would remove it."

"Of course I will help you. I will take it down myself, if you wish."

She shook her head. "No, Stanton. I want it to be my doing. Is there a ladder?"

There was, a stepladder lodged in one of the servants' closets by the entrance, which he removed and opened. "It's cold," he warned as he opened the door wide.

The January wind blew in, raw and biting, and pulling sleet with it. She gritted her teeth against more than the cold. It is a new year, she thought as Stanton moved the ladder to the door and steadied it for her. He held her hand as she climbed the two steps and unhooked the wreath. She was going to let it drop to the floor, but instead, she gripped it carefully around the center. Hanging on to Stanton's hand, she leaned away from the ladder and heaved the wreath through the front door and into the darkness. Ugly black streaks remained on the door, but the wreath was gone. Thank God, she thought. Thank God.

Without a word, she let him help her from the ladder, and made no objection when she just stood there in the circle of his arms, part of her empty, now that the wreath was gone, and part of her relieved. He must have pushed the door closed with his foot, because the sound of wind and rain grew faint. She thought it especially kind of him to pat her back, and then just hold her.

"I suppose I have used a butler for every possible purpose now," she said finally with a faint laugh as she stepped back. "Thank you, Oliver."

He merely nodded, and she thought it prudent not to comment on the tears in his own eyes. "I have certainly had my fill of war, and wounds, and death, and unkindness," she said.

"We all have, Miss Milton," he said, not moving from her side. He hesitated.

"Please speak, sir," she said.

"I have taken the liberty of arranging for a plasterer to fix the ceiling in Mr. Carruthers' room," he said, all business again. "I can as easily contact a painter for the front door."

She nodded. "And the trim around the windows, as well, Stanton." She looked around her at the entrance hall, as though seeing it for the first time. "We have gotten shabby this year, haven't we?"

He looked around, too, a smile on his face now. "We can change that."

As they started toward the stairs together, she remembered Mr. Butterworth's promise. "Stanton, Mr. Butterworth said that as soon as he can, he will send us a handyman from Huddersfield. There are so many little things that need to be done to prepare for the reunion."

"There are," he agreed. "We will find a place for him belowstairs when he arrives." He paused then, at the foot of the stairs. "February and March, Miss Milton, and then spring will be here."

"I am counting on it! I have so many plans."

He stepped back to observe her. "Then this is a different Miss Milton, indeed."

"Why, yes," she replied, surprised. "I suppose it is."

Chapter Sixteen

The plasterer arrived in the morning about the same time that Cecil, pale and on a stretcher, was quitting his room. I am continually amazed at the power of suggestion, Jane thought as she walked beside the stretcher, holding Cecil's limp hand in her own. Because Lady Carruthers appeared more intent upon arranging her luggage in the cart to follow, Jane saw that he was comfortably seated in Lord Denby's carriage with a shawl around his shoulders and a warming pan at his feet. I should own to a twinge of conscience, she thought, as she looked at her cousin's drawn expression and his body as limp as the lace on his nightshirt. Ah, well, no one is perfect.

"Did Mr. Lowe send you with more medicinal powders?" she asked, determined not to go into whoops before the carriage was out of earshot.

He nodded. "I am to take a diminishing dose over the next two days and check my piss carefully, cousin," he said, his voice hard to hear with Lady Carruthers booming out her orders regarding the stowage of bags and boxes.

"I am certain you will see a remarkable improvement by the end of the week, Cecil," she assured him without a qualm. Now if Stanton will not look at me until the carriage is out of sight, I think I will manage, she told herself.

To her relief, she noticed that Stanton was avoiding her eyes, as well, turning his full attention to Lady Carruthers as she worked herself into minor hysteria until the luggage was tied down to her complete satisfaction. He helped her into the carriage, nodding as she ordered him to have the chimneys checked before her return. "Stanton, there is something wrong when a person cannot have a hot bath for a month! And so I have been telling you! For a youngish man, you are remarkably deaf!"

"I am certain you are right, Lady Carruthers," he said. "How fortunate then, that the chimneys began to draw so well last night. One could almost call it providential."

She gave him a furious glance. "One could call it a lot of things!"

"Indeed, yes. Will we see you soon, my lady?"

"As soon as I recover from your mismanagement, Stanton!" she declared. "Oh, do hush, Cecil! You cannot be sick yet because we have not even started moving!"

Jane stepped forward. "Lady Carruthers, there is so much work to do here to prepare for the reunion that we will be glad of your prompt return."

"I will come when I have recovered, Jane, and not a moment sooner," she said, each word as sharp as icicles.

And that will be as soon as the work is done, Jane thought in triumph. "Very well, ma'am. Do have a pleasant journey with Cecil. Cecil, do you wish that basin closer to your mouth? Lady Carruthers, pardon my blushes, but I believe his urinal is handy so you can help him."

"Jane, you are a scoundrel beyond my wildest imagining," the butler murmured. They watched as the coachman shook his head and then climbed onto the carriage box.

"I confess it, Oliver. Not another word from you or I will disgrace myself."

"We could not have that." He nodded toward the baggage cart, which began to move behind the carriage. "Miss Milton, is that back wheel wobbling excessively? I would hate to have it fall off any sooner than . . . what do you say? Ten or fifteen miles?"

*   *   *

Thanks to Stanton, in the week that followed and the one after, Jane found herself too busy to repine much upon her own state of affairs. The painter had followed the plasterer, and when he was done with the front door, the trim, and a room or two, Jane could not overlook the general shabbiness of the entire estate. "Which means a return of the plasterer, the painter again, and then a visit to the cloth warehouse for new draperies and bed coverings in those chambers we are preparing for reunion guests," Jane wrote to Emma Newton. "I suppose all this effort would distress me, except that I seem to have no qualms about spending someone else's money!"

Indeed I do not, she thought, flexing her fingers and drawing her shawl closer about her as she sat in the bookroom at the end of the day. She added another paragraph about Andrew's progress through Gaul with Julius Caesar and Joe Singletary, but did not ask Emma if her brother had begun measures to sell his property near Denby. And I do not ask how he does, or if he seems tired, or what are his own plans, she thought. She read the letter again, wished she could say more without saying more, then sealed it.

She began her letters to Mr. Butterworth—the ones she never mailed—after she wrote that first letter to Emma. Her mind on Rumsey and the mill owner, it had been so simple to take out another sheet of paper and write him a letter. In the first letter, she assured him that she was sleeping well now, with the nightmare scarcely troubling her. Since she knew the letter was going nowhere, it was also simple to tell him how much she loved him, and then sign her name. That is what I would write if you were my husband and away from me, Mr. B, she thought as she folded the note and then dropped it in the waste basket. I would tell you what we did during the day, and how I missed you. She shook her head. No, it's more than merely missing you; I long for you.

This is probably not a good idea, she told herself as she wrote a similar letter the next night, and then the night after. Writing to Mr. Butterworth is fast becoming the best part of my day, which doesn't speak well to my state of mind, she thought the next day, when she should have been concentrating on the linen inventory. And yet, it is harmless, she decided, after the thought of no letter to write at day's end cast her into such glooms that even Stanton remarked on her low state.

When it was nearly March and the promised handyman had not materialized, she mentioned that fact in one of her late-night letters. "Mr. B, I will begin to think you do not care for me, because you have forgotten that one essential to a woman's total happiness: a handyman for the little jobs she cannot do herself," she wrote, when it was far too late and she was feeling both silly and ill-used. "One can always find a physician, and there are poulterers and solicitors a-plenty, but a handyman? My dearest love, a handyman is a pearl beyond price, more essential (discounting the necessaries) than a husband. I am desperate for a man who can hang a picture straight or level a table leg without turning it into furniture fit only for Lilliputians."

She read the letter and deposited it where all the others went. In the press of three mills to run, Mr. Butterworth has put you out of his mind, she told herself. For all you know, Jane Milton, he probably congratulated himself on helping a woman oppressed with excessive blame, and then moved on to another project. That would be entirely like him. Or so she told herself, but still she hoped for a letter.

None came, but then one day, long beyond when she had told herself not to look anymore, the handyman arrived.

It was one of those impossible days toward the end of March when the weather was so beautiful that she knew she could not bear to be indoors for one more linen inventory or silverware count. "Stanton, if I am virtuous and continue to count pillow covers on the assumption that tomorrow will be equally warm and sunny, I know that I am doomed to disappointment," she told the butler as she put down her list.

It was on the tip of her tongue to invite the butler to join her out-of-doors, but she resisted the impulse. There is no telling what additional rumors Lady Carruthers would circulate about me, if she knew that I already spend a large portion of my evenings belowstairs after Lord Denby is asleep, drinking tea with Stanton and the cook while Andrew does his Latin homework on the table, she told herself. She folded the last pillow cover, tossed in a handful of lavender, and shut the drawer with a finality that made the butler laugh.

She left Stover Hall with relief, walking first to the apple orchard to stare at the lower branches, and with squinting eyes, threaten the buds to hurry up and bloom. Enjoying the sun on her back, she strolled to the formal gardens that sloped away toward the lake. It is shabby here, too, she thought, itching to kneel down right then and pull weeds until dark. She could see the mill owner's house because the trees were still bare of leaves, and briefly considered releasing both Andrew and his teacher from its confines. This is no day to conjugate, she told herself. I cannot see Joe objecting if I were to spring into the room and demand Andrew's release.

She was walking toward the house when she noticed a gig slowing on the road. She stopped to watch as a man jumped down, then went around to pull out a traveling case. He stood a moment in conversation with the driver, who gestured toward Stover Hall, tipped his hat, and then continued down the road.

I wonder if this is Mr. Butterworth's handyman, Jane thought, hurrying back toward the estate. The man seemed in no hurry to walk any closer to the house, but remained where he was, as though he were taking the measure of the place. "I certainly know already that you do not rush into things," she murmured under her breath, "considering how long you have been getting here from Rumsey. Gawk a moment more, Mr. Handyman, and I will think you have never seen a great estate!"

She noticed that his clothes were plain, and looked much abused, as though he had traveled too long in them. She came closer and cleared her throat.

"This is Stover Hall," she said.

The man turned around at Jane's words and favored her with a wonderful smile. "Stover Hall?" he repeated.

"The very same," she answered. "I thought you would never get here."

If she thought the handyman would tug at his forelock and stumble through some apology, she was mistaken. "Came as fast as I could, considering," he replied, unruffled by her tone of voice. "So this is it?"

"Yes, indeed," she said, knowing it was best to be firm with the help, but quite unable to resist that smile. "I am Jane Milton, Lord Denby's relative, and I have such a list of things for you to repair. You are . . ."

"Dale," he said, holding out his hand. "Pleased to know you, Miss Milton."

She stared at his hand, wondering why on earth a handyman

would think she would ever shake it. When he did not withdraw his hand, she extended her own and let him give it a good shake. *Mr. Butterworth has sent me an eccentric,* she thought.

He picked up his traveling case and started toward Stover Hall. Jane watched him, a frown on her face. "See here, sir. You *do* repair things, do you not?"

He gave her a quizzical look. "I've been known to. Got something that needs doing here?"

"Of course I do!" she said, resisting the urge to stamp her foot. "Why do you think you were sent for?"

She could tell that he was paying no attention to her, but looking over her shoulder. His eyes widened and then he shook his head in amazement. "Miss Milton, that is the strangest chicken coop I have ever seen. And maybe the ugliest."

Mystified, she looked over her shoulder at Lady Carruthers' dreadful Greek temple. "It is a ruin," she explained.

"That's obvious. Probably pretty high on your repair list?" he suggested.

"It is supposed to look like that!" She took another look at the ruin, even worse than usual without the full leaf of ivy to offer merciful cover. "It *is* awful, isn't it?" she found herself saying, and added on impulse, "What would *you* do with it?"

"Burn it right down and build a proper coop," he said immediately. "I'll bet you can't keep a single chicken in there very long." He grinned at her with that same irresistible expression. "Bet they just stagger around, then flop over, dead with embarrassment."

Jane laughed and the handyman joined in. *How I would love to replace that horrid Greek temple with a chicken coop,* she thought. Lady Carruthers would go into spasms from which she would never recover. "It may go on my list of things to do. Shall we?"

They started for the house again. *Where is this man from?* Jane asked herself in amazement. *I have never heard such an accent, and he is so droll.* It was impolite to ask personal questions of a servant, so she knew there was no way to relieve her curiosity. Still . . . she did not know what Mr. Butterworth had told him.

"This is Lord Denby's estate," she explained as they walked up the lane. "I have been planning a reunion of his brother officers from the American Rebellion, and Mr. Butterworth—that is his house next door by that lake—promised to send me a handyman for those frustrating little odd jobs that need doing, but which always seem to be put off. I will pay you whatever Mr. Butterworth ordinarily pays you, and Stanton will find room for you belowstairs. Is that agreeable?"

He made no comment, but looked about him with a mild expression in his quite blue eyes.

"Well?" she asked.

He shrugged. "It never entered my mind that I would be making money here."

"We do not engage in slave labor!" she declared. "No matter what Mr. Butterworth with his republican ideas may have told you about us."

"Butterworth told me nothing. Don't you know when your leg is being pulled, Miss Milton?"

She had never heard that expression before, but the meaning was quickly obvious. "Perhaps I do not," she said. She stopped this time, even though Stanton—who possessed that butler's sixth sense—had already opened the front door. "Botheration, Dale, but I have gotten us off on the wrong foot." She simply could not resist smiling into his pleasant face. "It must have been the very leg you were pulling."

"You are quick, Miss Milton," he observed.

And you are surprisingly forward, she thought, but said nothing. And I need a good handyman too much to put you in your place. "There is a great deal to be done—just small things—and I need your help right now."

"I'm early for the reunion, though," he said.

"Well, yes," she replied, puzzled. "That's the whole point: that you would be here soon enough to get those things done before the guests arrive." Patience, Jane, she advised herself. Not everyone has prompt understanding.

She was rewarded with another dazzling smile. "I think I understand now," he said.

She started up the front steps. "Stanton, this is Dale. He has come from Mr. Butterworth to help us."

To her utter mystification, the handyman went through the handshaking ritual with Stanton, who seemed, despite his butler's demeanor, as puzzled as she was. Oh, Stanton, she thought, at least your manners are far better than mine. You don't look as totally dumbfounded as I felt.

"Stanton, is it?" Dale said, setting down his traveling case in the front entrance. "Do you have a first name?"

"Why, yes. It is Oliver."

"Oliver, then," the man said cheerfully. "I never can quite see calling someone by his last name without saying 'Mister.' Whoa there!" He looked over his shoulder at the footman, who had picked up the traveling case. "I can carry that. Just show me where."

"Follow me, uh, Dale," said the butler, his voice rather faint. Jane looked away to hide her smile. "We have a room below-stairs."

"Fine," he declared, looking around with pleasure. "Miss Milton, you could use a spot of paint on that wall to liven up things in here. Wouldn't a contrasting sort of Wedgwood blue be just right?"

She blinked and looked where he pointed. "I . . . I believe you're right," she said, after a moment's struggle within herself. "I didn't have that on my list but . . ."

To her further amazement, he set down the case and patted her shoulder. "Don't stew over that pot, Miss Milton. How about I just take your list and then look over the place, too?"

"If . . . if you wish," she replied.

"Two weeks until the reunion?"

She nodded.

"You'll be amazed what I can do in two weeks."

By the next afternoon she should have corrected him: She was amazed what he could do in one twenty-four-hour period. By the time she came downstairs in the morning, the treads that had squeaked since Andrew was a baby had been subdued somehow into silence, and the spot on the wall where a footman from years past had accidentally shoved a table corner was puttied now and waiting for paint. The author of all this magnificence was seated at the top of a tall ladder, casually inserting glazier's points into the frame where he had replaced a pane of glass. He had removed the draperies and bestowed them over the stair railing, and the 'tween stairs maid, seated on the floor, was rubbing soap over the curtain pole.

"Dale says it will make the draperies slide easier," she said as Jane knelt beside her to admire her work.

"I am certain he is right," Jane replied. "That *has* been rather a problem with these poles." She looked up at the handyman. "And here I thought I was the early riser."

"You have a long list of things for me to do before that reunion," he reminded her. "Hand me that putty, will you?"

She did as he said, reaching up with the can, and then standing back to watch him work. Now admit it, Jane, she told herself; you are admiring the handyman. She admired him without compunction, holding her breath at the casual way he leaned away from the ladder to apply the glazier points, and then smooth the putty on top. He had a handsome profile, with as straight a nose as a person could wish, and auburn hair somewhat the color of Blair's, but with a little curl to it. He needs a haircut, she thought, but possibly that is the fashion where he is from. He worked swiftly and with the assurance of the born handyman, whistling tunelessly under his breath, the picture of contentment on a tall ladder.

"I think that Mr. Butterworth has amply fulfilled his promise."

She jumped a little and then blushed to see Stanton at her side, looking up even as she was. "And more," she assured him. She lowered her voice. "Stanton, did you find out anything about him last night?"

"A very little," the butler replied in the same quiet voice. "Only that he is from Ohio, United States of America, not married, thirty-seven years old, and that he is in England visiting relatives."

"What is his connection with the factory at Rumsey?" she whispered back.

The butler shrugged. "We never got that far. Do you know, he has the most amazing stories about the wilderness and Indians, Miss Milton, and everything seems to remind him of something else. I believe we were all quite enthralled last night." He looked at her with a frown. "Now that I think of it, whenever I tried to bring the conversation round to Mr. Butterworth, it seemed to remind him of another story."

"Odd," she said, and returned her attention to the man on top of the ladder.

"Perhaps you could write a letter of thanks to Mr. Butterworth," the butler suggested.

I write a letter every night, she thought, and nearly said so, but stopped herself in time. No sense in advertising to the world what a ninny she was. "I could do that," she said softly.

And she would have, she told herself before she climbed in bed that night, except that it was far too late. She and Andrew had allowed themselves to be lured belowstairs, where they both listened with wide-open eyes to stories of Indians, and forest fires, and traveling by flatboat down the Ohio River. She could not deny that the handyman had a flair for a well-told tale, delivered in his peculiar flat American accent while he whittled a peg to repair a chair in the dining room. She wondered if he was ever idle, and decided that he was not.

After a moment's concentration, he gestured to Andrew. "All right, lad, pull that chair closer, and let us see if the peg fits."

It did. In another minute, Andrew had closed Caesar's *Commentaries,* and tongue out in concentration, was whittling a peg of his own while the handyman watched in that relaxed way of his. She could not help put compare him to Mr. Butterworth, who could look almost as casual, but who always seemed ready to move. Not Dale; she never saw a man relax so completely, and she envied him.

"Andrew, you can take it to the dining room," he said. Andrew picked up the chair, and Stanton opened the door for him. The handyman held up the peg. "He did a good job on this one, Miss Milton. You may have it as a spare."

She put the peg in her apron pocket, wishing there were some way she could bring the conversation around to Mr. Butterworth. *For no more reason than I long to hear him spoken of,* she thought. Nothing occurred to her, so she closed Andrew's Latin book and rose. She was ready to say good night, when the handyman patted the space beside him that Andrew had vacated.

"Sit a spell, Miss Milton. I have a confession."

This is different, she thought. *Most of us here are so reluctant to say anything.* She sat.

"I . . . I looked in on Lord Denby this afternoon. I hope you don't mind."

He looked so earnest that she decided she didn't mind at all. "We do talk about him in somewhat hushed tones, don't we?" she asked, wanting to put him at ease.

"Maybe that was it," he decided. "I guess I was curious."

"Did he invite you in?" she asked. "He spends so much time sleeping that I worry about him."

"He was awake. I sat down and told him I was the handy-man." He chuckled, and started whittling again. "I think he was surprised, but too polite to admit that he was." He leaned toward her. "I gather that here in England, handymen don't generally sit down and jaw with the lord."

"It is not precisely typical," she said, unable to resist a smile.

He whittled in silence, concentrating on the little circle he was carving, as though it demanded all his attention. She knew it did not, considering how free he had been with information about the United States when Andrew was sitting with him. If Mr. Butterworth were here, he would merely wait for the man to speak, she thought. I shall do the same.

"Lord Denby was not what I expected," the handyman said after he finished carving out the center of the wooden disk. He held up the disk, evening the sides, and then set it on the table and picked up a slender strip of wood. "I thought he would be imperious and rude; at least that is what I have imagined"—he hesitated—"a lord to be."

"He is kindness itself," she assured him. Except where he doubts, she added to herself, thinking of Andrew.

"I didn't expect that," he repeated, and then was silent. In a moment he finished shaping the skewer, then handed it to her with the disk. "For your hair," he said, then took it back. "I'll put some stain on it, and then give it to you again."

"Thank you," she said, suddenly shy. "Good night, Dale."

He winked at her and turned his attention to Stanton, who was coming toward him with a teapot and cups. "Oliver! Did I tell you last night how I watched the Battle of Lake Erie from the deck of Captain Perry's flagship? His name was Oliver, too."

So it is "Oliver" and "Dale," Jane thought as she went up-stairs. Lord Denby would call that far more democracy than the law permits. She went to Andrew's room, thinking to see him asleep with a book on his chest. Instead, she found him sitting cross-legged on his bed with shavings all around him, carving a small block of wood. "Did Dale loan you a knife?" she asked.

Andrew nodded, his eyes on the wood. "It will be a bird," he announced.

"Eventually," she agreed.

"And I will send it to Mr. Butterworth, along with a letter, telling him that I miss him," he continued.

You, too? she thought in dismay. Oh, we are a sad lot, if we cannot manage without the mill owner. "I do, as well," she said after a moment's consideration.

"Stanton thought I should write him a letter," Andrew said, putting down the knife and getting into bed when she pulled back the covers. "We could both do it."

"Stanton seems determined that we write to Mr. Butterworth," she told him as she pulled up the covers, and shook off some of the wood shavings onto the floor.

"Then let us do it, Miss Mitten," Andrew said. He raised up on his elbow to look at her. "I do not think we have enough friends to waste one, do you?"

"I do not think so, either," she said. "I will do it tonight."

It is a simple thing, she told herself as she went back downstairs to the bookroom. The main floor was dark, and she knew that Stanton must consider his charges safely abed now, so he could sleep. She moved quietly, sure of herself in the house she knew so well, letting herself into the bookroom and closing the door without a sound. "Thanks to Dale," she said. "Nothing in this house creaks now." She sat a moment at the desk, mentally going down her list of reasons why it was perfectly unobjectionable to mail a letter to the mill owner. The list was short; nothing in her upbringing advised her to write even the briefest note, thanking him for the handyman.

"I will do it anyway," she said out loud, as she reached for the sulphurs and stood up to light the other branch of candles on the desk. "I told Andrew that I would and Stanton seems to expect it." She thought about Lady Carruthers, who had already announced her arrival in a day. "I will invite him to the reunion, as well."

It was a short note, unlike the long letters she wrote and never mailed, businesslike even, thanking him for sending Dale to make the place right and tight before the reunion. Writing faster, before she lost all her nerve, she invited him to the reunion dinner. I can hope that Lady Carruthers will not be rude if he appears, although there is no guarantee, she thought. She sealed the letter and backed it, carrying it carefully to the table in the front hallway, as though it were eggs balanced on top of each other.

You are being foolish, Jane, she told herself. It is merely a note of thanks for the handyman, and you are enlarging upon it in the same way that you imagined that he cared for you. I suppose this is the fantasy of old maids.

Deep in reflection, she walked down the hall again, touching the familiar tables, running her hand along the leather-tooled wallcovering which had seemed so grand when she came from the workhouse years ago, but which was stained now, and old. She knew that Stover Hall had gone to seed as surely as the formal garden was now a mass of weeds and choked plants, and it pained her heart. She knew also that Lady Carruthers was right. Stanton and I should never have planned a reunion, she thought. I wonder if it is not too late to call it off.

She sat on the stairs, chin in hand, to think about the matter, and realized with a chill that she was not alone. She couldn't help herself; she thought first of Blair. When that panic passed, she forced herself to stand up and listen. Someone was humming.

On silent feet, she moved back down the hall until she stood outside the sitting room. She pressed her ear against the door. I know that tune, she thought, and whispered, " 'If buttercups buzzed after the bee, If boats were on land, churches on sea . . .' Oh, my dear Lord Denby."

She opened the door, careful not to make sudden noises, and stood there. Her eyes were already accustomed to the darkness, and she had no trouble seeing Lord Denby seated in a chair that was pulled up to the open window. You'll be cold, she almost told him, and then she just stood there, enjoying the blessed fragrance, so delicate, of lilacs. I would have planted those in the front of Mr. Butterworth's house in Rumsey, she thought, closing her eyes and breathing deep.

" 'If summer were spring, and the other way round, then all the world would be upside down.' 'Tis a sad little tune, Jane," Lord Denby said without turning around. "It isn't supposed to be."

"How do you know it is I?" she countered, coming closer, relieved to see that he had covered his legs with a blanket, even though the air was mild.

"Who else?" he asked simply. He pushed out the footstool. "Sit down, my dear."

She did as he said, and made no objection when he raised the blanket to cover her lap as well as he could. She leaned against his knees, something she had never done before, and sighed when he rested his hand on her head.

"The fifers played that tune when we surrendered at Yorktown to Washington and Rochambeau," he murmured. "No one sang, Jane, because the heart was ripped from our bodies. We were the best in the world, and we surrendered to rabble! What a damnable business."

She nodded, unable to think of anything to say. He was silent for a long moment, and she heard him humming again. "I am reminded of defeat, Jane," he said, when he finished.

"I should not have organized a reunion, should I?" she asked. "Say the word, my lord, and I will call it off." She felt the pressure of his hand increase on her head, but it was not unpleasant.

"No, my dear, it is precisely right," he replied. "I only wish all of my comrades in arms could be here next week. Oh, Jane!" The words seemed torn from him. "Lord Cornwallis is dead in India these twelve years. Henry Clinton gone; Reich, that dreadful Hessian who could beat us all to flinders at whist, drowned off Malta; Palmerton and Riggs carried off by Caribbean fevers. We were young once together, and it pains me, Jane."

"You know Lord Ware will come," she reminded him, "and I have heard from Banastre Tarleton, who said he would not miss this opportunity. And the others: I do not remember their names, but you know them well. Oh, Lord Denby, what can I do for you?"

She raised up to look at him, and to her surprise, he was smiling. But such an odd smile, she thought, feeling again the same little chill.

"When I told you and Mr. Lowe that I wanted to die, I meant it, Jane," he told her, and then put his finger to her lips when she tried to speak. "But that is the coward's way, and I do not choose it now. I have something to tell my brother officers, and with this gathering, you have given me the opportunity."

"What, sir?" she asked, thoroughly alarmed now by the oddness of his smile, which was no smile.

He shook his head. "It will keep awhile longer, my dear, and so will your regard for me, I trust."

"Long after," she insisted.

"I fear not," he said. "But it will keep a few more days." He sighed then, and shifted his weight, and his mood seemed to change. "Do you know what it is to regret something with all your heart, and to know that there is nothing you can ever do to make amends?"

Oh, I do, she thought. Mr. Butterworth may excuse me, and I have made my peace, but there will always be that moment—maybe when I am tired, or disappointed, or in some low state—when I will wonder if I could have saved Blair's life. I deeply regret that Mr. Butterworth decided that someone with my background just wouldn't do. "I . . . I have some little idea of what it means to regret, my dear Lord Denby," she whispered.

"Well, then, we understand each other," he said. He shifted his legs. "I am certain it is late, but stay here with me awhile longer."

She nodded, and he patted her head. "I am glad you are not wearing those frumpy old caps anymore," he told her.

"I don't need them. There is nothing wrong with my hair," she said, smiling into the dark. "Maybe I even think it is beautiful."

"Just stay awhile longer," he repeated, even as she heard a drowsy tone to his words. "Do you know, that handyman just came and sat by my bed this afternoon."

"How odd," she murmured. "He said nothing?"

"Well, he told me he was Dale, and that he wanted to tell me about America, if I felt like it." He chuckled. "According to Stanton, this handyman is fixing everything in sight, so I decided, in fairness to all your efforts, to humor a lunatic." He touched her head again. "Truth to tell I liked having him there, and so I want you here for a moment more."

"And so I shall be," she said, her voice low.

He was quiet a long time, and his hand grew heavier on her head. Her eyes were starting to close when he began to hum again. "I regret," he whispered, when he finished the tune.

So do I, she thought. Is there a worse taskmaster than regret? After another long period of silence, she sat up. "Lord Denby, may I help you back to your room?"

"No, my dear," he said. "I can find my way. Good night now." He sighed. "If my sister is returning tomorrow, we will both need all our energy."

She stood for a moment with her hands on his shoulders. "I hope you will not take to your bed again because Lady Carruthers will be here."

"I think not," he replied. "Of course, it is one thing to face

Mahrattas in India and rabble in America, and quite another to deal with one's relatives."

Jane smiled into the darkness and kissed his cheek. "Good night, my lord." She left the room and paused at the entrance foyer, wondering if she should retrieve the letter to Mr. Butterworth. There is nothing in it but a thank you, and yet I am reluctant to intrude where I obviously have no place, she thought. Life would be so easy if I did not care.

She stood a moment in great indecision, then left the letter where it was. She started for the stairs, then turned in surprise when the front door opened. She knew it was Stanton by his silhouette, even though she could not see his face in the dark. She walked toward him and he waited at the door.

"It is a lovely night, Stanton," she said, standing with him in the doorway.

"Indeed, Miss Mitten," he replied.

She could sense his hesitation more than hear it, and put her hand on his arm. "We have been through a great deal together, sir," she said.

"We have," he agreed. "Miss Milton, despite all of it, I would miss this place."

"You do not plan to leave, do you?" she asked, startled.

"I would hope not," he said.

It was not an answer that satisfied her. She waited for him to say more, but he did not. "Stanton, do you have any regrets?" she asked on impulse.

He considered the question at length. "Fewer than I did last week, Miss Milton," was all he said.

"Then you are among the lucky."

Chapter Seventeen

She waited, half in hope, and half in dread, for a response to her letter, but none came. Her heart leaped when Stanton delivered a letter to her at the breakfast table two days later, but it was just a letter from Emma, recounting the latest exploits of her brood, and stating that Olivia was now laughing.

She was returning the letter to its envelope when she noted a postscript on the back of the last page. "Jane, I have been forwarding your letters to Scotland, where my brother is at present visiting Robert Owen in New Lanark," she read.

And so I shall not hear from him, she thought, frowning at the letter. But I only sent one letter, unless Andrew has been writing as well, and that is entirely possible. I shall ask him when he returns from Joe Singletary's tutelage today. Better still, I will meet him at the lake and walk him home. It has been so long since I have done even that. Surely I can bear to walk that close to Mr. Butterworth's home now, after this much time.

She wandered Stover Hall that afternoon, noticing with pleasure all the final touches administered by the handyman, from the gleaming wall of paint in the entrance, Wedgwood blue as he suggested, to the new hinges on the French doors that opened onto the terrace, with its view of Mr. Butterworth's lake. Content despite her qualms about the guests due to arrive tomorrow, she went belowstairs, where the cook pronounced everything ready, and the footman polished silver as though kingdoms would fall if he did not. She chose not to disturb Stanton, who was in deep conversation with the upstairs maids, and went back to the terrace.

She smiled to see the 'tween stairs maid and the groundsmen weeding diligently in the formal garden, and watched as Andrew, coming up from the mill owner's house, dropped his books on the flagstone path, waved to her and started pulling weeds, too. I should help, she thought, but was content to sit where she was, the sun on her face. Tomorrow there will be reunion guests, and Lady Carruthers will have arrived to preside and claim all my own hard work as her own. I need to marshal my forces for this ordeal of my own creation.

She could not have closed her eyes for long, but when she opened them, there was Mr. Butterworth approaching the terrace, his arm around Andrew. She passed her hand before her eyes, sure that he would disappear, but he did not. You have returned, you dear man, she thought, as she straightened her dress and rose to greet him. She looked closer. It would be good if you were smiling, she told herself. Or if you did not look thinner, somehow.

"Hello, sir," she said, putting out her hand and having the pleasure of finding it grasped in both of his. "You have been long away."

"Aye, Miss Milton, I have."

He seemed content to stand there and hold her hand, and she could not think of a single reason to distract him from such a pleasant occupation.

"See here, Mr. Butterworth, you are to shake her hand and then let it go," Andrew said with a laugh. "Besides, sir, I have much to tell you."

The mill owner released her hand, his face serious. Think of all the conversation I should be making, she thought in confusion, as she merely stood and admired him. No question that he was thinner; his collar was loose, and his coat seemed to hang a little off his tall frame. He wore a terribly ordinary waistcoat, which told her more about him than words could ever convey. Perhaps he does not care anymore, she thought.

"Mr. Butterworth, I think you must be far too busy with your mills," she scolded, seeking for the right tone, and wondering if she was even close.

"Em calls me a skeleton," he said, then turned to Andrew. "Lad, I think it would be sporting if you would continue helping that charming little lady in the rose patch"—he looked at Jane, with the first actual hint of a smile in his eyes—"the formal gardens. We can talk later." He watched Andrew return to the garden, then turned his attention to her again. "You may say those things about me, but I have to ask in turn if you need to be reminded to eat."

"Sometimes," she said. "Stanton reminds me."

"Not enough, I should think." He indicated the chair she had vacated. "Could we talk a moment, my dear?"

She sat, and after another moment spent watching Andrew, he joined her. He started to speak, and then stared at his hands. "I do not know how to say this, Miss Milton, but it needs saying, before much more time has passed."

She waited, a cold coming into her bones that she would not have expected, considering that it was April now. "Perhaps it can keep."

"No, it cannot," he declared with some force. "I would not for the world mislead you."

"You never have, sir," she interrupted. Say no more, sir, she thought, not while you look so sad.

"Your letters were forwarded to me in Scotland," he began finally, the words pulled from him by pincers it seemed.

"It was just one letter, Mr. Butterworth, and totally unobjectionable," she said in apology. "I cannot believe there was anything in it to cause distress on your part or warrant a visit! I merely wanted to thank you for sending us the handyman." How low I must be in his estimation now, she reflected, when he never asked for correspondence from me. He must think I have no more propriety than an opera dancer.

When she nerved herself to look at his face again, she could see nothing but perplexity there. "The handyman," she repeated, wondering why he stared at her.

The mill owner strode to the French doors, flinging them open. "Miss Milton, I sent no handyman," he said.

"Of course you did," she argued, propelled from her chair by a sense of urgency, even as she strove to keep her voice calm. "He said he came from you . . ." She stopped and stared at him. "No, he never said anything of the sort! I assumed . . . You did not send a man of about thirty-seven or thirty-eight? He is from Ohio. He has fixed everything on my list, just as you said he would."

"Never," the mill owner said. "In the press of everything, I forgot to send Jonathan."

"Dale."

They stared at each other.

"Good God," she exclaimed. "Who is upstairs?"

Her mind on Lord Denby, she picked up her skirts and ran down the hall, taking the stairs two at a time, to the astonishment of the upstairs maids. She heard Mr. Butterworth right behind her, shouting for Stanton in that factory voice of his.

"For the last week, he has been sitting with Lord Denby in the afternoons," she called over her shoulder as she ran to the chamber and threw open the door.

He sat there now, rising in surprise from the chair by the bed when the door banged against the wall. "Miss Milton!" he exclaimed, his voice filled with alarm. "Is something wrong?"

Staring at him, unable to say anything because of her exertions, Jane shook her head. Never taking her eyes from his face, she sat on Lord Denby's bed and took his hand in hers. The mill owner, breathing heavily, hurried to her side, his eyes on the handyman as well. "Should I throw him out, Jane?" he asked. "Say the word."

She almost did not hear him, but she shook her head, puzzled by the slight smile on Lord Denby's face.

"Sit down, Dale," the old man said. "She's not slow, lad, although she has been preoccupied of late."

The handyman did as he was told. Jane looked from one to the other, and then back again, her eyes wide in amazement. "I do not understand," she said finally, and reached behind her to touch the mill owner, who sat beside her, leaning forward and intent.

"I think you do, Jane," Lord Denby said. "Hand her the book, Dale."

The handyman picked up the essays from the bedside table and turned to the first one, holding it out to her, and then placing it on her lap when she made no move to take it. Without a word and scarcely breathing, she looked down at the familiar essay about Lieutenant Jeremy Dill and his lusty New York landlady.

"Jane, how good of you to come just now," Lord Denby said, his lips quivering. "I have only just been properly introduced to someone I would like you to meet."

"Good God," Mr. Butterworth whispered, looking over her shoulder at the essay, and then from Lord Denby to the handyman. "Jane, you did not notice the resemblance? Jane?"

"Jane!"

She wondered why he kept calling her name, and then she realized that for the first time in her life, she must have fainted. She opened her eyes to find herself lying on Lord Denby's bed and staring at the plaster cherubs in the ceiling. She could not have been unconscious long, because Mr. Butterworth was still unbuttoning her bodice and the handyman was fanning her with the book. She started to breathe again, and put up her hand to stop the mill owner. "I think I am all right, sir," she said, her face flaming with embarrassment. "Do help me up."

"No," said the mill owner firmly. "You will stay right where you are, Jane."

"At least button me again," she ordered, then put up her hand to stop him when he obliged her, his fingers warm against her chemise. "No! I will do it."

She lay there with her eyes closed and her mind whirling about, waiting for the room to quit dipping and revolving. When her breathing returned to normal again, the mill owner lifted her into a sitting position. "I have never fainted before," she assured Lord Denby. "Truly I have not."

No one said anything as she looked from Lord Denby to the handyman. Why did I not notice, she asked herself in astonishment. True, Lord Denby's hair is long past auburn, but that portrait from his younger days hangs in the gallery, and his hair is glorious and abundant like Dale's, with just that same curl to it. Discounting the years, I have never seen two men who look so much alike. "I must be an idiot," she admitted finally.

"Not at all," Dale said, putting down the book. "Why would you look for a resemblance where none was even dreamt of? And tell me truly: have you been this close to both of us at the same time?"

He was right, of course. She shook her head, and regretted the sudden motion. "I only looked in on you each afternoon, when I wondered where you were," she told him, her fingers pressed to her temple. "Dale, who are you? And how could I be so dense?"

"I am Dale Bingham, and you're not dense."

"Bingham." She looked at the mill owner for confirmation. "Mr. Butterworth, Edward Bingham of Connecticut!" she said slowly, fixing her gaze again upon the handyman. "The name on the list. He is your . . ."

"My stepfather," the handyman said. "Along with Lord Denby here, he served on Sir Henry Clinton's staff in New York City during the rebellion."

She looked at the book. "And Edward Bingham was quartered in the same house with Lord . . . with Lieutenant Dill?" she asked. "But you say you are from Ohio."

"I didn't lie to you, Miss Milton," he said. "I *am* from Ohio. I live in the Western Reserve and Kirtland. I was in Connecticut visiting my parents when your letter arrived."

"And you came all this way?" she asked.

He nodded, and looked at his father. "I was on my way to Scotland anyway to buy surveyor's transits. Miss Milton, I am a land agent in the Western Reserve. The best surveying supplies and transits in the world come from Abercrombie and Mackey in Edinburgh and I am chary about spending that much money sight unseen."

"You said you were a handyman," she accused him.

Patiently he shook his head. "No, Miss Milton, *you* asked me if I could fix things. I happen to be good at fixing things."

"But why didn't you tell me who you were?" she persisted.

"You didn't give me a chance." He smiled at her indignation. "To be honest, Miss Milton—are we cousins of some sort?—I was not so sure that I wanted anyone to know who I was anyway." He seemed to lose his confidence for a moment. "You can appreciate the . . . the delicacy of this situation."

She considered his artless statement and could not disagree. "I suppose I can," she murmured. She touched Lord Denby's hand. "Can I assume that you did not part on precisely good terms with Edward Bingham, all those years ago?"

"He was in New York, and by the time Dale was born, I was in Yorktown with Cornwallis, ready to be shipped back to England." He looked at Dale, a long, hungry look that brought sudden tears to Jane's eyes. "Edward wrote me a scathing letter and demanded to know what I was going to do about this situation of my own creation." He sighed. "I ignored his letter and left Dale's mother to suffer considerable abuse, taunts, and mistreatments from her neighbors and relatives. When I speak of regret, Jane . . ." He could not finish.

Still pressing her hand to her temple, she leaned forward and kissed him. "You don't need to say any more, my lord."

"But I do," he insisted. "Edward Bingham—the second son of an earl, I might add—evacuated New York after the Treaty of Paris, returned to England, and resigned his commission immediately."

"And returned to New York?" she asked.

"By way of Canada, where I was then on duty. He gave me a tongue lashing for deserting a good woman, called me out, and nearly killed me in a duel," he said. His face grew red. "It was long before you came here. You know my war wounds that Blair liked to tease about? He had no idea. In all my years of active duty in India, Canada, America, and the Caribbean, I was only wounded in a duel instigated by a outraged man in love with the mother of my American son. A pretty picture, eh, Jane? Any wonder it never came up in conversation over whist or cigars?"

She was silent then, leaning back against Mr. Butterworth,

who put his arm around her. "I'm sorry for both of you," she said at last.

"No need," Dale said, "at least on my part. I realize that now." It was his turn to look away, but she could still see the struggle on his face. "Pa married Mama and adopted me, and we moved to Connecticut where no one knew us. He's a farmer, and a good one, I might add. I have five brothers and two sisters. My little sister and her family live in Ohio, and I stay with her when I am not surveying."

"Your parents?" she asked gently.

"Mama has never regretted my birth, and Pa loves me," he replied simply. "I have a good life." He looked at his father. "I wouldn't change it, but I think I needed to know that there wasn't any point in hating you, sir." He took the old man's hand and kissed it, then twined his fingers through Lord Denby's. "On the voyage over here, I rehearsed what I was going to say at that reunion banquet. I was all ready to stand up tomorrow night and expose you as a hypocrite and a fraud."

"I would not blame you if you did," Lord Denby said.

The handyman shrugged. "What would be the point? My stepfather knows, and he chose not to say anything. Lord Ware—they have been corresponding for years—seems to suspect, but he is a gentleman. And if your essays have served a useful purpose . . ." He looked down at his father's hand in his. "I can forgive. If there is anything to forgive."

She sat up suddenly, as another thought occurred to her. "Will you . . . can you make Dale your heir, my lord? And what about Andrew? I *know* he is Blair's son."

"I know he is not. Miss Milton, although you are too kind to consider it, sometimes rumors are true."

Jane gasped and turned around to stare at Stanton, who stood in the doorway. She held her breath, and wondered if everyone else in the room was doing the same thing. The silence seemed to thunder in her ears.

"I . . . do not think we need you now, Stanton," Mr. Butterworth said slowly, intruding upon the quiet. "There really wasn't an emergency after all."

"I believe there is, sir, if you will excuse me," the butler said, as imperturbable as usual.

"I will not!" the mill owner exclaimed. "Damn you, Stanton. I did not ask for this!"

"No, you didn't," he replied, all serenity. "I have taken it entirely upon myself." He turned to Jane. "I should have done so years ago." He gave an apologetic look to Dale Bingham, who was glancing from the mill owner to the butler, his eyes lively with interest. "Dale, this is what comes of too many tales belowstairs of initiative and Yankee know-how. I shall blame you."

"Go right ahead, Oliver," Dale said, grinning.

"Since everyone else is free enough with the truth this afternoon, I intend to speak my mind, Miss Milton," the butler said. "It is a long time overdue, wouldn't you say, Mr. Butterworth?"

Without a word, the mill owner got up from the bed and sat himself in the window seat, looking no one in the face. "Does it matter what I think?" he said finally.

"Right now? Probably not, sir," Stanton replied. "I like you too well to see you flog yourself one more minute. Shall I tell these good people, or will you do it, sir? It would come better from you, I believe."

He is so alone there, Jane thought. Quietly she got to her feet, swayed a little, and sat beside Mr. Butterworth. "I can return a favor," she said simply, taking his hand onto her lap. "Andrew is your son, is he not?" She looked at Lord Denby and Dale. "God help me, Mr. Butterworth, but that afternoon at Rumsey when you and Andrew and Jacob—oh, heavens, Jacob is his cousin!— came back from the factory with grease on your faces and identical smiles!" She pressed his hand. "But Dale would only say I was not looking for a resemblance, and therefore saw none."

When he still said nothing, she nudged his shoulder gently. "The empty miniature frame on your desk, Mr. Butterworth. Was it Lucinda?"

To her horror, he began to cry, gulping sobs that came from a place she had no idea existed in the mill owner, that man of competence and ability. Without a word, she wrapped her arms around him and held him while he cried. "Oh, sir," she murmured as she ran her hand over his back. "Rumor said he was an older man and a ne'er-do-well. None of us ever actually knew who she loved before she married Blair," Jane said, when he was silent in her arms. "It was you, wasn't it?"

He nodded, taking out his handkerchief and then blowing his nose. "I loved her too much, obviously." He still could not look at anyone. "These things happen, don't they, Lord Denby?" he said, with just a touch of his old humor.

"It seems to be the way of the world, Mr. Butterworth," the marquis replied. "Why didn't you marry Lucinda? You are certainly a man of principle, even if you will not sell me your lake."

He looked at them then, and Jane could only bite her lip at the sight of so much anguish in one man's eyes. "She wrote a note telling me that I had got her with child. I came right there and proposed." He tightened his grip on Jane's hand. "I was not a scoundrel, Jane, not precisely."

"Of course you were not. She . . . she did not accept?"

His eyes grew bewildered, as though he were going through the experience all over again. "Turned me down flat." He released her hand and got to his feet, unable to keep still. "My God, I wanted to do the right thing! I was on my knees before her! There she was, pale as whey and worn from puking, and all she could say was that I was a mill owner and my father had come from a pig farm! Even in that extremity, she would not marry me." He walked over to the bed. "She chose to dupe your son instead, my lord." He leaned closer and touched the old man's shoulder. "I think he knew, but he loved her and thought that would be enough. I think it might have been enough, too, if she had not died."

Jane nodded. "After she died, Blair seldom came home." She leaped to her feet. "But why did you not say something then? It would have been a scandal, Mr. B., but people forget! You could have had your son all these years!"

He attempted a smile, but it barely crossed his lips before it vanished. "I thought about it, Jane, I really did, but as far as anyone knew, Andrew was Blair's son. I thought that my son's life as a marquis would be better than anything I could offer him. Lucinda certainly thought so, anyway, because she rejected me. Why should I upset that apple cart, when no one had an inkling?"

"Even after the rumors started?" Jane persisted.

Lord Denby chuckled. "Won't my sister be amazed to know that she was right after all? Oh, Lord, what webs we weave, Dale."

"I knew my son had a worthy advocate in you, Jane," Mr. Butterworth said. "I put all my trust in you." He smiled. "All those years ago, when I sought you out at town gatherings and . . . and parties when someone condescended to include me, I became such a master at monopolizing you and pulling the conversation around to my son. You were always so pleased to talk abut him, and I thank you for that." He took a deep and shaky breath. "It was all I lived for."

Jane sat on the bed again, overwhelmed by the enormity of what she was hearing. "And Stanton?"

The mill owner looked at the butler, who had come into the room now. "Stanton's father was my father's partner in the pig farm, and that was all just good fortune, on my part. When I learned that he was footman here at Stover Hall and then butler, I knew that I could count on him to keep me totally informed about Andrew." He touched her hair. "Between the two of you—one of you knowing, and the other totally convinced that Andrew was Blair's son—I managed."

Jane took a deep breath, wondering for a moment if so much revelation had sucked the very air out of the room. She looked around at the others. How much time you have all wasted, she thought.

"When you would do a kindness for me and then say you were only doing it to thank me for the way I was taking care of Andrew, you really meant it, didn't you?" she asked, her voice soft.

"More than you know, my dear." He chuckled. "Except that you *do* know now."

"And when you helped me through my own particular crisis?" she asked.

"That was for you, alone," he replied, his voice equally soft.

"Thank you."

And now comes the moment I am dreading, she thought. No sense in putting it off another second. "Mr. Butterworth, I am certain that Lord Derby and Dale will excuse us all. I know that you have a conversation in the formal garden that has been post-poned far too long."

He nodded. "It scares me a little bit."

It kills me, she thought. You are taking the child I raised from infancy far out of my reach. "I do not doubt that you will find just the right touch."

"Come with me," he asked, taking her hand.

She let him pull her from the room. Stanton closed the door and stood in the hall with them. "Miss Milton, I have one more confession."

"I am certain it cannot be any more difficult that anything we have heard yet," she said. "And then I do insist that Mr. Butterworth tell me why he came back, if he has not yet received my letter about the handyman."

"Don't, Stanton," Mr. Butterworth said.

"I have to," he said simply. "Miss Milton, I forwarded all of your letters—the ones you wrote late at night in the bookroom—to Mr. Butterworth at Rumsey. Mrs. Newton must have sent them on to Scotland."

She stared at him, unable to speak. "Those were not meant for anyone's eyes," she managed to say finally, not even daring to look at the mill owner.

"You did not mean what you wrote?" Mr. Butterworth asked, his voice low.

"Of course I did!" she exclaimed, stung to irritation. "I meant every word!"

"That is what I came to speak to you about," he said. "I suppose your thank you letter about the handyman is somewhere between Rumsey, Edinburgh, and here. It is not what brought me back."

She closed her eyes, near to tears. "You needn't concern yourself about it now, Mr. Butterworth, especially since I think you owe your son a long conversation."

"Miss Milton . . ."

"It can keep, Mr. Butterworth. Excuse me, please, both of you."

Shaking her head when Stanton called her name, she hurried down the hall to the sanctuary of her own room. Her head throbbing, she sank onto the window seat, fit for nothing more than to stare out at the trees. *He has never recovered from his passion for Lucinda,* she told herself, *and thanks to Stanton, I have bombarded this intensely private soul with love letters he never wanted.* "Dear me," she said, resting her forehead against the cool glass of the window. "I know it's good to speak one's mind, but perhaps some things are better left unsaid."

Her mind on her own misery, she stared out the window, then sat up straighter to watch as Mr. Butterworth walked across the terrace. He stood there so long, hands behind his back, rocking back and forth on his heels in that familiar manner, that she felt herself growing impatient. "Do not waste one more minute," she told him firmly through the glass.

To her gratification, he left the terrace and walked with real

purpose toward the formal garden. "The rose patch," she said
with her lips against the window. "Dear Mr. Butterworth, you
are such a commoner. How I will miss you both."

Andrew sat on his haunches, pulling weeds. "Sit down there
next to him, Mr. Butterworth," she whispered. "Ah, that is the
way. Tell him everything; hold nothing back. He is my own
dearest child—heaven knows I raised him—and he will make
you . . . us . . . proud."

She knew it was a long story, but she was patient to wait there
at the window, watching their heads close together, and then the
mill owner's arm around his son, and then their fierce embrace.
"Oh, God, I would feel so good if this did not hurt so much," she
whispered against the glass as they rose, hugged again, and
started arm in arm down to the lake, and then to the mill owner's
house beyond.

She watched them until they were gone, and then sat there in
the window seat until the room was dark. She was aware that
Stanton knocked on her door once, and said he was leaving a
tray outside. She was silent, and he went away. Dale came by
later, but she had nothing to say to him, either.

Hours later, hollow-eyed with staring into the darkness and
feeling far older than her years, she dragged herself to bed, only
to spend the night staring at the ceiling and wishing for dawn.
Dale, you would call this a fine how-de-do, she thought as the
sun finally rose on the day of the reunion. I spoke my mind—
we all did, for heaven's sake—and everyone is happy now, except me.

Chapter Eighteen

She sat in the window seat all night and watched the clouds blot
out the stars. She flinched from the lightning, thinking of Andrew at Mr. Butterworth's home, and hoping that he would not
mind if the boy came into his room and sat on his bed until the
storm passed. You could sing, Mr. Butterworth, if you are so inclined. Andrew knows my entire repertory of rain songs.

The rain came as a relief, hurling itself against the panes until the storm moved away. Still she sat there, watching the rain slide down the panes now, a murmur instead of a threat, the thunder only a faint growl, nature's afterthought. A little while longer, and then dawn came, the sky clear and hopeful.

Breakfast interested her no more than dinner the night before, so she went onto the terrace instead, stepping around the pools of water to stand finally at the stone railing and gaze down on the formal garden and Mr. Butterworth's lake beyond. She discovered quickly that it was not a view she wanted anymore.

She turned to look at the house, thinking of all the times in her life that she would have left it willingly, if Andrew had not tied her there, and then Blair, with his final illness. Except that I never would have left Andrew, she told herself. Or Blair, even if that burden did prove too heavy. And if I did not acquit myself as I would have wished, I did my best. Some regrets just have to be borne.

It was a thought to console her, she decided, as she looked at the lake again. If you would ask me, Mr. Butterworth, I would tell you that at any point in our lives, we are only doing the best we can. I have become so wise this year. A pity no one ever wants advice.

"Miss Milton, Stanton has sent me to find you and force you—with whips and cudgels if necessary—to the breakfast table."

She turned around to see Dale Bingham standing by the French doors. "I don't know, sir, that anyone has the power to force me to do anything now. And please call me Jane, cousin."

He laughed and joined her at the balustrade. "I suppose we are cousins," he began.

"Oh, why not?" she said. "I think I am cousin to half of England, Dale." She touched his arm lightly. "I was asking myself earlier this morning—did someone think to move you upstairs to a guest room?"

"Lord Denby offered me Blair's room, but I prefer belowstairs, Jane," he replied, his eyes merry. "My dear, I have grown up in kitchens and nothing will change that now." He was silent a long time, looking at the view. "A storm clears away a lot of things, doesn't it?"

More than you know, she thought.

Dale perched himself on the railing. "Jane, he has offered to make me his heir, if I will repudiate my adoption and remain here in England. What do you think of that?"

"I think it would be a mistake for you," she said.

He sighed. "And so I told him. I am an American, and I would miss my country and my family." He shrugged. "Why would I want to be a marquis, own extensive land, be richer than Croesus, and sit in the House of Lords? Not when I can have mud and mosquitoes and Indian alarms, no indeed!"

Lady Carruthers arrived from London first, barely acknowledging Jane and going right to her brother's room, to emerge all smiles a short time later. Jane stood by Stanton and watched her come down the hall, the picture of triumph. "Of all things, this is the worst," she murmured to him.

"Then thank Almighty Providence that you are not going through it alone, Miss Milton," he replied as Lady Carruthers bore down on them. "Lovely day, isn't it, my lady?"

She ignored him as though he were a violet in the wallpaper and took Jane's arm, shaking her. "You were always so certain you were right!"

Before Jane could speak, Stanton stepped between them, forcing Lady Carruthers to let go. "My lady, Miss Milton was right up until yesterday afternoon when Mr. Butterworth's claims were made plain," he said, each word distinct. "We could all wish for such a champion."

"But she was wrong!"

"Wrong to believe the best and cherish the Canfields' son? You are mistaken, Lady Carruthers."

Jane stared at the butler. "Bless you, Oliver," she murmured.

Stanton glanced at her and she could not mistake the regard in his eyes, full of expression now, and not masked in the usual way of those who serve.

"But she was wrong!" Lady Carruthers repeated, stamping her foot, as her turban quivered like a live thing.

"She was kind," he said, putting on his careful demeanor again as some men shrug into a coat. "Heaven knows how she became that way, considering her example in this household. It must have been her good training in the Leeds workhouse."

Lady Carruthers gasped and her face took on a peculiar mottled color. "I will see that you are dismissed without a character!" she stormed.

"Not in this lifetime," he said simply. "Your brother has assured me that I have his entire confidence. And when you and your brainless boy assume control here someday, as you will, you will walk onto a totally deserted estate, Lady Carruthers."

Her silence was terrible, and then she turned her attention to Jane. "I can ruin you," she stated finally.

"I do not see how," Stanton said.

"I am not talking to you! Jane, you aren't aware, but the night Blair died, I looked in the room and saw you sleeping in the chair. I call that gross neglect, and so I will tell anyone who will listen."

Jane sucked in her breath and reached for Stanton, who grasped her hand. "Never mind it now," he said softly, then as she watched, turned his full attention to Lady Carruthers.

"I wouldn't do that," he told her, his voice firm, but with an edge to it that Jane had never heard before. "The more gross neglect is yours, for not waking her. *She* was exhausted; *you* were cruel. Did that never occur to you, Lady Carruthers? I am surprised."

Lady Carruthers could only gape like a fish, her mouth opening and closing with no sounds coming out. "Perhaps I should find her some smelling salts," Jane whispered, her eyes on the woman.

The butler frowned. "My dear Miss Milton, are you doomed forever to be far too kind?"

"I suppose I am," she replied, totally in charity with him.

He took her arm and turned his back upon the woman, speechless with rage, who gasped for breath. "Jane, I have often wondered through the years why she was so unkind to you. I have a theory now."

"I would be the last one to keep you from speaking your mind, Oliver," Jane said.

"Some people are just unpleasant. Perhaps we must leave it at that. Do excuse us, Lady Carruthers, but I believe our guests are arriving. Could you take your spasms elsewhere? London would be nice; Venice even better. St. Petersburg?"

They came all morning, elderly men, some of them carrying parts of faded uniforms, most still erect with the military bearing that Jane admired. Dale helped his father down to the sitting room, made sure that Lord Denby was comfortable, and left him

to the tender mercies of his comrades. "I think they are all growing younger by the minute," he whispered to Jane later as he
peered through the door.

Younger men came, too, the sons of officers unable by death
or distance to attend. They introduced themselves, and then
joined the others in the sitting room, content for the most part to
listen, and whisper among themselves about the old warriors
swapping reminiscences before them. Jane circulated among her
guests until she noticed, to her amusement, Dale sitting by the
door, staring at his hand.

"You look as though you have been bitten," she declared, sitting next to him, happy for the moment to be off her feet.

"I don't know what you would call it," he said. "Jane, this will
mean nothing to you, but this hand just shook the hand of Major
Patrick Arnold. Great God Almighty, Lord of Battle!"

"I do not understand," she replied, mystified. "Whoever he is,
he cannot be contagious. Do you mean that rather handsome
gentleman with the red hair?"

"His father's name was Benedict, my dear," Dale replied, his
voice still faint. "Not a favorite colonial son, let me hasten to
add."

She recognized one of Lord Cornwallis's sons, a thin, pop-
eyed man who had not yet acquired his father's full flesh, and
pointed him out to Dale. The handyman's eyes grew wider.
"Dear Jane, these are the bogeymen who frighten American
children into good behavior!" He managed a chuckle. "I suppose you will tell me next that Banastre Tarleton—damn his evil
hide—is skulking in here somewhere."

She leaned her face against his shoulder to hide her laughter.
"Next to your father, my dear cousin!"

She felt him start in surprise. "Jane, he looks so ordinary. No
horns, no fangs, no cloven hoof." He managed a laugh of his
own. "Am I foolish?"

"No! You're just an American, Dale. Please don't change."

With a grin, he looked around and then kissed her quickly. "I
wouldn't dream of it, my dear."

She spent the afternoon hovering about the edge of the gathering, unwilling to leave it, not because Lord Denby seemed in
any danger of exhaustion, but because she had seen Marsh arrive from Mr. Butterworth's and whisper a few words to Stan-

ton. She knew he was collecting Andrew's things; armies could not have dragged her to watch.

She went belowstairs finally, to put on an apron and blanch almonds until her face was rosy and her hair curling in tendrils around her face. I am comfortable in kitchens, too, she thought, with no feelings of pity or dismay. I will never tell her, but Lady Carruthers is more right than she knows: I have the common touch.

At peace with herself, she arranged almond crescents on a glass plate, then applied herself to the macaroons until Cook pronounced her efforts good enough. When she was sure Marsh must be gone, she went upstairs again. I will not look in the room, she told herself as she hurried upstairs to change for dinner. It will only be empty, with that look of total abandonment that all vacant rooms seem to have, whether the occupant has been gone fifteen minutes or five years.

She stuck to her resolution, dressing quickly, giving up on her hair because the steam from belowstairs had curled it beyond help, and then seating herself before the cold hearth. She thought of a little book she used to read to Andrew about an enchanted mole whose only solace was to pull the earth over himself when the day was gloomy. It was the wrong memory, bringing with it the vivid image of Andrew with a blanket over his shoulders, giggling and dropping down to cover himself like the mole, while she chased him around the lawn.

"Mr. Butterworth, you are taking my child," she said out loud. "How can you be so cruel?"

She could only count her blessings that the banquet in Lord Denby's honor exceeded her modest expectations to such an extent that no attention came her way. Lord Denby was the man she remembered, his dignity restored one hundredfold by the good wishes of his comrades. Once during the evening, she caught his eye on her, and it was easy to smile and blow him a kiss.

She was startled at first to see Mr. Butterworth, impeccable in evening clothes and brilliant waistcoat again, seated among the celebrants. He belongs here, she thought, after her first surprise. If ever a man was a good neighbor, he is, even if he has broken my heart in more ways than I would have thought possible. The wonder of it is that I love him still.

Despite the most acute misery that filled her whole body, she rejoiced in the tributes that came with each toast after dinner, as

Lord Denby's comrades rose to tell story after story of his qualities that made him such an example to the officer corps. I hope your regrets are gone, my lord, she thought, happy to rise and applaud with the others.

Then Dale rose, glass in hand. She held her breath for just a moment, then released it slowly when Lord Denby's son spoke of his father Edward Bingham's regard for the adjutant he had served with so many years before. "It is certainly my privilege to echo whatever sentiments my father would have expressed, had he been able to attend this reunion," Dale said. "Lord Denby, long life and good health from America to you, still the best among us!"

He sat down and Jane smiled at him across the table. She watched Lord Denby, his eyes on his son, and she felt the familiar scratching in her throat, the dryness behind her eyelids. Dale, you could have said such terrible things, she thought. Thank goodness we have all spoken our minds—or nearly all of us. And thank you for keeping that one secret.

The thoughts were not out of her mind when Lord Denby rose, and looked at his guests. "Gentlemen," he began, "and, lady," he said, with a nod to her, "I could not finish this evening without a confession to you, who think you know me best." He paused and gripped the table, and Jane held her breath. She watched Dale half rise from his chair, concern etched on his face, and then sit down again.

As she listened, scarcely breathing, Lord Denby told his guests his well-kept secret. His voice did not waver as he spoke of his own hypocrisy in ignoring a son of his body and leaving the mother to suffer shame. He expressed his own gratitude for Edward Bingham, "a far better man than I," he said, "for he did the right thing, where I did not, and earned the loyalty of a son as truly his as those of his own making." He paused, as if gathering strength, and looked down the length of the silent dining table. "Gentlemen, I aim to rewrite that story of Lieutenant Jeremy Dill, not as a joke this time, but as an honest reminder of the responsibility we bear for all our actions."

He sat down to silence. "I can tell I have disappointed you, my brothers-in-arms and colleagues," he said, his voice old again. "I suppose there is no remedy, but it was time to speak my mind, before night closes in and it is too late to make amends."

She closed her eyes with relief when Dale stood up and began to applaud. In a moment the others were on their feet. She rose, too overwhelmed to applaud, her hands clasped together. She smiled at Dale, and then could not resist a glance at the mill owner, who applauded with the rest. To her surprise, he was looking at her, as though it were her tribute.

As the guests gathered around Lord Denby, it was an easy matter to excuse herself. With a sigh of relief, she hurried outside and away from the odor of food and gentlemen's cologne. This day will end soon, she reminded herself, as she walked to Mr. Butterworth's lake. She sat down on a bench, pressing her hands to her face to wish away the warmth. With any luck at all, I will find employment in Scotland, she reminded herself. And if I am really lucky, I will think of Andrew only on the stroke of every hour, and Mr. Butterworth on the half stroke.

"Pretty night, isn't it?"

She recognized Dale's voice, and patted the bench beside her. "You did the right thing," she told him, as he took hold of her hand.

"I think so," he agreed. Suddenly he pressed her fingers to his lips. "Jane, you can come to Ohio with me. In fact, I wish you would."

"Mr. Bingham, do you love me?"

He grinned at her. "I like you quite a bit, and you are, after all, what my pa calls a 'cuddlesome woman.' "

She laughed and pulled her hand away. "It's a kind offer, and I shall think about it." She nudged his shoulder. "Go on back to the party, sir."

"You love that mill owner, don't you?" he asked.

"With all my heart."

"Damn the man," he said with some feeling. "If I did not like him so well myself, I could grow weary right now! Ah, me." He kissed her cheek with a loud smack, laughed, and strolled back inside.

Well, at least I can go to my grave knowing that I have been asked, Jane thought, even if he was not precisely serious. He does have the makings of an excellent husband. She smiled into the darkness. But probably not mine.

She heard footsteps on the terrace, familiar ones, but she did not turn around. I owe you such an apology, she thought. Please come sit by me, Mr. Butterworth. The wind was blowing against her back so she breathed the pleasant fragrance of his cologne before he sat down.

"Did Dale propose to you?" he asked without any preliminaries.

His question startled her, delivered as it was in that dry, matter-of-fact tone not even remotely sentimental, but dearer to her than anyone else's voice. "Sort of," she replied, after a pause to push her thoughts together.

"Miss Mitten, one does not 'sort of' propose," he informed her. "One either does or doesn't." He stopped, and when he continued, his voice sounded less confident. "At least, that is what I think, but my experience, as you know, is limited."

"Less limited than mine, sir," she said, in no rush to ease his path, and more concerned with her own train of thought. "Mr. Butterworth, please accept my apology for those dratted letters. I never intended them to be sent, even if Stanton thought he was doing you—or me—a favor." Her hands felt cold all of a sudden, and she clasped them tightly together in her lap. "Since yesterday I . . . I think I understand better the depth of your love for Lucinda. Please forgive me for what happened."

"You're off the mark there, Miss Milton," he said, moving closer. "Would you mind terribly if I put my arm around you? The benches on this side of *my* lake are somewhat stingy in length and my rump is hanging off the edge."

She laughed and scooted over. "You could ask Dale to survey the property and determine once and for all whose lake this is, sir."

"I could, but then, what would Lord Denby have to argue about?"

His arm was warm around her waist, and she felt herself relaxing against him. "That was my last confession to you, Mr. Butterworth," she told him. "This may even be our last conversation, for all I know. I am so heartily sorry for any embarrassment I have caused you."

He started to speak, but she put her fingers to his lips. "Hush now! It's my turn. I have apologized to you now, I have told you awful truths and you have borne them. I suppose now that the payment is my own son. Andrew *is* mine, sir, in all ways but birth. I raised him; you did not." She stopped, unable to say more on that subject. "I have an offer of Ohio now, which I might accept."

"And do you know, I think that if Stanton can work up the nerve, you will have another offer there, Miss Milton," Mr. Butterworth said, his voice as spare as ever. "He doesn't appear to know his place any better than the rest of us. I blame it entirely on this modern age we live in."

"You would! He is dear to me," she said simply, putting her arm around the mill owner, and feeling a certain gratification when he sucked in his breath and then ran his finger around his collar.

"Warm night," he offered.

"Not really," she replied, then sat up with a start. "Mr. Butterworth, you said I was 'off the mark' about Lucinda?"

He chucked and pulled her close again. "Wondered if you were listening, dear Jane. Yes, I loved her, but you would be amazed what a change can result from a flat turndown of a heartfelt proposal."

"But you said . . ."

"I said nothing. What a blow she dealt my pride! Do you think I was about to forget my origins again?"

"It would put a damper on things," she agreed.

He got up and walked to the lake. Intrigued, she followed, taking the hand he held out to her and circling the water with him until they were on his side. "Oh, Jane! I took my broken heart to Egypt and studied cotton like I meant it, and then I went to Georgia and even picked the stuff because I wanted to know what it felt like. I took my hurt pride back to Huddersfield and threw myself into work, to the total relief of my dear father. And along the way, I suppose I discovered that helping people became my substitute for a family." He put his arm around her waist again. "Lucinda I could forget eventually, but Andrew . . . never. He was my son."

She moved away to look at his face. "You could have married."

He shook his head. "Impossible. I wanted to punish myself. I mean, why should I be happy?"

"Mr. Butterworth, I always thought you were such a sensible man," she chided him.

"Now you know I am not," he replied with a serenity that reminded her of his sister Emma.

"Well, why on earth did you keep that empty miniature frame on your desk all those years?" she persisted.

He looked at her, and what she saw in his eyes made her take his hand. "Because I couldn't for the life of me figure out how to get a likeness of you and put it there, Jane! I think I have been in love with you since that first gathering in Denby when I coaxed you into telling me about Andrew and his first steps!"

She gasped at such an outburst from a rational man and would have stepped back, except that the mill owner was pulling her in close to him—too close, really, but she couldn't think of an objection. She clung to him when he kissed her, and returned his affection with all the fervor she possessed. She didn't want to let him go, but after he kissed her once more with a loud smack of his own, she took a deep breath, and then another.

"Were your ribs in any danger, my love?" he said softly.

She shook her head.

"Mine were," he replied frankly. "Jane, I always thought you had a fragile air about you! What a fool I am with women. You had better be my wife, and soon, or there is no telling what kind of trouble I will get into." He sat her down with him and pulled her onto his lap. "Did I just propose? Well?"

"Yes, yes of course," she answered. "But you could have courted me—oh, let us see—ten years ago, and asked me then!"

"And risked another rebuff from a lady? Oh, no! You may be a poor relation, my dearest Jane, but we still don't run in the same social circles." He hugged her. "Think of the people we are going to absolutely scandalize. I am too old for you, and I am a mill owner, and I wear loud waistcoats. Good Lord, they will think you were desperate."

She thought about what he meant, then put it from her mind forever and kissed him. When they paused, he held her close. "I thought I would be content to admire you from a distance."

"What changed your mind?" she asked, her voice soft as she kissed the angle of his jaw.

"You needed me," he said simply, and kissed her fingertips. "And maybe, just maybe, I needed you. Could it be?"

They sat together on the ground by the lake until the lights across the water in Stover Hall started to wink out. "I had better go," she said, making no move to rise.

"I suppose," he agreed, but made no move, either, his hand warm on her knee.

With a laugh, she pulled herself away from him. "Stanton will be up all night if I do not appear."

He shrugged and took hold of her ankle when she tried to stand up. "Tongues will wag, Lady Carruthers will spread all sorts of rumors—by the way, did she return to London? What could have happened?—the vicar will make you the subject of a sermon." He lay on his back. "Amanda will be so pleased, Richard will pat me on the back, and Emma will cry." He turned over on his side to look at her. "Em had a hard enough time at Christmas, seeing her nephew Andrew for the first time."

"I did wonder," Jane said. "Unhand me now, sir. I will see if my legs . . ."

". . . nice legs, by the way," he interrupted.

"You *are* a scoundrel. I will see if my legs will get me back to Stover Hall. And you will return to your house before I accuse you of being a bad parent by leaving Andrew alone so long."

"Yes, indeed," he said, pulling her down beside him again. "Alone with a butler, two footmen, a cook, a housekeeper, two upstairs maids, a parlor maid, and two or three gardeners." He kissed her. "I do have one more question of some importance, my love, so pay attention and leave off kissing me for a moment. Well, not entirely! Tomorrow I will go to York for a special license and then the morning after, we will stand up in all fear and trembling before the vicar."

"Your question?" she reminded him, sitting up again.

"It is this: When we are belly to belly a couple of days or nights from now—probably even shy of our clothing—are you going to persist in calling me Mr. Butterworth?"

She blushed, and was grateful for the dark. "I promise you—only in the throes of deepest passion, sir! Otherwise you will be Sippy . . ."

"Merciful heaven!"

". . . or perhaps Africanus."

"Worse and worse!"

"What do you suggest? *I* didn't name you!"

He pulled her to her feet, kissed her soundly, and gave her a push toward the Stover side of the lake.

"Just call me husband. Good night, Jane."

I can do that, she thought. I can.

AUTHOR'S NOTE

With the beginning of the Industrial Revolution, factory owner Robert Owen and philosopher Jeremy Bentham, who appear briefly in this narrative, reflected the changing values of English society. The period of George IV's regency saw England begin the transformation from a nation of cottage industries to a world manufacturing power. Factories in Britain's industrial north supplied the world with cotton cloth. Enlightened men like Owen and Bentham worked to relieve abuses of women and children in factories, and to institute some regulation in factory operation. The British Factory Act of 1847 restricted the working day for women and children ages thirteen to eighteen to ten hours a day. Other European nations followed the lead of Britain. In the 1840s—America's "Reforming Forties"—various U.S. state legislatures began to regulate the employment of minors in textile factories. Not until FDR's Fair Labor Standards Act of 1938 were children under sixteen prohibited by law from working in most U.S. industries.